How ...

Boggar...

Beta for Boggart

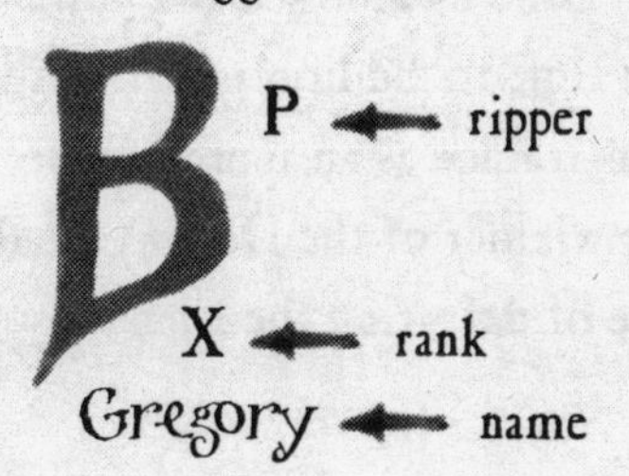

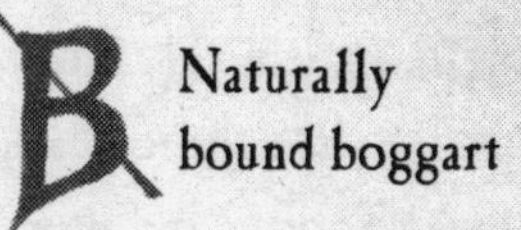

Artificially bound boggart

I – dangerous

X – hardly detectable

Ghosts/Ghasts

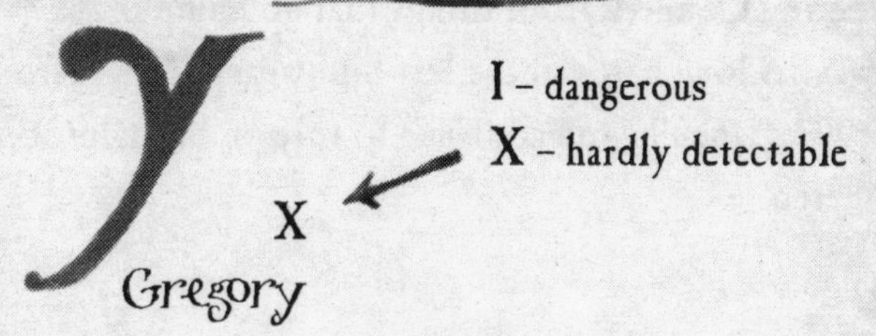

Witches

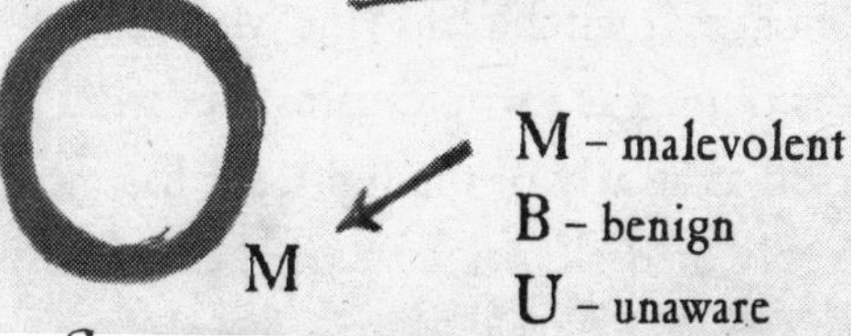

Gregory

CHARACTER PROFILES

TOM

Thomas Ward is both the seventh son of a seventh son and the child of a powerful Lamia witch. He has abilities beyond those of a regular spook: as well as being able see and hear the dead, he can also slow down time to aid him in battle. For more than three years he has trained as an apprentice to the local Spook, and now as the wielder of the Destiny Blade he may be the world's only hope of defeating the Fiend.

THE SPOOK

The Spook is an unmistakable figure. He's tall and rather fierce-looking. He wears a long black cloak and hood, and always carries a staff and chain. For over sixty years he has protected the Country from things that go bump in the night, but his long battles have left him weary. Tom fears that the days when he can continue to rely on his mentor may be numbered.

ALICE

Tom can't decide if Alice is good or evil. She is related to two of the most evil witch clans (the Malkins and the Deanes) and was trained as a witch against her will. While she counts herself as an ally of the light, she has increasingly been forced to rely on dark magic to save her friends. Tom fears that every time she does will draw her closer and closer to the dark.

MAM

Tom's mam always knew he would become the Spook's apprentice. She called him her 'gift to the County'. There always were quite a few mysterious things about Mam, but even Tom never suspected the truth: that she was a Lamia witch, and that she had planned for Tom to battle the Fiend since before he was even born. Tom's mam fell in the battle against the Ordeen, but he hopes that she might still be watching over him somehow . . .

GRIMALKIN

Grimalkin is the current assassin of the Malkin witch clan. Very fast and strong, she has a code of honour and never resorts to trickery. Although honourable, Grimalkin also has a dark side and is reputed to use torture. Recently she has forged an unlikely alliance with Tom Ward against their common enemy, the Fiend. But can a true servant of the dark ever really be trusted?

THE FIEND

The Fiend is the dark made flesh, the most powerful of all its denizens and the very oldest of the old Gods. He has many other names, including the Devil, Satan, Lucifer and the Father of Lies. Together, Tom Ward and his allies managed to sever the Fiend's head in battle, but their fight to destroy him once and for all has only just begun . . .

THE WARDSTONE CHRONICLES

BOOK ONE:
THE SPOOK'S APPRENTICE

BOOK TWO:
THE SPOOK'S CURSE

BOOK THREE:
THE SPOOK'S SECRET

BOOK FOUR:
THE SPOOK'S BATTLE

BOOK FIVE:
THE SPOOK'S MISTAKE

BOOK SIX:
THE SPOOK'S SACRIFICE

BOOK SEVEN:
THE SPOOK'S NIGHTMARE

BOOK EIGHT:
THE SPOOK'S DESTINY

BOOK NINE:
SPOOK'S: I AM GRIMALKIN

BOOK TEN:
THE SPOOK'S BLOOD

BOOK ELEVEN:
SPOOK'S: SLITHER'S TALE

ALSO AVAILABLE

THE SPOOK'S STORIES:
WITCHES

THE SPOOK'S BESTIARY

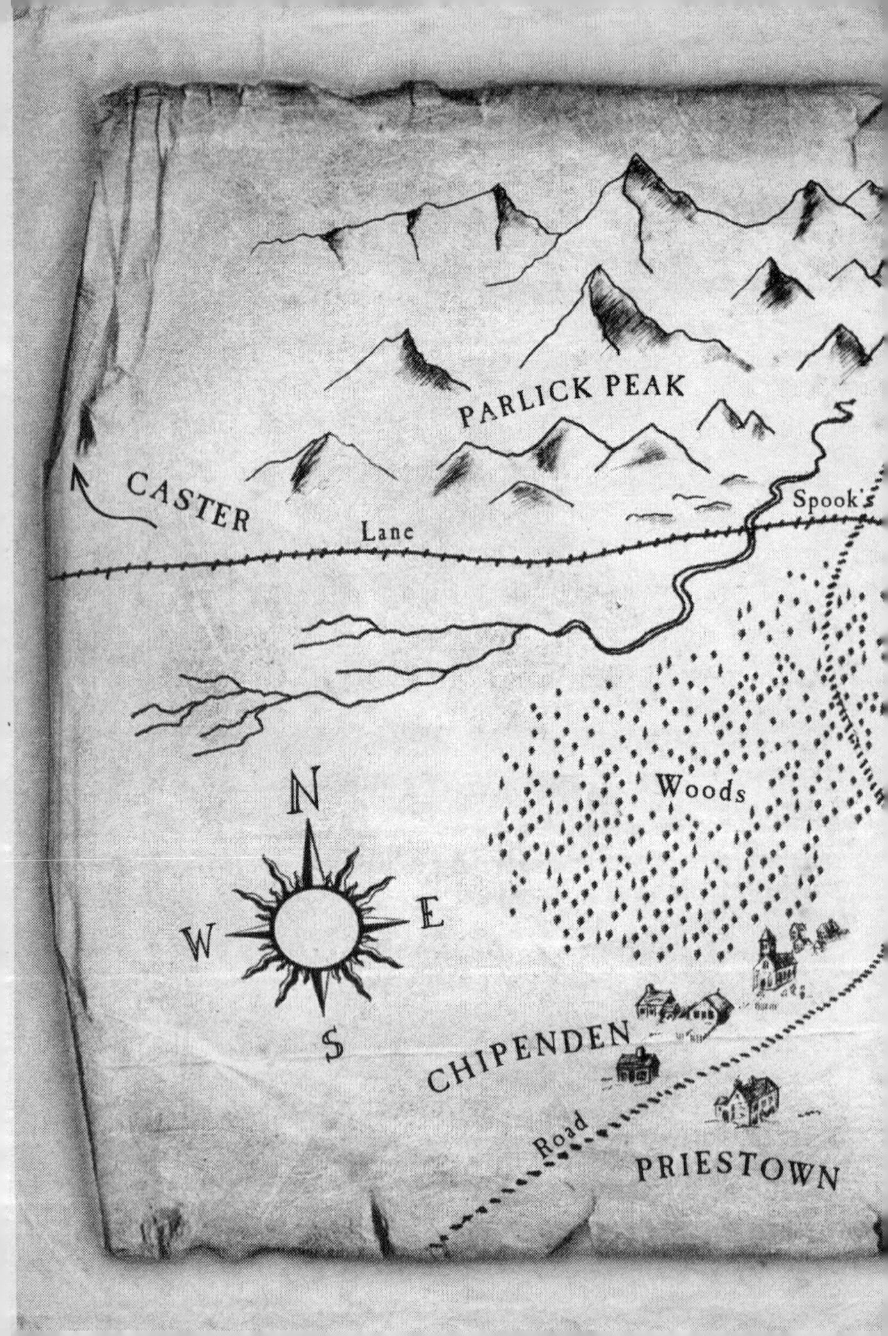
PARLICK PEAK
CASTER
Lane
Spook's
Woods
N
E
W
S
CHIPENDEN
Road
PRIESTOWN

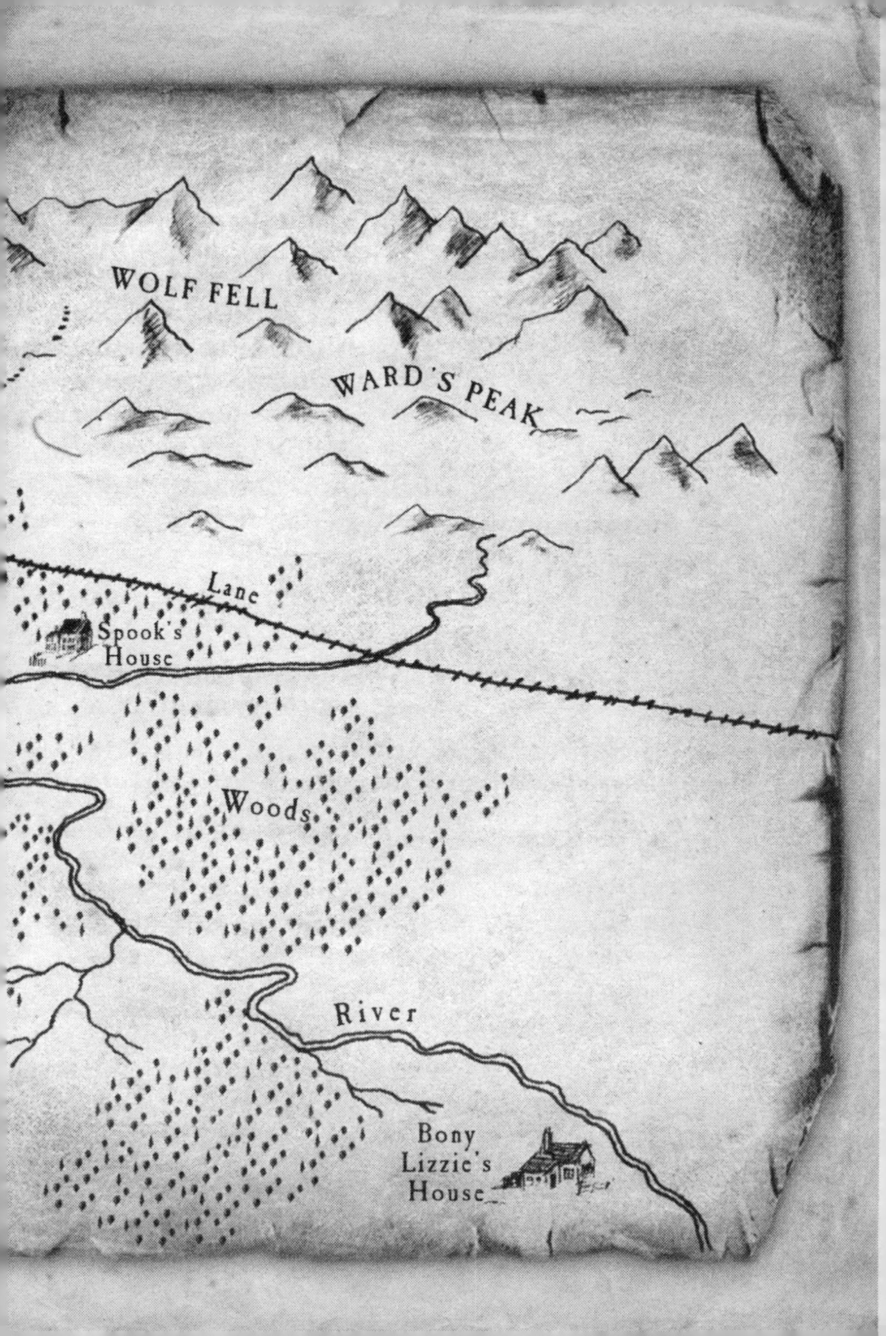
WOLF FELL
WARD'S PEAK
Lane
Spook's House
Woods
River
Bony Lizzie's House

JOSEPH DELANEY

Illustrations by David Wyatt

RED FOX

THE SPOOK'S BLOOD
A RED FOX BOOK 978 1 849 41107 3

First published in Great Britain by The Bodley Head,
an imprint of Random House Children's Publishers UK
A Random House Group Company

Bodley Head edition published 2012
Corgi edition published 2013

1 3 5 7 9 10 8 6 4 2

The Random House Group Limited supports the Forest Stewardship Council (FSC®), the leading international forest certification organization. Our books carrying the FSC label are printed on FSC®-certified paper. FSC is the only forest certification scheme endorsed by the leading environmental organizations, including Greenpeace. Our paper procurement policy can be found at www.randomhouse.co.uk/environment.

Set in 10.5/16.5 Palatino by Falcon Oast Graphic Art Ltd

RANDOM HOUSE CHILDREN'S PUBLISHERS UK
61–63 Uxbridge Road, London W5 5SA

www.**randomhousechildrens**.co.uk
www.**totallyrandombooks**.co.uk
www.**randomhouse**.co.uk

Addresses for companies within The Random House Group Limited can be found at:
www.randomhouse.co.uk/offices.htm
THE RANDOM HOUSE GROUP Limited Reg. No. 954009

A CIP catalogue record for this book is available from the British Library.

Printed and bound in Great Britain by CPI Group (UK) Ltd, Croydon, CR0 4YY

for Marie

The highest point in the County
is marked by mystery.
It is said that a man died there in a
great storm, while binding an evil
that threatened the whole world.
Then the ice came again, and when it
retreated, even the shapes of the
hills and the names of the towns
in the valleys changed.
Now, at that highest point on
the fells, no trace remains of what
was done so long ago,
but its name has endured.
They call it –

The Wardstone.

CHAPTER 1
TIME TO REBUILD

The Spook was perched on a log in his garden at Chipenden, the sun singing through the trees and the air bright with birdsong. It was a warm spring morning in late May – as good as it got in the County. Things seemed to be changing for the better. I was sitting on the grass wolfing down my breakfast and he was smiling to himself and looking quite contented for a change as he gazed back towards the house.

From it came the sound of sawing; I could smell the sawdust. My master's house was being repaired, starting with the roof. It had been burned out by enemy soldiers, but now the war in the County was over, and it was time to rebuild and get on with our lives as a Spook and his apprentice dealing with all manner of things from the dark – boggarts, ghosts, ghasts and witches.

'I can't understand why Alice would leave like that without saying anything,' I complained to the Spook. 'It's not like her at all. Especially as she knows we'll soon be setting off east and will be away for at least a couple of days.'

My friend Alice had disappeared three nights earlier. I had been talking to her in the garden and had left briefly to tell the Spook something, saying I'd be back in a few moments. On my return she had gone. At first I hadn't been too worried, but then she'd missed supper and hadn't reappeared since.

The Spook sighed. 'Don't take this too hard, lad, but maybe she's gone for good. After all, you've been bound together for quite some time by the need to use that blood jar. Now she's free to do as she pleases. And she's a different person after being dragged off to the dark and held there for so long.'

My master's words were harsh. Despite the fact that she had been helping us for years, he still didn't trust

Alice. She'd been born in Pendle and had spent two years being trained as a witch; John Gregory would be glad to see the back of her. When we were in Greece, Alice had created a blood jar to keep the Fiend at bay; otherwise we would both have been snatched away into the dark. Now it was no longer needed. We had bound the Fiend and cut off his head – which was now in the possession of Grimalkin, the witch assassin. She was on the run from his servants. Were the two halves of his body ever reunited, he would be free again and his vengeance would certainly be terrible. The consequences would be dire, not only for the County, but for the whole world beyond it; a new age of darkness would begin. But we had bought a little time in order to seek a way to destroy him permanently.

My master's final words hurt me most of all. The Fiend had taken Alice off into the dark; on her return she'd changed dramatically. Her hair had turned white: that was merely physical, but I feared that her soul had been damaged – that she'd moved closer to the dark. Alice had expressed that same concern. Maybe she would never return? Maybe she could no longer be close to a spook's apprentice? After four years of facing dangers together, we had become close friends and it saddened me that we were now drifting apart. I remembered something my dad had told me when I was younger. Although just an ordinary farmer, he'd been wise, and as I was growing up he'd taught me lots of truths about life.

'Listen, Tom,' he'd once said. 'You have to accept that in this world things are constantly changing. Nothing stays the same for ever. We have to learn to live with that.'

He was right: I'd been happy living at home with my family. Now Mam and Dad were both dead and I could never go back to that life. I just hoped that my friendship with Alice wasn't coming to an end too.

'What sort of place is Todmorden?' I asked, changing the subject. There was no point in arguing with my master about Alice.

'Well, lad, my duties have never taken me to that town but I do know a bit about it. Todmorden straddles the eastern County border, which is marked by the river Calder. So half the town is in the County and half is beyond it. No doubt the folk across the river will have different customs and attitudes. We've travelled a bit in the past two years – firstly to Greece, next to the Isle of Mona, and finally to Ireland. Each of those lands presented us with new problems and difficulties to overcome. The fact that our destination isn't far from home doesn't change the fact that we need to be on our toes.'

The Spook's library had been destroyed in the fire – the legacy of generations of spooks, filled with knowledge of how to fight the dark. Now we had heard of a collection of books about the dark in Todmorden. After ringing the bell at the withy trees crossroads late one night a week earlier, a mysterious visitor had left a note for us. It had been short but to the point:

Dear Mr Gregory,
I learned with deep sadness of the loss of your Chipenden library. I offer my condolences. However, I hope to be of assistance because I own a large collection of books about the dark. Perhaps some might be of use to you? I am prepared to sell at a reasonable price. If you are interested, please visit me soon at Todmorden. I live in the house at the top of Bent Lane.
Mistress Fresque

Only one book from my master's original library remained – the *Bestiary* that he had written and illustrated himself. It was more than just a book. It was a living, working document annotated by his other apprentices – including me. It was a record of his life's work and what he had discovered with the help of others. Now he hoped to start restocking his library. However, he refused to take any books from the small collection in the watermill north of Caster that had been occupied by Bill Arkwright, one of his ex-apprentices. He had hopes that one day the mill would become a spook's house once more; if that happened, the new incumbent would need those books. John Gregory anticipated that the visit to Todmorden would be the first step to replacing his own library.

My master had originally intended to set off right away but, as interested as he was in acquiring books, the rebuilding of his house came first, and he had spent hours going over plans and schedules with the builder. He had a list of priorities, and the completion of a new library to house books was one of them. I'd encouraged him in that because I wanted to delay our departure to give Alice time to return.

'What's the point of getting new books if we haven't a library ready to put them in?' I'd argued.

He'd agreed, and it had bought me more time, but at last we were off to meet Mistress Fresque.

In the afternoon, about an hour or so before we were to set off on our journey, I wrote a note of my own. This one was for the absent Alice:

Dear Alice,

Why did you go off like that without a word? I am worried about you. This morning my master and I will set off for Todmorden to look at the library we heard about. We should be back in a couple of days.

Take care. I miss you.

Tom

But no sooner had I pinned it to the new back door than I suddenly sensed a coldness – the warning I sometimes get that something from the dark is nearby. Then I heard someone coming up behind me. My staff was leaning against the wall, so I snatched it up and spun round to face the danger, holding it in the defensive diagonal position.

To my surprise, Alice was standing before me. She was smiling but looked tired and dishevelled, as if she'd been on a long wearisome journey. The coldness quickly faded. She wasn't an enemy, but that brief warning worried me. To what extent had she been contaminated by the dark? I wondered.

'Alice! I've been really worried about you. Why did you leave like that without saying anything?'

She stepped forward and, without answering, gave me a hug. After a few moments I held her at arm's length.

'You look like you've had a hard time of it, but it's really good to see you,' I told her. 'Your hair's returning to its usual colour. It'll be back to normal soon.'

Alice nodded, but the smile slipped from her face and she looked very serious. 'I've something really important to tell you, Tom,' she said. 'It's best if Old Gregory hears it too!'

I'd have liked a little more time to talk to Alice alone, but she insisted that we see my master immediately. I went to fetch him, and as it was a sunny afternoon, he led the way to the bench in the western garden.

The Spook and I sat down but Alice remained standing. I had to stop myself from laughing because it reminded me of the occasions when the Spook would stand there giving me a lesson while I took notes. Now my master and I were like two apprentices!

But what Alice had to say soon wiped the smile off my face.

'While she was on the run with the Fiend's head, Grimalkin took refuge in Malkin Tower,' she told us. 'It's a long story, and no doubt she'll eventually tell you the details of what happened herself—'

'Is the Fiend's head still safe in her possession?' interrupted the Spook.

'It's been hard, but Grimalkin's kept it safe so far. Ain't going to get any easier, though. There's some bad news. Agnes Sowerbutts was killed by the Fiend's supporters.'

'Poor Agnes,' I said, shaking my head sadly. 'I'm really sorry.' She was Alice's aunt and had helped both of us in the past.

'One of the two lamia sisters was killed as well, and now only one – Slake – is left defending the tower. She's under siege and can't hold out indefinitely. From what Grimalkin said, it's important that you go there as soon as possible, Tom. The lamias studied your mam's books and found out that she was the one who hobbled the Fiend. Slake thinks that by looking more closely at the hobbling process you might be able to work out how to finish him off for good.'

The hobble had limited the Fiend's power in certain ways. If he was able to kill me himself, he'd reign on in our world for a hundred years before being forced to return to the dark. Of course, for an immortal being, that wasn't long enough. But if he got one of his children to do the deed, the son or daughter of a witch, then the Fiend could rule the world indefinitely. There was also a third way to achieve this end: he could simply convert me to the dark.

'I always thought it was likely that Mam did the hobbling,' I said. After all, I was her seventh son born to Dad, another seventh son, and thus her chosen weapon against the Fiend. The hobble concerned me, and which other of his enemies could have been powerful enough to do it?

The Spook nodded in agreement but didn't look at all happy. Any use of magic made him very uneasy. At present an alliance with the dark was necessary but he didn't like it.

'I thought the same,' said Alice. 'But there's one more thing, Tom. Whatever's needed, whatever it takes, you have to do it at Halloween. There's a seventeen-year cycle, and it's got to be next Halloween – the thirty-fourth anniversary of the hobble carried out by your mam. That leaves little over five months . . .'

'Well, lad,' said the Spook, 'you'd better get yourself to Malkin Tower as soon as possible. That's more important than books for my new library. Our visit to Todmorden can wait until you get back.'

'Aren't you coming?' I asked.

My master shook his head. 'Nay, lad, not this time. At my age the County damp starts to rot your joints, and my old knees are playing up worse than I can remember. I'd only slow you down. With the girl to guide you, you'll be able reach the tower without being seen. Besides, you've got years of training behind you now; it's time you started to think and behave like the spook you'll soon become. I have confidence in you, lad. I wouldn't send you off like this if I didn't think you could take care of yourself.'

CHAPTER 2
SACRED OBJECTS

After that, I spent an hour with the dogs. Claw and her fully grown pups, Blood and Bone, were wolfhounds trained to hunt water witches. They'd belonged to Bill Arkwright, a spook who had died fighting the dark with us in Greece. Now I considered them to be my dogs – although my master had still not agreed to give them a permanent home. While we were away he had promised to look after them, but I knew he was busy planning repairs to the house; moreover, his knees were playing up, so the dogs would no doubt spend most of their time chained up. I took them for a long walk, letting them run free.

Within an hour of my return we were setting off on our journey. We walked fast. Carrying my staff and bag, I followed Alice east towards Pendle. Our aim was to arrive just before sunset, enter under cover of dark and then head directly for Malkin Tower.

Under my gown, in the scabbard crafted for me by Grimalkin, I was carrying the Destiny Blade, a weapon given to me by one of Ireland's greatest heroes, Cuchulain. The witch assassin had trained me in its use and it would prove a valuable additional weapon.

We crossed the river Ribble with hours to spare and, heading north, kept to the west of that huge, ominous hill, feeling the chill of its brooding presence. Pendle was a place that was particularly conducive to the use of dark magic. This was why so many witches lived here.

However, we were on the safer side of Pendle; the villages of the three main witch clans lay to the south-east, beyond the hill. We knew that the clans were divided amongst themselves; there were those who supported the Fiend and those who opposed him. The situation was complicated but one thing was certain – a spook's apprentice would not be welcome anywhere in the district.

We skirted Downham, then rounded the northern edge of the hill, before heading south once more. Now, with every stride, we were moving closer to danger, so we settled down in a small copse to wait for nightfall.

Alice turned to face me, her face pale in the gloom. 'I've more to tell you, Tom,' she said. 'I think this is as good a time as any.'

'You're being very mysterious. Is it something bad?' I asked her.

'The first part ain't – though the second might upset you, so I'll start with the easy bit. When your mam hobbled the Fiend, she used two sacred objects. One of 'em is in the trunk in Malkin Tower. The other could be anywhere, so we need to track it down.'

'So we have one – that's a start. What is it?'

'Grimalkin doesn't know. Slake wouldn't let her see it.'

'Why not? Why should the lamia decide that? She's the guardian of the trunk, not the owner.'

'It wasn't Slake's idea – it was your mam's. She said nobody but you could know what it was or see it.'

'This was in Mam's writings that Slake found in the trunk?'

'No, Tom,' Alice said, shaking her head sadly. 'Your mam appeared to Slake and told her that directly.'

I looked at Alice in astonishment. Since Mam died I'd had contact with her once, on the ship on the way home from Greece – but I hadn't seen her; it had just been a feeling of warmth. At the time, I'd been certain that she'd come to say goodbye to her son. But as time had passed I'd become less and less sure that it had really happened. Now it seemed more like dreaming than waking. But could she really have been talking to Slake?

'Why would she tell Slake that? Why not tell me directly? I need to know – I'm her son!' Suddenly I felt angry. I tried to suppress the feeling but I felt tears prickling behind my eyes. I missed Mam terribly. Why hadn't she contacted *me*?

'I knew you'd be upset, Tom, but please try not to let it bother you. It might be easier for her to talk to Slake. After all, they are both lamias. There's something else I should tell you. Grimalkin said the lamia sisters talked about her as if she were still alive. And they worship her. They call her *Zenobia*.'

I took a deep breath to calm myself. It made sense.

Mam had been the very first lamia, a powerful and evil servant of the dark. But she had changed: after marrying Dad she'd finally turned her back on her former life and become an enemy of the Fiend.

'Perhaps she'll talk to me when I get to the tower?' I suggested.

'Ain't good to build up your hopes too much, Tom. But yes, she might. Now, there's something else I'd like to ask. It's important to me, but if you say no I'll understand.'

'If it's important to you, Alice, I won't say no. You should know me better than that.'

'It's just that, on our way to the tower, we'll be passing by Witch Dell. Grimalkin said that part of it was burned by the Fiend's supporters as they pursued her, but that Agnes Sowerbutts might have survived. She was my friend as well as my aunt, Tom. She helped me a lot. If she's still in there, I'd like to talk to her one last time.'

'I thought it was best to stay away from dead witches: the longer they stay in the dell, the more they change, forgetting their past life, their family and friends.'

'That's mostly true, Tom – their personalities change for the worse, which means that living and dead witches don't mingle much. But Agnes ain't been dead for long and I feel sure she'll still remember me.'

'If she did survive, how will you find her? We can't just wander through the dell with all those dead witches around. Some are really strong and dangerous.'

'Grimalkin told me that there's probably only one strong one around at the moment. But there's a call I sometimes used to contact Agnes. She taught it to me herself. It's the cry of the corpsefowl. That'll bring her out.'

The sun went down and the copse grew darker. It was a clear moonless night – the moon wouldn't rise for several hours – but the sky was sprinkled with stars. Keeping to the shelter of hedgerows, we began a meandering journey south towards the tower, finally skirting the eastern edge of Witch Dell. We could see the devastation caused by the fire – a wide swath of burned trees cut it in half. It must have destroyed a lot of dead witches, many of them with allegiance to the Fiend. I realized that his supporters would do anything to retrieve his head.

We stopped about fifty yards from the dell's southern tip. There were signs of the terrible battle between Grimalkin and her witch opponents. She was formidable, but I wondered at the size of the forces that were hunting her down – and about Alice's part in all this.

Alice cupped her hands around her mouth and sent an eerie call out into the darkness. The corpsefowl – or nightjar – flies by night, and the cry sent shivers down my spine. The powerful water witch, Morwena, had used a corpsefowl as her familiar, and I had some scary memories of being hunted by her. I remembered the time she had surged up out of the marsh, hooked me with a talon and tried to drag me down to drain my blood.

I couldn't tell the difference between Alice's cry and the real thing, but she told me she modulated it slightly so that Agnes would know it was her and not just a bird.

Every five minutes, Alice repeated that cry. Each time, that eldritch call, echoing amongst the trees of the dell, made me shudder. Each time it went out into the darkness, my heart beat harder: the bad memories came flooding back. Claw had bitten off the witch's finger and saved me. Otherwise I'd have been dragged down into the marsh, my blood drained before I'd even had time to drown. I pushed these thoughts to the back of my mind and tried to stay calm, slowing my breathing as my master had taught me.

Alice was about to give up when, after the eighth attempt, I suddenly felt cold. It was the warning that something from the dark was approaching. Everything became unnaturally still and silent. Then there was a rustle of grass, followed by low squelching noises. Something was approaching across the soggy ground. Soon I could hear snuffling and grunting.

Within moments, we spotted a dead witch crawling towards us. It could have been any dead witch out hunting for blood, thinking we were likely prey, so I tightened my grip on my staff.

Alice quickly sniffed twice, checking for danger. 'It's Agnes,' she whispered.

I could hear the witch sniffing the ground, finding her way towards us. Then I saw her: she was a sorry creature indeed, and the sight brought a lump to my throat. She had always been such a clean, houseproud woman; now she wore a tatty dress that was caked in dirt and her hair was greasy and wriggling with maggots. She smelled very strongly of leaf mould. I needn't have been concerned that she might have forgotten us: as soon as she came close she began to sob, the tears running down her cheeks to drip onto the grass. Then she sat up and put her head in her hands.

'Sorry to be so maudlin, Alice,' she cried, wiping away her tears with the back of her hand. 'I thought it was bad when my husband died – I missed him terribly for many a long year – but this is far worse. I just can't get used to being like this. I wish the fire had taken me. I can never go back to my cottage and live my old comfortable life. I'll never be happy again. If only I'd been a strong dead witch. At least then I'd have been able to travel by night and hunt far from this miserable dell. But I'm not strong enough to catch anything big. Beetles, voles and mice are the best I can hope for!'

Alice didn't speak for quite a while. I couldn't think of anything to say, either. What comfort could I give to poor Agnes? No wonder most living witches kept away from their dead relatives. It was painful to see someone you liked in such a terrible state. There was nothing to be said that would make her feel better.

'Listen, Tom, I'd like to have a few words alone with Agnes. Is that all right?' Alice asked me eventually.

'Of course it is,' I said, getting to my feet. 'I'll wait over there.'

I walked well out of earshot to allow Alice a bit of privacy with her aunt. In truth I was more than happy to get away. Being close to Agnes made me feel sad and uneasy.

After about five minutes Alice came towards me, her eyes glittering in the starlight. 'What if Agnes was a really strong witch, Tom . . . Just think what that would mean. Not only would she have a much better existence, which she deserves, she'd be a really useful ally.'

'What are you saying, Alice?' I asked nervously, knowing she wasn't much given to idle speculation.

'Suppose I make her strong . . . ?'

'Using dark magic?'

'Yes. I can do it . . . Whether I *should* is another matter. What do you think?'

CHAPTER 3
LOTS OF BLOOD!

'I thought that all the magic drained out of a dead witch, leaving only a need for blood? So how can your magic help?' I asked Alice.

'It's true that a dead witch no longer has her own magic in her bones. But I can use mine and just make her stronger for a while,' she replied. 'Her new strength will lessen with time, but her existence in the dell could be better for years to come. By the time she weakens, her mind will have started to disintegrate anyway, so she will no longer pine for her old life. Ain't nothing wrong with that.'

'But what about her victims? What about those she'll

kill because she needs their blood? At least she's feeding on insects and small animals now – not people!'

'She'll only take the blood of the Fiend's servants – there are plenty to keep her satisfied for a long time! And each one she kills will lessen the danger to us and make it more likely that we'll succeed in destroying him for all time.'

'Can you be sure she'll limit herself to them?'

'I know Agnes. She'll keep any promise she makes – I'll get that commitment before I do anything.'

'But what about you, Alice? What about *you*?' I protested, raising my voice a little. 'Each time you use your magical power it brings you closer to the dark.'

My argument was exactly the one my master would have used. I was Alice's friend and was worried about her, but it had to be said.

'I use it so we can survive, so that we can win. I saved you from the witch, Scarab, and the goat mages back in Ireland, didn't I? I used it to stop the witches getting away with the Fiend's head; and I gave Grimalkin some of my power so she could kill our enemies. If I hadn't done so, she would be dead, I'd be dead and the Fiend's head would have been reunited with his body.

It had to be done, Tom. I did what was necessary. This could be just as important.'

'Just as important? Are you sure you're not helping Agnes because you feel sorry for her?'

'And what if it *was* only because of that?' Alice retorted angrily, her eyes glittering. 'Why shouldn't I help my friends just as I helped you, Tom? But I promise you it's more than that, much more. Something's going to happen, I feel sure of it. I can sense something moving towards us from the future – something dark and terrible. Agnes might be able to help. We'll need a strong Agnes just to survive. Trust me, Tom, it's for the best!'

I fell silent, filled with a terrible unease. Alice was using dark magic more freely than ever. She'd given Grimalkin power, and now she wanted to make a dead witch stronger. Where would it end? I knew that whatever I said, she'd go ahead and do it anyway. Our relationship was changing for the worse. She no longer valued my advice.

We glared at each other, but after a few seconds Alice spun on her heel and went back to Agnes. She crouched down, placed her left hand on the head of the dead witch and spoke to her softly. I couldn't hear what she was saying, but Agnes's reply was clear as a bell. She spoke just three words: 'Yes, I promise.'

Alice began to speak in a sing-song voice. It was a dark spell. Louder and louder, faster and faster she began to chant – until I looked around uneasily, sure that every dead witch in the dell would hear her and come towards us. We were now deep in witch territory; the three villages set in the Devil's Triangle lay just a few miles to the south. There could be spies around and the noise would alert them to our presence.

Agnes suddenly let out a blood-curdling scream and jerked backwards, away from Alice. She lay in the grass, moaning and whimpering, limbs thrashing and body spasming. Alarmed, I went over to Alice. Had the spell gone terribly wrong? I wondered.

'Be all right in a few minutes, she will,' Alice said reassuringly. 'Hurts a lot because it's such powerful magic, but she knew that before I started. Accepted that, she did. Agnes is very brave. Always was.'

After a few moments Agnes stopped writhing about and got to her hands and knees. She coughed and choked for a few moments, then lurched to her feet and smiled at us in turn. There was something of the old Agnes in her expression. Despite her filthy face and tattered, blood-stained clothes, she now seemed calm and confident. But in her eyes I saw a hunger that had never been present in the living Agnes.

'I'm thirsty!' she said, looking about her with an intensity that was really scary. 'I need blood! I need lots and lots of blood!'

We headed south, with Alice in the lead and Agnes close on her heels; I brought up the rear. I kept glancing about me and turning my head to look behind. I expected to be attacked at any time. Our enemies – the witches who served the Fiend – might well be following us or lying in wait ahead. Despite his predicament, the Fiend could still communicate with them. He would take every opportunity to have us hunted down. And Pendle was a dangerous place at the best of times.

We were making good progress, and Agnes, who had been able to crawl only with difficulty, was now matching Alice stride for stride. The moon would rise soon – it was vital that we reached the tunnel beneath the tower before its light made us visible to all in the vicinity.

I wondered about Slake, the surviving lamia. How far had she progressed towards the winged form? She might well have lost the power of speech – which meant that I would be unable to question her properly. I needed to know as much about the sacred objects as possible. I also hoped to be able to communicate with Mam in some way.

Soon the three of us were walking along beside Crow Wood; the way into the tower was now close: the dense tangled copse that had grown over an old abandoned graveyard. The entrance to the tunnel was to be found roughly at its centre. You reached it by entering a sepulchre, built for the dead of a wealthy family. Although most of the bones had been removed when the graveyard was deconsecrated, theirs remained in place.

Alice suddenly came to a halt and raised her hand in warning. I could see nothing but a few tombstones amongst the brambles, but I heard her sniff quickly three times, checking for danger.

'There are witches ahead, lying in wait. It's an ambush. They must have scryed our approach.'

'How many?' I asked, readying my staff.

'There are three, Tom. But they'll soon sniff out our presence and then signal to the others.'

'Then it's best that they die quickly!' Agnes said. 'They're mine!'

Before Alice or I had time to react, Agnes was surging forward, bursting through the thicket into the small clearing that surrounded the sepulchre. Witches have varying levels of skill when long-sniffing approaching danger; while Alice was very good at it, some are relatively weak. Moreover, an attack that is improvised and instantaneous rather than premeditated can take the enemy completely by surprise.

The screams that came from the clearing were shrill and ear-splitting, filled with terror and pain. When we caught up with Agnes, two witches were already dead and she was feeding from the third: the woman's limbs thrashed as Alice's aunt sucked the blood from her neck in great greedy gulps.

I was appalled by the speed with which Agnes had changed; she no longer bore any resemblance to the kindly woman who had helped us so many times in the past. I stared down at her in horror, but Alice just shrugged at my look of disgust. 'She's hungry, Tom.

Who are we to judge her? We'd be no different in her situation.'

After a few moments Agnes looked up at us and grinned, her lips stained with blood. 'I'll stay here and finish this,' she said. 'You get yourselves to safety in the tunnel.'

'More enemies will be here soon, Agnes,' Alice told her. 'Don't linger too long.'

'Don't you fear, child, I'll soon catch you up. And if more come after these, so much the better!'

We could do no more to persuade Agnes, so, very reluctantly, we left her feeding and headed for the sepulchre. The building was almost exactly as I remembered it from my last visit – getting on for two years ago – but the sycamore sapling growing through its roof was taller and broader, the leafy canopy that shrouded this house of the dead even thicker, increasing the gloom within.

Alice pulled the stub of a candle out of her skirt pocket, and as we walked into the darkness of the sepulchre, it flickered into life, showing the cobwebbed horizontal tombstones and the dark earthen hole that gave access to the tunnel. Alice took the lead and we crawled through. After a while it widened and we were able to stand and make better progress.

Twice we paused while Alice sniffed for danger, but soon we'd passed the small lake once guarded by the killer wight – the eyeless body of a drowned sailor who'd been enchanted by dark magic. This one had been destroyed by one of the lamias and now no trace was visible, his dismembered body parts long since lost in the mud at the bottom. Only a faint unpleasant odour was testimony to the fact that this had once been a very dangerous place.

Before long we reached the underground gate to the ancient tower and were walking past the dark, dank dungeons, some still occupied by the skeletons of those tortured by the Malkin clan. No spirits lingered here now: on a previous visit to this place, my master had worked hard to send them all to the light.

We soon found ourselves in the vast cylindrical underground hall – and saw the pillar hung with chains; there were thirteen chains in all, and to each was attached a small dead animal: rats, rabbits, a cat, a dog and two badgers. I remembered their blood dripping down into a rusty bucket, but now it was empty and the dead creatures were desiccated and shrunken.

'Grimalkin said that the lamias created the gibbet as an act of worship,' Alice said, her voice hardly more than a whisper. 'It was an offering to your mam.'

I nodded. On our previous visit, the Spook and I had wondered what the purpose of the gibbet was. Now I knew. I was dealing with things that had very little to do with the warm caring person I remembered. Mam had lived far beyond the normal human span, and her time spent on the farm as a loving wife and the mother of a family of seven boys had been relatively short. She had been the very first lamia; she had done things that I didn't care to think about. Because of that I'd never told my master her true identity. I couldn't bear the thought of him knowing what she'd done and thinking badly of her.

CHAPTER 4
SHE WHOM YOU MOST LOVE

There was no sign of the lamia so we began to climb the steps that spiralled up around the inner walls. High in the ceiling above, the lamias had enlarged the trapdoor into an irregular hole to allow themselves easier access. We clambered through this and continued up more stone steps, worn concave by the pointy shoes of many generations of Malkin witches, our footsteps echoing off the walls. We were still underground, and water was dripping from somewhere in the darkness far above. The air was dank, the light of Alice's candle flickering in a cold draught.

We began to pass the cells where the witches had once incarcerated their enemies. On our last visit to the tower, we had spent some time in one of them, fearing for our lives. But when two of the Malkins had come to slay us, Alice and Mab Mouldheel had pushed them off the steps and they had fallen to their deaths.

There was a noise from inside and I saw Alice glance at the door of our former prison. She raised her candle and headed for the entrance. I followed, staff held at the ready, but it was just a rat, which darted past us and scampered down the steps, long tail trailing after it like a viper. As we started to climb again, Alice looked down to the place where her enemies had died. She shuddered at the memory.

In a strange way, that natural reaction gladdened my heart. By exerting her magical power, Alice might have moved closer to the dark, but she was still able to feel emotion and was not so hardened that she had lost herself, finally surrendering her innate goodness.

'It was a bad time, that!' she said, shaking her head. 'Don't like to be reminded of what I did there.'

My brother, Jack, his wife, Ellie, and their young child, Mary, had also been prisoners in that cell. As they'd opened the cell door, a witch had uttered words that chilled me to the bone:

Leave the child to me, she'd said. *She's mine . . .*

At that moment Alice and Mab had attacked them.

'You did what you had to do, Alice,' I reassured her now. 'It was them or us. And don't forget that they came to kill a child!'

At the top of the steps we emerged into the storehouse, with its stink of rotting vegetables. Beyond this lay the living quarters, once home to the Malkin coven and their servants. Mam's trunk was there – the one that contained her notebooks and artefacts. It was open, and beside it stood the lamia, Slake.

The trunks had been stolen from our farm and brought here by the Malkin witches. Mam's two lamia sisters had been hidden in the other two trunks. I had released them and they'd driven the witches from the tower. Since then, it had been safer to just leave the trunks here, guarded by the lamias.

Slake's face was now bestial in appearance, and her body was covered in green and yellow scales. Her wings were almost fully formed and folded across her shoulders. Was she still able to speak? I wondered.

Almost as if she had read my mind, she spoke, her voice harsh and guttural. 'Welcome, Thomas Ward. It is good to see you once more. Last time we met I was unable to speak; soon I will lose that ability once more. I have much to say to you and we have little time.'

I bowed before replying. 'My thanks for guarding the trunk and its contents and keeping them safe for me. I was sorry to learn of the death of Wynde, your sister. You must feel very lonely now.'

'Wynde died bravely,' the lamia rasped. 'It is true that I am lonely after spending so many long happy years in the company of my sister. I am ready to leave the tower and find others of my kind, but your mother has commanded me to stay until you have learned all there is to know here. Only when you have destroyed the Fiend will I be free to fly away.'

'I was told that there is an artefact in the trunk – a sacred object that might help my cause. May I see it?' I asked.

'It is for your eyes only. The girl must leave while I show it to you.'

I was about to protest when Alice spoke up.

'It's all right, Tom. I'll go back and meet Agnes,' she said with a smile.

'There is another with you?' asked Slake, extending her talons.

'Remember the witch who was slain below the tower? Her name is Agnes Sowerbutts and her body was carried to Witch Dell by your sister,' Alice explained. 'She is still an enemy of the Fiend. As a powerful dead witch, she will be a strong and useful ally.'

'Then go and guide her to us,' the lamia commanded.

Alice left the room and I heard her pointy shoes descending the stone steps. Alone with the lamia, I suddenly felt nervous, my senses on full alert. She was dangerous and formidable, and it was difficult to be at ease in the presence of such a creature.

'In all, there are three sacred objects which must be used to destroy the Fiend,' hissed the lamia. 'The first is already in your possession – the Destiny Blade given to you by Cuchulain. It is fortuitous that it came into your possession – otherwise you would have needed to journey to Ireland again in order to retrieve it.'

Slake had used the word 'fortuitous', suggesting that

the blade had come into my hands by chance. But the name alone told the truth of the matter. It was destiny that had united me with it. We were meant to be together; intended to bring about the final destruction of the Fiend. Either that, or I would die in the attempt.

'This is the second object,' she went on, reaching down into the trunk. Her clawed hand emerged clutching a dagger. One glance told me that its slim blade was crafted from a silver alloy, a material particularly effective against denizens of the dark.

The lamia held it out to me handle first, and the moment my fingers touched it I knew instinctively that I had also been born to bear this weapon. Although far smaller, visually it was the twin of the Destiny Blade, its handle shaped in the form of a skelt's head, the blade taking the place of the bone-tube used to take its victims' blood. The skelt was a deadly creature that lurked in narrow crevices close to water. When somebody passed by, it would dart out and thrust that long bone-tube into their neck. When I went to work with the spook Bill Arkwright, I had been attacked by such a creature and he saved me by smashing its head in with a stone.

No sooner had I gripped the handle of the dagger than the two ruby eyes began to drip blood.

'Was this also forged by Hephaestus?' I asked. He was the Old God who had crafted special weapons for his peers – the greatest blacksmith who had ever existed.

Slake nodded her fearsome head. 'Yes, he forged all three of the sacred objects. They are known as "hero swords", although in truth two of them are just daggers. Some say that they were once used as swords by the Segantii, the little people who once dwelt in the north of the County.'

I remembered seeing the small stone graves chiselled out of rock to hold the bodies of the Segantii. In their hands the daggers would have indeed seemed as large as swords.

'Do I need all three?' I asked.

'All three must be used together. I know where the other is to be found – though it lies in a place that is inaccessible to mortals. It is hidden within the dark, but it could be brought forth by one who is brave, powerful and resourceful.'

'I'm not that brave,' I said, 'and I doubt I have the

power, but if someone has to venture into the dark it must be me.'

The Old God Pan had told me that. Each powerful dark entity had its own private dwelling within the dark – a huge place with many domains, the most powerful and dangerous belonging to the Fiend.

'Your mother, Zenobia, knows precisely where it is to be found. She will tell you herself and explain what must be done.'

'What? Mam will speak to me. When?' I asked excitedly. 'When will that happen?'

'She will appear tonight within this chamber – but to you alone. Her words are for your ears only.'

That night I waited in the chamber, sitting beside Mam's trunk. A single candle flame danced on the table nearby, sending grotesque shadows flickering up onto the far wall.

I had spoken to Alice and explained the situation and she hadn't seemed put out. 'It's natural, Tom, that after all this time apart your mam would want to speak to you alone,' she'd said. 'It is family business, after all, ain't it? I'll just settle down here with

Agnes. You can tell me all about it in the morning.'

Thus Alice, Agnes and Slake were somewhere in the lower part of the tower, leaving me to a lonely, excited but nervous vigil. I wondered what form Mam would take to visit me. Would she be the fierce lamia with snow-white wings like the angels of myth, or the warm understanding Mam who had cared for me as a child?

There had been another surprise. I was prepared to make an immediate start, sifting through the materials in the trunk, hoping to learn more about the ritual I must perform – how the hobbling of the Fiend could be extended to destroy him for ever. But Slake had told me that this would no longer be necessary. It seemed that with Mam's guidance she had already done the necessary decoding and had written down the instructions to be given to me after Mam had made contact.

At first I was excited, longing to see Mam again, and couldn't sleep. But gradually I grew weary and my head began to nod. I kept jerking awake and opening my eyes, but finally I must have fallen into a deep sleep.

Then, very suddenly, I was wide awake again, my

heart thudding in my chest. The candle had gone out but there was another light – a pale, bright column – in the room beside me. Standing before me was Mam – in the shape she had assumed back in Greece just before the final battle with her terrible enemy, the Ordeen. Her cheekbones were high and sharply defined; her cruel eyes those of a predator. I felt nervous and upset, and a small cry escaped my lips as my heart began to beat more rapidly – I didn't like seeing her in this form. She was nothing like the woman who had been a mother to me and my brothers. Her body was covered in scales very similar to Slake's, and sharp talons sprouted from her fingers and toes, but her folded wings were exactly as I remembered them – covered in white feathers. Then, as I watched, to my relief, she began to change.

The wings shrank rapidly, withering back into the shoulders; the scales melted away, to be replaced by a long dark skirt and blouse and a green shawl. The most significant change was to the eyes: they softened, lost their cruelty and were filled with warmth; then she smiled, radiating love.

It was Mam just as she had been back on the farm;

the woman who had loved my dad, raised seven sons and been the local midwife and healer. And it seemed to me that she wasn't simply an apparition; she looked as solid a presence here as she'd ever been in our farmhouse kitchen.

Tears were running down my cheeks now, and I stepped forward to embrace her. The smile slipped from her face, she stepped backwards and held up a hand as if to ward me off. I stared at her, baffled, as my tears of joy changed to those of rejection and hurt.

Mam smiled again. 'Dry your eyes, son,' she said softly. 'More than anything in the world I would love to give you a hug, but it just isn't possible. Your spirit is still clothed in human flesh, whereas mine has a very different covering. Were we to touch, your life would be over. And you're needed in this world. You still have much to do. Maybe even more than you realize.'

I rubbed my eyes with the backs of my hands and did my best to smile back. 'Sorry, Mam – I understand. It's just so good to see you again.'

'And it's good to see you too. But now we must get down to business. I cannot remain in this world for more than a few minutes at a time.'

'It's all right, Mam. Just tell me what I have to do.'

'You now have the dagger and also, through your own endeavours, the sword in your possession. The third artefact is to be found in the dark. It is hidden right at the heart of the Fiend's lair – under the throne within his citadel. Slake will instruct you on the ritual that needs to be performed, and with those three sacred objects in your possession you will be able to destroy the Fiend for all time. I had only two but was still able to hobble him. You will complete what I began.'

'I'll do my best,' I told her. 'I want you to be proud of me.'

'Whatever happens, Tom, I'll always love you and be proud of you – but now we come to the really difficult part . . . Even if I'd had all three objects, I would still have failed – because the most important part of the ritual is the sacrifice of the person you love best on this earth. In your case it is *she* whom you most love.'

I was appalled and opened my mouth, but no words came out. Finally I managed to speak. 'You, Mam? I have to sacrifice *you*?'

'No, Tom,' she replied. 'It must be a living person, and although I know you still love me, there is one now living in this world whom you care for even more.'

'No, Mam!' I cried. 'That's not true!'

'Look into your heart, son, and you will see that it is true. Every mother must face the time when her son cares for another woman more.'

She was telling me something that, deep down, I already knew. The full import of her words dawned on me.

'No! No! You can't mean that!' I protested.

'Yes, son, it grieves me to say so but there is no other way. In order to destroy the Fiend, you must sacrifice Alice.'

CHAPTER 5

ANOTHER USE FOR THE GIRL

'I must take Alice's life?' I cried. 'Is there no other means?'

'It is the only way, Tom – the price that must be paid – and she must offer her life willingly. So I leave it to your own judgement when you tell her what must be done.

'I faced something very similar but was unable to do it,' Mam continued. 'My sisters tried to persuade me to kill your father or give him to them to devour. Then, later, they begged me to use him as a sacrifice to enhance the power of my magic. Without all three sacred objects, it would not have succeeded in destroying the Fiend, but I would have increased the limitations on his power. I decided against it because there was already a spark of love between me and your father – and I saw the future: how I could give birth to you, the seventh son of a seventh son, and forge you as a weapon to destroy the Fiend.'

Mam's words disturbed me. She was describing me as if I were an asset, something to be used against our enemy, rather than a cherished son.

'But I think you will prove to be more disciplined than I was: you have a strong sense of duty, its seed planted by your father and nurtured by John Gregory. Not only that – my powerful blood flows within your veins, along with my gifts. Use everything that I have bequeathed to you. You *must* destroy the Fiend, whatever the cost, or the consequences will be terrible. Imagine a world completely in thrall to the dark! There would be famine, disease and lawlessness. Families would be divided; brother would kill brother. The Fiend's servants would be unchecked, preying on men, women and children, devouring their flesh and drinking their blood. And where would you be, son? You would know that it was your failure that had brought about that horror. Even worse – you would no longer care because you would have lost yourself; yielded your soul to the Fiend. All that could come to pass unless you act decisively. The people of the County and the wider world beyond need you to perform this deed. I am sure you won't let them down – despite the cost to you personally. I'm sorry, son, but I can stay no longer. Destroy the Fiend – that's what is important. It is your destiny! It is why you were born.'

Mam began to fade and I called out desperately. 'Please, Mam, don't go yet. We need to talk some more. There's got to be another way. This can't be right! I can't believe what you're asking me to do!'

As she faded, she changed back into the fierce lamia with the feathered wings. The last thing I saw was her cruel eyes. Then she was gone.

The room was immediately plunged into darkness so, with shaking hands, I eased the tinderbox out of my pocket and managed to light the candle. Next I sat down on the floor beside the trunk and examined the tinderbox, turning it over and over in my hands. It had been the last thing Dad had given me when I left home to become John Gregory's apprentice. I could see him now in my mind's eye and I remembered his exact words:

I want you to have this, son. It might come in useful in your new job. And come back and see us soon. Just because you've left home, it doesn't mean that you can't come back and visit.

The tinderbox had certainly proved useful in my line of work and I'd used it many times.

Poor Dad! He'd worked hard on the farm but had not lived to enjoy his retirement. I thought back to the story of how he'd met Mam in Greece. Dad was a sailor then, and he'd found her bound to a rock with a silver chain. Mam had always been vulnerable to sunlight, and her enemies had left her to die on a mountainside. But Dad had saved her, shielding her from the sun.

Before sailing back to the County with her to begin his new life as a farmer, Dad had stayed at her house in Greece. Something he'd told me about his time there made sense now. Mam's two sisters sometimes came after dark, and the three of them danced around a fire in the walled garden; he'd heard them arguing and thought that the sisters had taken against him: they used to glare at him through the window, looking really angry, and Mam would wave him away.

The two sisters were the lamias Wynde and Slake, who'd then been transported to the County hidden in Mam's trunks. They continued to argue with her, and now I knew why. They had been trying to persuade her to strengthen the hobble on the Fiend by sacrificing Dad.

I was roused from my thoughts by the sound of someone coming up the steps into the storeroom. I realized that it was Slake, who no longer walked and moved like a human being. The sight of her in the flickering candlelight chilled me to the bone. Her wings were folded but her claws were extended, as if ready to attack me. Instead she smiled and I rose to my feet.

'Has Zenobia spoken to you?' she asked, her voice harsher than before. I had to concentrate hard to understand what she was saying.

'Yes, but I don't like what I've been asked to do.'

'Ah! You mean the sacrifice. She said that it would be hard for you, but that you were a dutiful son and had the strength to do what was necessary.'

'Strength and duty – they're just words!' I said bitterly. 'Mam couldn't do it; why should I?'

I stared at Slake, trying to control my anger. Had the lamia and her sister had their way, Dad would have died in Greece, and my brothers and I would never have been born.

'Calm yourself,' she said. 'You need time to think – time to meditate upon that which must be done. And you cannot deal with the Fiend unless the third sacred object is in your possession. To find that must be your priority.'

'That artefact lies in the dark – and, moreover, under the very throne of the Fiend,' I responded, full of rage now. 'How am I supposed to lay my hands on that?'

'It is not you who must do it. We have another use for the girl. Alice has spent time in the dark already. Not only will she find it relatively easy to return there, she will be familiar with the Fiend's domain. And so long as his head remains separated from his body, the danger will be much reduced.'

'No!' I shouted. 'I can't ask her to do that. After her first visit she almost lost her mind.'

'The second one will be easier,' insisted Slake. 'She will gradually become immune to the adverse effects.'

'But at what cost?' I retorted. 'By becoming closer

and closer to the dark until she belongs to it entirely?'

The lamia did not reply. Instead she reached into the trunk and handed me a piece of paper. 'Read this first,' she said. 'It is written in my hand but was dictated to me by your mother.'

I accepted the paper, and with shaking hands began to read:

The Dark Lord wished that I return to his fold and make obeisance to him once more. For a long time I resisted while taking regular counsel from my friends and supporters. Some advised that I bear his child, the means used by witches to be rid of him for ever. But even the thought was abhorrent to me.

At the time I was tormented by a decision that I must soon make. Enemies had seized me, taking me by surprise . . .

Mam then went on to repeat what I already knew – how she'd been bound to a rock with a silver chain and rescued by a sailor. That sailor had been Dad, of course – he'd told me the story not long before he died. I knew the rest of it too – how Dad had been given shelter in her house. But her next words chilled me to the bone.

. . . It soon became clear that my rescuer had feelings for me. I was grateful for what he had done, but he was a mere human and I felt no great physical attraction to him.

I felt a pain in my heart at those words. I thought Mam and Dad had loved each other from the beginning. Dad had made it sound that way, anyway. It was what he'd believed. I had to force myself to keep on reading.

However, when I learned that he was the seventh son of his father, a plan began to take shape within my mind. If I were to bear him sons, the seventh would have special powers when dealing with the dark. Not only that, the child would carry some of my attributes, gifts that would augment his other powers. Thus, this child might one day have the ability to destroy the Fiend. It was not easy to decide what to do. Bearing his seventh child might give me the means to finally destroy my enemy. Yet John Ward was just a poor sailor. He came from farming stock. Even if I bought him a farm of his own, I would still have to live that life with him, the stench of the farmyard forever in my nostrils.

Thinking of poor Dad, I stifled a sob. There was no mention of love here. All Mam seemed to care about was destroying the Fiend. Dad was just a means to achieving that end. Maybe that's all I was too?

My sisters' counsel was that I kill him or give him to them. I refused because I owed him my life. The choice was between turning him out of my house so he could find a ship to take him home or, returning with him.

I glanced up from the sheet of paper and glared at Slake, who extended her claws in anger at my reaction. This was one of the two lamias who had argued that Dad should be killed! I continued reading.

But to make the second option a possibility, I first had to hobble my enemy, the Fiend. This I did by subterfuge. I arranged a meeting on the Feast of Lammas – just the Fiend and me. After choosing my location carefully, I built a large bonfire, and at midnight made the necessary invocation to bring him temporarily into our world.

He appeared right in the midst of the flames, and I bowed to him and made what seemed like obeisance – but I was already muttering the words of a powerful spell and I had the two sacred objects in my hand. Despite all his attempts to thwart me, I successfully completed the hobble, paving the way for the next stage of my plan, which began with my voyage to the County and the purchase of a farm.

And so I became the wife of a farmer and bore him six sons and then, finally, a seventh whom we named Thomas Jason Ward; his first name chosen by his father, the second by me after a hero from my homeland of whom I was once fond.

We lamias are accustomed to shape-shifting, but the changes that time works on us can never be predicted. As the years passed I grew to accept my lot and to love my husband. I moved gradually closer and closer to the light, and eventually became a healer and a midwife, helping my neighbours whenever I could. Thus it was that a human, John Ward, the man who saved me, moved me down a path I had not foreseen.

The end of the letter made me feel a little better. At least Mam was saying now that she'd loved Dad. She'd gradually changed and become more human. I gave a sudden shiver, realizing that now the opposite was true: she was leaving her humanity behind and had evolved into something very different to the mother I remembered. What she was asking was unthinkable.

'Mam said she held *two* sacred objects,' I told Slake. 'Why is the second one of those now in the dark?'

'Do you think it was easy to hobble the Fiend?' she

hissed, once more extending her talons. She opened her mouth very wide, showing me her teeth, and saliva began to drip from her jaws. For a moment I thought she intended to attack me, but then she slowly let out her breath and continued to speak.

'There was a great struggle despite Zenobia's magic. The Fiend snatched up one of the objects as he was hurled back into the dark. These are Zenobia's instructions for the ritual . . . Read them now!' she commanded, handing me a second piece of paper.

I took it, folding it and putting it in my pocket. 'I'll read it tomorrow,' I said. 'I've already learned too many things that aren't to my taste.'

Slake growled deep in her throat, but I turned my back on her and went up the steps to the battlements. I didn't want to see Alice yet. I had to think things through first.

CHAPTER 6
HALF A TALE

I paced the battlements of Malkin Tower, backwards and forwards, backwards and forwards, like someone demented. As I walked, my mind twisted this way and that, trapped in a labyrinth; no matter which avenue of escape I explored, I always returned to the two questions that tormented me.

Should I tell Alice that she had to go into the dark again? And after that, was I prepared to make such a sacrifice? Could I really take Alice's life?

The night passed slowly as I agonized over what I should do. Finally I leaned on the parapet, staring west over the trees of Crow Wood. Gradually the sky began to lighten, until the massive bulk of Pendle Hill was visible. There, in that pale dawn light, I began to read the letter outlining the ritual by which the Fiend could finally be destroyed.

The destruction of the Fiend may be achieved by the following means. Firstly the three sacred objects must be to hand. They are the hero swords forged by Hephaestus. The greatest of these is the Destiny Blade; the second is the dagger called Bone Cutter, which will be given to you by Slake. The third is the dagger named Dolorous, sometimes called the Blade of Sorrow, which you must retrieve from the dark.

The place is also important. It must be one especially conducive to the use of magic. Thus the ritual must be carried out on a high hill east of Caster, which is known as the Wardstone.

That was a strange coincidence. I was to attempt to destroy the Fiend on a hill that bore my own name! I shivered as if someone had walked over my grave – then continued to read.

First the blood sacrifice should be made in this precise manner. A fire must be constructed – one capable of generating great heat. To achieve this it will be necessary to build a forge.

Throughout the ritual the willing sacrificial victim must display great courage. If she once cries out to betray her pain, all will be lost and the rite will fail.

Using the dagger Bone Cutter, the thumb-bones must be taken from the right hand of the victim and cast into the flames. Only if she does not cry out may the second cut be made to remove the bones of the left hand. These also are added to the fire.

Next, using the dagger Dolorous, the heart must be cut out of the victim and, still beating, cast into the flames.

The full implications of what was being asked

suddenly became clear in my mind. Alice was being asked to retrieve the blade Dolorous – which would then be used in the disgusting ceremony to cut out her heart. She was being asked to venture into the dark to seize the very weapon that would slay her!

It was appalling. I shuddered at the thought of carrying out such a task.

Then I heard someone climbing the steps towards me. I recognized the click of Alice's pointy shoes and hastily stuffed the letter into my breeches pocket. Seconds later she emerged onto the battlements behind me.

'Did you see your mam?' she asked, placing her hand on my shoulder. 'How did it go? You seem upset. I can feel you trembling.'

'I am upset,' I admitted. 'She's changed terribly. She doesn't seem at all like the mam I remember.'

'Oh, Tom!' Alice cried. 'Everybody changes. If you were to step into the head of your future self years from now, you'd no doubt be appalled by how different you were and how much your thoughts and feelings had altered. We're changing all the time, but it's so gradual we don't notice it happening. And for lamias it's much more rapid and marked. Your mam can't help it, Tom. It's in her nature – but she still loves you.'

'Does she?' I said, turning to face her.

She stared at me. 'What is it, Tom? There's something wrong, isn't there? Something you haven't told me.'

I gazed into Alice's eyes and made a decision. I would tell her *part* of what I knew – that she was being asked to go into the dark again. But there was no way I could tell her that she would have to be sacrificed to finally defeat the Fiend. That was impossible. The ritual was horrible, and I knew I was incapable of carrying out such an act on my worst enemy, let alone my best friend.

So there on the battlements, in the grey light of dawn, with the raucous cries of crows in the background, I gave her half a tale.

'There's something I've got to tell you, Alice,' I said. 'It's terrible but you have to know. There are three sacred objects needed to bind the Fiend for all time. I already have the first two – my sword and a dagger called Bone Cutter. But the third of the hero swords is also a dagger and it's hidden in the dark under the Fiend's throne. They want *you* to go into the dark and get it, Alice – but I said I wouldn't let you.'

For a moment Alice was quiet, all the while staring intently into my eyes. 'What do you know about the ritual itself, Tom? What has to be done?'

'I'll be told that later – once we have the three objects,' I lied.

After I'd finished we were both silent for a long time. I stared up at the sky, watching the small clouds race eastwards, their edges tinged with red and pink from the rising sun. Then suddenly Alice rushed into my arms and we hugged each other tightly. As we did so, I knew that I could never sacrifice her; there *had* to be another way.

When we finally broke apart, Alice looked up at me. 'If it's the only way, then I'll go into the dark and get what we need,' she said.

'No, Alice! Don't even think of it. There must be something else we can do!'

'But what if there isn't, Tom? Grimalkin can't keep the Fiend's head out of the hands of our enemies for ever. They'll never give up. Everywhere we go is dangerous because they're always at our heels. They waited for us here, didn't they? And eventually the Fiend will return with all his power. We'll be snatched away into the dark for an eternity of torment. At least this way only one of us has to go. I have to venture into the dark whatever the cost. And I'll be coming back. Ain't going to stay there for ever, am I?'

'No, you can't go into the dark,' I insisted. 'I won't let you.'

'It's my decision, Tom, not yours. There's still more than five months till Halloween, but the sooner I get that dagger, the better.'

'You can't go back there, Alice!' I cried. 'Remember what it did to you last time.'

'That was different, Tom. I was snatched away by the Fiend. Well, he ain't there now, and the dark is weakened because of it. And I've a lot of power of my own. I can look after myself, don't you worry!'

I didn't reply. Even if Alice succeeded, she would only have moved things nearer to the point where she was supposed to die. Mam's second letter was in my pocket, and there it would stay.

We stayed in the tower for the remainder of the daylight hours, planning to leave after dark, when it would be easier to slip away unseen.

While Alice went down into the tunnel to pay another visit to Agnes, I had a short conversation with Slake. In her presence I read through the remainder of Mam's letter and was able to question her about things that were unclear. The more I learned, the worse it got. By the end of our discussion I was close to despair.

At last it was time to leave. While Alice waited for me, I turned to the lamia. 'I may never return here,' I told her. 'You are free to go.'

'It is not for you to dismiss me,' Slake hissed. 'I will stay here until after Halloween. Then, when the Fiend has been dealt with, I will burn the trunks and leave to seek out others of my kind.'

'And if he is not dealt with?'

'Then it will go badly for all of us. If you fail, the consequences do not bear thinking about. You *must* do what is required.'

'It is not for you to tell me what to do!' I retorted. 'I make my own decisions. However, you have my gratitude. If ever you need my help, call me and I will stand at your side.'

As we left the lamia, Alice stared at me in astonishment. I knew why: those final words had flown out of my mouth without thought, but I realized that I meant every word. That night on Pendle Hill, when the Fiend had been summoned by the covens, Slake and her sister had fought to save us. We would have died there but for their intervention. Here, guarding the tower, Wynde had been lost. And although it was difficult to accept, she was distant kin – a descendant of Mam's – so I owed her no less than what had been promised.

'Do you know what I think, Tom?' Alice said as we began to descend the steps. 'You talked about your mam having changed, but you've changed too. You made that promise to Slake without any thought of what Old Gregory might say. You're more of a spook than he is now.'

I made no reply. It saddened me to think of my master in decline, but I knew that Alice was right. As he had told me the previous day, I needed to act and think like the spook that I would become. We were heading into an uncertain future, but things were approaching a climax. Soon, for good or ill, it would be over.

Agnes was waiting for us near the exit of the tunnel. There were flies buzzing about her head and dried streaks of blood around her mouth. She smelled of loam and things that slithered underground.

'We're going back to Chipenden,' Alice told the dead witch. 'I'll come back and see you when I can.'

Agnes nodded, and a grey maggot fell out of her hair and writhed at her feet. 'Come and see me in the dell when your need is great. You too, Thomas Ward. You also have a friend amongst the dead.'

Alice gave the witch an affectionate pat on the shoulder and we crept along the tunnel cautiously, emerging through the sepulchre to stand amongst the thickets that covered the graveyard.

Alice sniffed three times. 'There are half a dozen witches here but they're all dead. Agnes has been busy!'

So we hurried north, then west, skirting the edge of Pendle to head directly for Chipenden. Agnes was our ally and friend, but I noticed that Alice had not bothered to tell her about her journey into the dark. Dead witches changed, moving away from human concerns, and Agnes was no longer someone Alice could confide in.

CHAPTER 7
CROSSING IT IS DANGEROUS

As we crossed the Spook's garden, the dogs raced towards us, barking excitedly, and I had to spend a few minutes patting them and being licked in return. I thought the disturbance would have brought my master out to greet us, but there was no sign of him. Was there something wrong? I wondered. Had he gone off on spook's business?

But then I saw the smoke rising from the kitchen chimney and was reassured. When I led the way inside, I saw a stranger sitting by the fire talking to John Gregory. Both men rose to their feet and turned to face me.

'This is Tom Ward, my apprentice,' said the Spook.

'And that's the girl, Alice, who I've been telling you about. And this is Judd Brinscall, lad, one of my ex-apprentices. He's come all the way from Todmorden to escort us back there.'

'Mistress Fresque is a friend of mine, Tom,' Judd said with a smile. 'She's a Romanian, but now lives in Todmorden, and she sent me to find out what's delayed your master's visit to her library.' Judd Brinscall was shorter than my master and slight of build. He appeared to be in his mid-forties, but his face was lined and weather-beaten, suggesting that he had spent most of his life outdoors. His blond hair was starting to recede, but his eyebrows were black, making a strange contrast. He wore the hood and gown of a spook, but unlike ours, his was green with streaks of brown and yellow.

I remembered his name because it was amongst the most prominent ones scratched upon my bedroom wall here at Chipenden – the room used by all the boys my master had trained.

'You're staring at my gown,' he said with a faint smile. 'Once I wore one almost identical to yours, Tom. But there's a reason for it. When I'd finished my time here with Mr Gregory, he offered to let me work with him for a couple more years to develop my skills as a spook further. That would have been the sensible thing to do, but I'd endured five long years learning my trade in the County and I had the wanderlust. I needed to visit new places while I was still young – particularly Romania, the land my mother's family come from.

'I travelled far, crossed the sea and eventually ended up there. I spent two years studying under one of the local spooks in the province of Transylvania and substituted this gown for my own. It provides n-ecessary camouflage when journeying through the forest.'

'Well, lad,' interrupted the Spook, turning to me, his face filled with concern. 'How did things go at Malkin Tower? Sit yourself down and tell me all about it.'

So, while Alice remained standing, I took my place at the table and began my tale. At first I was hesitant, feeling a little uncomfortable about revealing so much in front of a stranger.

My master must have noticed my disquiet. 'Spit it out, lad! You needn't clam up in front of Judd here. We go back a long way.'

So I told my master part of what I had learned – though nothing of the ritual itself, which he would not have countenanced. I told the same lie I'd given Alice – pretended that the next course of action would be revealed only when all three hero swords were in my possession. And, of course, I did not reveal the worst thing of all – that I must sacrifice Alice to achieve our aims.

It saddened me to lie by omission in that way, but perhaps not as much as it might once have done. I was becoming harder, and I knew that what I did was for the best. A great burden of responsibility was being thrust upon my shoulders and I had to learn to bear it alone.

When I'd finished, both spooks stared hard at Alice. 'Well, girl?' asked my master. 'It's asking a lot, but are you prepared to attempt what's required? Will you go back into the dark?'

'There's got to be another way!' I said angrily. 'We can't ask Alice to do this.'

Neither spook said a word; both cast their eyes down and stared at the table. Their silence said everything. I felt bitter. Alice was nothing to them. Judd Brinscall had only just met her, and my master had never learned to trust her, despite what she'd been through with us; despite all those times she'd saved our lives.

'I'll do what's necessary,' Alice said in a quiet voice, 'but I want to be sure that it's the only way. I need time to think. And I need to talk to Grimalkin. She ain't that far away, so I'll go and find her. I shouldn't be away more than a few days.'

The next morning Alice headed north to find the witch assassin. I gave her a hug at the edge of the garden.

'Whatever you decide, Alice, don't go off into the dark until we've spoken again. Do you promise?'

'I promise, Tom. Wouldn't go without saying goodbye, would I?'

I watched her walk off into the distance, my throat constricting with emotion.

Within the hour, after leaving the three dogs in the care of the village blacksmith, my master, Judd Brinscall and I had departed too. Although he'd cried off from the journey to Pendle, the Spook seemed happy enough to head for Todmorden. His knees were feeling better and his stride showed its usual energy. As we walked, the three of us talked.

'Do you know what I miss about the old house?' Judd said.

'For me, it's the roof and the library,' the Spook joked, 'and it gladdens my heart to see that both are being attended to!'

'Well, I miss the boggart!' exclaimed Judd. 'It might have burned the bacon occasionally, but it always did the washing-up and kept the garden safe from intruders. It scared me at first but eventually I grew quite fond of it.'

'It scared me too,' I said. 'It gave me a clout behind the ear when I came down to breakfast too early on my first day. But my memories of it are mostly good.'

'Aye,' my master agreed. 'It warned us of danger and saved our lives on more than one occasion. It will certainly be missed.'

We broke our journey in the village of Oswaldtwistle, the Spook leading us directly to its one and only tavern, the Grey Man.

'Money might be short at present but my old bones are begging for a warm bed tonight, lad,' he told me.

'I can pay for our accommodation,' Judd said. 'I know you've had a hard time of it.'

'Nay, Judd, put your money away – I won't hear of it.'

Our finances were limited because my master needed most of what he had recently accumulated to pay for the repairs to his house. Whenever he did a job, he often had to wait to be paid; sometimes until after the next harvest. That he was willing to pay for rooms now showed how weary he must still be feeling. During the last couple of years our struggles against the dark had taken a lot out of him. But he was proud as well, and wouldn't let an ex-apprentice pay for his lodgings.

A few locals sat gossiping in the corner by the huge fire, sipping ale from pint tankards, but we were the only diners. We tucked into huge plates of beef and roasted potatoes swimming in delicious gravy.

I looked at the Spook. 'You said your work had never taken you to Todmorden, so I wonder how Mistress Fresque knew about your library and what happened to it . . . Did *you* tell her, Judd?' I asked.

'Aye, that I did. I've not been back in the County for more than a few weeks. I wanted to return months ago, but it was still occupied by enemy troops. As soon as I arrived, I looked up Cosmina Fresque, an old friend from Romania, who kindly provided me with a roof over my head while I found my feet. She said she had some books to sell – so, of course, I told her about you. She travelled to Chipenden herself, and en route found out about the sad loss of your library.'

'She should have visited us rather than just leaving a note,' said the Spook.

'She didn't want to disturb you when you were busy with all the rebuilding,' Judd explained.

'She'd have been very welcome,' my master said. 'You too, Judd. Why didn't you bring her up to the house?'

'As much as I'd have loved to visit, I can't afford to pass up the chance of paid work. There was a boggart to be dealt with just over the County border, so duty called!'

'It's an unusual name, Todmorden,' I commented. 'I wonder where it came from. Does it mean anything?'

'All names mean something,' said the Spook. 'It's just that some are so old that their origins have long been forgotten. Some say the name is derived from two words from the Old Tongue: *tod*, which means death, and *mor* – which also means death!'

'But others dispute that,' Judd said. 'They claim the name means the Valley of the Marsh Fox.'

The Spook smiled. 'Human memory is fallible and the truth is sometimes lost for ever, lad.'

'Was your dad from the County, Judd?' I asked.

'That he was, Tom, but he died in the first year of my apprenticeship, and then my mother returned to Romania to be with her family there.'

I nodded in understanding. My own dad had died during the first year of my apprenticeship and my mam had gone back to Greece. We'd endured similar things and I knew how he felt.

I'd previously met three of my master's ex-apprentices. All of them were dead now. First there was Morgan, who'd served the dark and had been killed by Golgoth, one of the Old Gods. Secondly, there'd been Father Stocks, murdered by the witch Wurmalde. Most recently, in Greece, Bill Arkwright had died fighting a heroic rearguard action while we made our escape.

I'd hated Morgan, who'd been a bully, but had grown to like Father Stocks – and even Bill eventually, though he'd given me a difficult time at first. And now

I felt the same way about Judd. He seemed an amiable man. The life of a spook could be very lonely. I hoped that I was about to make a new friend.

The next day we strode east across the moors until late in the afternoon. Then, after we'd passed through another small village, three steep-sided valleys came into view below us. In the middle lay the small town of Todmorden. I saw that it was hemmed in by dense woods which extended up the slopes. The Spook had told me that the place had a river running through it; the far bank lay beyond the County border. There was something odd about the layout of the town though. Not only was it divided by the river but there was a swath of trees on either bank, as if nobody had wanted to build a house too close to the water.

'Well, I'm sorry, but this is where we part company,' Judd said.

'After coming all this way I thought you'd have been guiding us to Mistress Fresque's door and introducing us,' the Spook said, evidently surprised.

'Regretfully, I have to decline. You see, I have unfinished business across the moors to the south. It's that boggart I told you about. I drove it out of one farmhouse and it immediately made its home in another. But you'll have no trouble locating the Fresque house. Just ask anyone for Bent Lane. The mistress is expecting you.'

'What's she like, this Mistress Fresque?' asked the Spook. 'How did you come to meet her?'

'She's a kind woman, but with a good head for business and practical matters,' Judd replied. 'I'm sure you'll get along fine. I met her on my travels. She gave me my first taste of Romanian hospitality.'

'Ah, well, spook's business comes first,' said my master. 'But we hope to see you again before we leave. I expect we'll be here for one night at least.'

'Of course, I'll see you tomorrow. Give my regards to Mistress Fresque!'

Judd gave us a nod, then set off southwards, and without further ado the Spook led the way down the steep track towards the town.

The narrow cobbled streets were bustling with people going about their business. There were market stalls, and street hawkers selling food and trinkets from trays. Todmorden seemed just like any other small

County town, but there was one difference: its inhabitants all looked grim-faced and unfriendly.

The first man my master sought directions from ignored him and walked straight past us, with the collar of his jacket turned up against the wind. At the second attempt he had a little more success. He approached an elderly, florid-faced gentleman who was walking along with the aid of a stick. He looked like a farmer, with his broad leather belt and big heavy boots.

'Can you please tell us the whereabouts of Bent Lane?' my master asked.

'I could – but I'm not sure if I should,' said the man. 'You see, it lies across the bridge on the other side of the river. The people over there are foreigners and best kept well clear of!' With that he nodded and continued on his way.

The Spook shook his head in disbelief. 'You wouldn't credit it, lad,' he said. 'Just a few paces across a river and you become a "foreigner"! They're just folks like us that happen to be from another county, that's all!'

We walked as far as the narrow wooden bridge, which was the only obvious point at which the river could be crossed. It was falling into disrepair – a few of the planks were missing and others were partially rotted through; it was just wide enough to accommodate a horse and cart, but only the foolhardy would risk taking one across. It seemed odd that nobody had thought to mend it.

From here, the part of the town on the other side of the river looked no different to the part on the County side. Beyond the trees I saw the same small stone houses and cobbled streets, though they seemed deserted. I thought we were about to cross, but the Spook pointed back to a tavern on the County side.

'Let's save ourselves some trouble, lad, and ask someone who might be able to give us precise directions. We could kill two birds with one stone by finding somewhere to spend the night.'

We entered a small tavern whose sign proclaimed its name: THE RED FOX. The room was empty, but there was a fire in the grate and a balding sour-faced man in a leather apron was washing pewter tankards behind the bar.

'We're looking for the house of Mistress Fresque,' said the Spook. 'I believe that she lives at the top of

Bent Lane somewhere across the river. Could you be so kind as to give us directions?'

'It's on the other side of the river, all right,' said the man, not answering the question. 'And crossing the river is dangerous. Few do so from this side. You'll be the first this year.'

'Well, it's certainly in need of urgent maintenance,' said the Spook. 'But I don't think it's quite ready to fall into the river yet. Are you the innkeeper?'

The man put down the tankard he'd been drying and stared hard at the Spook for a few seconds. My master returned his gaze calmly.

'Yes, I'm the innkeeper. Do you require food and drink, or maybe a bed for the night?'

'We might need all three,' said the Spook. 'A lot depends on how our business goes.'

'Cross the bridge,' the man said at last, 'then take the third street along on your left. It leads to Bent Lane. The house of Mistress Fresque is the big one right at the end of the lane up in the woods. It's hidden by trees so you won't see it until you're very close. And stay on the path. There are bears in the vicinity.'

'Thanks for that.' The Spook turned to go. 'It may well be that we'll see you later.'

'Well, if you do require rooms, make sure you're back before sunset,' the landlord called after us. 'The doors are locked and barred then, and I'll be safe in my bed well before dark. If you have any sense, you'll follow my example.'

CHAPTER 8
A STUDY OF THE MOROI

'What kind of tavern shuts its doors so early?' I asked my master as we strode towards the bridge.

'It's obviously one that doesn't really welcome strangers, lad! That's clear enough.'

'I didn't think there were any bears left in the County,' I said.

'They are certainly rare. The last time I glimpsed one was over twenty years ago. It sounds like most of 'em have crossed the border to live here!' the Spook said with a smile.

'So what's that innkeeper scared of?' I asked. 'Why

does he need to get to bed before the sun goes down and make so much fuss about locking his doors?'

'Your guess is as good as mine. But this town doesn't seem a very friendly place. Maybe there are robbers lurking after dark. Maybe they don't get on with the people across the river. Sometimes there are grudges and feuds between families. It wouldn't take much for folk from different counties to imagine all sorts of grievances.'

We turned into Bent Lane, which soon started to rise steeply. The few houses were, without exception, unoccupied, their windows boarded up against the elements. Soon the trees took over, and the further we walked, the closer they crowded in until they formed a claustrophobic leafy archway over our heads that shut out the sun and made everything very gloomy.

'I wonder why they call it Bent Lane,' I said. 'It's not the slightest bit crooked.'

The Spook nodded. 'You seem very interested in words and their meanings today, lad.'

'I do find place names interesting,' I told him. 'Especially County ones, and the way their meaning sometimes changes over time. It's funny how the word

Pendle once meant "hill". But now we use that word with it and call it Pendle Hill.'

There was another place name that had been lurking in my mind since I first read it in Mam's instructions – the Wardstone, a hill that lay to the east of Caster, which I hadn't even known existed. Why did it carry my name? Was it just a coincidence that the ritual to destroy the Fiend had to be carried out there? My mind immediately turned to Alice and the terrible things that had to be done to her. Shuddering, I thrust the thought to the back of my mind and forced myself to concentrate on what the Spook was saying.

'That's true enough. And you're right – places sometimes have very old names from an era when the word meant something totally different. Their origins are lost in the mists of time.'

Suddenly I realized that it was very quiet; unnaturally so. I was about to mention it to my master, but before I could speak he halted and pointed ahead to what must surely be the home of Mistress Fresque.

'Well, lad, I've never seen anything quite like that before. I'm no architect, but I know what's pleasing to the eye, and that house is a very odd mixture of styles.'

It was large, with the central part built in the shape of a letter E, like many grand County mansions. But other sections had been added in a higgledy-piggledy manner, as if each new owner had felt compelled to build on, giving no thought to what already existed; many different types of stone and brick had been used, and the towers and turrets lacked any symmetry – there was no sense of balance and harmony at all. But there was something else that added to my sense of disquiet.

It was the trees, which crowded in around the house as if demanding entry. Most people would have cleared the saplings when they first started to sprout, or at least cut them back. But nothing had been done at all. Trees draped their branches over the roof or leaned against the walls as if trying to push them over. One had even grown right out of the path outside the front door. Anyone leaving or entering the house would have to step around it. It was gloomy too; the sun could not find a way through the leaf canopy.

'The place has been badly neglected,' said the Spook. 'I hope the library is in better condition! Anyway, we'll find out soon enough.'

It was surprising to see the house in such a state.

Judd had said that Mistress Fresque was a practical woman. So why would she allow the trees to grow up like that? It didn't make sense.

There was no surrounding wall or gate; the path we'd been using continued right up to the front door. Walking round the tree that blocked his path, the Spook went up and rapped on it twice.

There was no answer so he tried again. Once more I noticed how quiet it was. It was a real contrast to my master's house at Chipenden which, at this time of year, was surrounded by birdsong. It was as if something huge and threatening was lurking nearby, sending all the forest creatures into hiding.

I was just about to comment on this to my master when I heard footsteps approaching the door. Then a key was turned in the lock and it slowly opened inwards. A girl was standing before us, holding a candle in one hand and a big bunch of keys in the other. She was slim and pretty and couldn't have been more than eighteen or nineteen years of age. She was dressed simply in a black dress that came down to her ankles; it contrasted with her long, reddish fair hair, which was pulled back from her forehead by a coronet in the current fashion of well-to-do County women. Her face was very pale but her lips were painted red, and at the sight of us they widened into a smile and all my former unease evaporated away.

'Good afternoon,' she said in greeting. 'You must be John Gregory and his apprentice, Thomas Ward. I have heard so much about you. I am Mistress Fresque, but please use my first name. Call me Cosmina.'

I was immediately struck by her accent. She spoke English well but undoubtedly came from Romania, as Judd had explained. And despite her obvious youth, her eyes seemed to hold the experience and assurance of a much older woman.

'We are pleased to be here,' said the Spook, 'and are very much looking forward to examining your store of books. Judd Brinscall guided us here but had to leave on business.'

'Well, he is my guest, so we'll see him later – and you are most welcome. I bid you enter . . .' With those words she stepped aside, and the Spook and I crossed the threshold into the gloomy interior.

'Come with me,' she said. 'I will show you to the library.'

She turned on her heel and led us down a passageway lined with a wainscot painted a dark glossy brown. Right at the end, directly facing us, was an oval door. She selected a key from the bunch and turned it in the lock, and we followed her inside. Immediately I heard the Spook gasp in astonishment.

We were in a vast round tower and its walls were fitted with curved wooden shelves whose every inch was occupied by books. In the centre was a round oaken table, its surface highly polished, and three chairs. There was another door directly opposite the one we had come through.

This was an atrium, a circular space that extended right up to the conical roof. I glimpsed other floors – maybe six or seven – each furnished with books in the same way. The library must have contained thousands of books, and it was many times larger than the Spook's one at Chipenden.

'You are the owner of this vast library?' he asked in astonishment.

'Nobody can ever truly *own* a library such as this,' Mistress Fresque replied. 'It is a legacy from the past. I am just its keeper and preserver.'

The Spook nodded. He understood that. That was exactly the position he had taken towards his own library. It wasn't about ownership; it had been about keeping it safe for the use of future generations of spooks. Now it was gone, and he felt its loss keenly. I was really pleased for my master: now he might be able to start restocking it.

'I am the librarian, but I have the right to lend books or sell any which I consider surplus to requirements,' the girl went on.

'May I ask what percentage of this large collection of books actually relates to the dark?' asked the Spook.

'Approximately one seventh,' Mistress Fresque replied. 'In fact, the whole of this lowest floor. Why don't you examine the books at your leisure? I will bring you some refreshments.'

With these words she gave a little bow and left the room by the second door, closing it behind her.

'Well, lad,' said the Spook enthusiastically. 'Let's get to work.'

So we went to opposite sides of the circular room and began to look at the titles on the spines. Many were intriguing: a large leather-bound tome caught my eye: *Speculations on the Dark: Its Achilles Heel.*

I knew that Achilles was a hero from Greek history. At birth his mother had dipped him into a cauldron to bestow upon him the gift of invulnerability. Unfortunately she had held him by the heel, so this part was not immersed in the liquid. In later life an enemy had fired an arrow into that heel and he'd died. So this book probably told the reader how to find the secret weaknesses of creatures of the dark, which could lead to their destruction. I thought that might be well worth dipping into.

I was just about to lift it off the shelf when the Spook called me over. 'Come and look at what I've found, lad!'

In his hand was an open book. It was quite slim, but obviously its size was not linked to its importance. My master closed it and pointed to its cover. Engraved into the brown leather, high on the cover in silver letters was one word:

Doomdryte.

Below it, also embossed in silver, was an image that I instantly recognized. It was the head and forelimbs of a skelt.

'It's a grimoire, lad,' my master told me. 'In theory the most dangerous one that has ever existed. No doubt this is just a copy, but if accurate, its text could still bestow incredible power upon a practitioner of the dark arts. Some say it was dictated by the Fiend to a mage who tried to use its magic but was killed in the process. If one word of the incantation is wrong or mispronounced, the speaker is instantly destroyed. However, if a mage ever does manage to read it aloud accurately at one go – and that takes many hours – then he'd achieve god-like powers. He'd be invulnerable, and able to do terrible things with impunity.'

'Why has a skelt's head been used on the cover?' I asked.

The hilts of my sword, the Destiny Blade, and Bone Cutter, the dagger given to me by Slake, were formed in the likeness of a skelt's head. The sight of such an image on the cover of the most dangerous of all grimoires made me feel uneasy about the sword. At times it almost seemed sentient. Immediately before combat, blood dripped from the ruby eyes. Even though it was supposedly a 'hero sword', there was something of the dark about it, forged as it was by one of the Old Gods.

'Well, as you know, lad, the skelt has long been associated with witches who use blood magic – especially water witches. They keep one in a cage and let it loose to drain their prisoners. Once the creature is bloated with blood, they rip its living body to pieces with their bare hands and then devour it. This triples the power of the blood magic. I've always considered that a particularly nasty ritual – a creature that is most appropriate, don't you think, for the very worst of the grimoires?'

'You'd think such a dangerous book would be hidden away – not just placed casually on a shelf here. I wonder if Mistress Fresque knows what it is?'

'A librarian hasn't necessarily read all the books in her library, lad.'

'So you'll want this one for your own library?' I asked, more uneasy than ever.

'Nay, lad, not for my library. I want this book so that I can destroy it and prevent it from falling into the wrong hands.'

At that moment the far door opened and Mistress

Fresque backed into the room holding a tray, which she set down on the table. It was laid with a knife, three tankards of water, and a large plate with thick slices of bread and cold chicken, and two wedges of cheese; one was from the County but the other I didn't recognize.

I saw her glance at the book the Spook was holding, and it seemed to me that a flicker of annoyance briefly twisted her pretty face. It disappeared so quickly that immediately afterwards I wondered if I'd just imagined it. My master certainly didn't notice it; he had turned and was already replacing the *Doomdryte* on the shelf.

'You must be hungry after your journey – please help yourselves,' Mistress Fresque said, gesturing to the tray.

I sat down next to the Spook; our host sat some distance away, facing us across the table.

'Aren't you going to join us?' my master asked.

She shook her head and smiled. 'I've already eaten. Later I will prepare supper – you're welcome to stay for the night.'

The Spook neither accepted nor declined her invitation. He simply smiled, nodded and cut himself a piece of County cheese. I helped myself to some chicken. I often had more than my fill of cheese: this was the only thing I was allowed to nibble on when we were preparing to deal with the dark.

'What do you think of my library after your first brief inspection?' she asked.

'It's an astonishing collection,' my master said. 'There are so many books to choose from – which leads me to two questions. Firstly, how many books are you prepared to let go, and secondly, would you accept payment in stages? I'm involved in the expensive business of rebuilding my house at the moment.'

'The number of books you can take is, of necessity, limited. But I could see my way to selling maybe three hundred or so. The price of each will vary – some are rare indeed, while others could be replaced from other sources. There are just a few that I cannot allow to leave this library, but make your selection and we will see. It may not be a problem. As for price – we will negotiate, but I'm sure we can reach a compromise that will make us both happy. You needn't worry about paying for them all immediately. Indeed, the cost could be paid over the course of a couple of years if you wish.'

There was a question that had been bothering me. It was an impressive library, so why did she want to reduce the stock?

'Do you mind if I ask why you're selling some of your books? Is it just to help Mr Gregory?' I asked.

Mistress Fresque smiled and nodded. 'It is partly to help your master rebuild his own library. He has done much good work and deserves help in restocking that resource to leave to his heirs. But I must confess that I am also driven by a need to carry out repairs to my own house. I inherited it just five years ago when my uncle died. He was an old man who was set in his ways – he had a great love of trees. He could not bear to break a single twig, never mind cut down anything that encroached upon the house. There has been some damage done to the foundations, and I need to enlist the services of a forester to deal with the roots. I also need a stonemason to carry out repairs to the structure of the building.'

'Thank you, Mistress Fresque. Your offer to stagger the payments is kind and of necessity I must accept it,' said the Spook, 'but I can make a payment up front – one that will enable you to begin to attend to your own needs.'

I noted that my master had not addressed her by her first name, Cosmina, even though she had invited us to do so. Her superior manner and air of assurance made it seem inappropriate to be on first-name terms with her.

After we had finished our meal, Mistress Fresque took the tray and prepared to leave the room so that we could get on with our search. When she reached the doorway, she pointed to a cord hanging down beside one of the bookshelves. 'Pull that and it will ring a bell in my quarters. Do not hesitate to summon me if there if anything you need,' she said, giving us a smile as she left.

'Well, lad, what I suggest is that we place any books that take our fancy on the table. It doesn't matter if we take too many. We can make a final selection later and then return the remainder to the shelves.' He sighed and shook his head.

'What's the matter?' I asked. 'Aren't you happy to be able to choose from so many books?'

'Aye, lad, that's good – it's just that I know that some things can't be replaced. Just think of all those note-books written by past spooks that I had at Chipenden;

the history of their endeavours, how they solved problems and discovered new things about the dark . . . That's all gone for ever. We won't find such materials here.'

But the Spook was quickly proved wrong, for I soon found a book by one of his ex-apprentices – none other than Judd Brinscall!

'Look at this!' I cried, handing the book to him. It was a slim volume entitled *A Study of the Moroii*.

My master nodded in appreciation. 'He was a good apprentice, lad, one of the few who completed his time to my satisfaction. And during his travels abroad he's added to our store of knowledge. Moroii are Romanian elemental spirits. And I can tell that he knows his business because he's spelled moroii with two "i"s at the end, which is correct for the plural. He must have given this to Mistress Fresque. I'd certainly like it for my new Chipenden library.'

After more than three hours of debate and selection we had piled about three hundred and fifty books on the table. 'It's getting late, lad. I think it's time we were off. We'll come back first thing tomorrow,' said the Spook, putting his hand on my shoulder.

'Aren't we going to take up Mistress Fresque's offer to stay the night?'

'I think it's best if we get back to the tavern. There are a few things that I need to think through,' said the Spook, pulling the cord twice. I could hear nothing but knew that somewhere a bell would be ringing.

Within a minute Mistress Fresque had joined us; she smiled when she caught sight of the books on the table. 'I see that you have been busy.'

'That we have, but now we're tired,' said the Spook. 'So we'll come back in the morning, if you don't mind.'

'Won't you stay here tonight?' she said, looking very disappointed. 'You really are most welcome. I get so few visitors and would love to offer you further hospitality.'

'Your offer is very kind, but we don't want to put you to any trouble. Before we go there is one thing I'd like to ask . . .'

The Spook went over to the table and picked up the book by Judd Brinscall. 'This book by Judd – how would you feel if I bought it?'

'Judd gave it to me knowing that it would be safe here. But it is probably better suited to your new collection,' she replied. 'I have looked at the book – it is an excellent study of the elementals of my homeland.'

'You have lived most of your life in Romania?' my master asked.

'Yes, I was raised there. But my uncle left the country as a boy and spent most of his life in your land. On his death I came here to claim what he left me – this house and library and a very small income from his investments. I cannot draw on the capital – hence my need to sell books.'

After taking our leave we walked back through the trees towards the river. My master seemed lost in thought.

'Is there something wrong?' I asked.

The Spook nodded. 'It's just my instincts – they're telling me to be on my guard. Tell me, lad, when we were talking to Mistress Fresque, did you have any sense of a warning coldness? Anything at all?'

The Spook was asking if I had experienced the chill that told me something evil was close by. As seventh sons of seventh sons, we had the ability to sense witches, mages and other servants of the dark.

I shook my head. 'I felt nothing. Not the slightest hint.'

'Neither did I, lad. But some types of witch have the power to block our sensitivity to such things.'

'But earlier, just before we entered the house, I did sense something wrong. A feeling that we were being watched; that something dangerous was lurking close by,' I told my master.

'Well, that's one more reason to be alert and ready for anything.'

'Do you think she *might* be a witch?' I asked.

'I'm not jumping to conclusions, lad, but there are a few things bothering me. Why were there such a large number of books about the dark in that library? What would be the motive for acquiring them? Did her uncle have a special interest in such matters? If it weren't for the fact that Judd is a friend of hers, I'd be more than suspicious.'

'Do you trust Judd?'

The Spook nodded. 'He was a good apprentice, and once I'd have trusted him with my life. But folks can change . . .'

'There's something else too,' I told him. 'She saw you

holding the *Doomdryte* and I'll swear that, for a moment, she looked furious.'

'Then let's see how she reacts tomorrow when we tell her it's one of the books we've selected.'

CHAPTER 9
SEVENTH SONS

We left Bent Lane, made our way down to the riverbank, crossed the bridge and walked on until we reached the tavern. The sun was an orange orb sitting on the horizon, but it was already closed and locked. The Spook hammered on the front door with his staff several times. It was a while before the innkeeper unlocked it. He glanced towards the setting sun.

'Another five minutes and you'd have been too late,' he remarked. 'And you're certainly too late for supper.'

'We've eaten already,' my master told him. 'Two

rooms will do. And we'd like breakfast at the crack of dawn.'

Muttering to himself, the landlord locked and bolted the door behind us and then showed us to our rooms. As he was about to leave us, the Spook asked him a question.

'We hope to conclude our business with Mistress Fresque tomorrow and need to transport quite a large quantity of books. Do you know of anyone who might have a horse and cart for hire?'

The man scowled and shook his head. 'Nobody this side of the river will want to cross that bridge. We keep ourselves to ourselves.'

Before we could question him further, he left the room, still muttering under his breath.

'Well, that's a job for you tomorrow, lad. But first you can come up to the house and help me make a final choice.'

We retired to our own rooms, and it wasn't long before I drifted off into a dreamless sleep. However, for some reason I kept waking up. It seemed a very long night.

* * *

We had to wait over an hour for our breakfast because the innkeeper didn't rise until the sun was well up over the horizon.

The Spook wasn't best pleased but he didn't complain. We left our bags in our rooms and, clutching our staffs, were soon walking up Bent Lane once more.

'The service at the tavern isn't very good,' I remarked.

'That's very true, lad,' my master replied. 'But we have to make allowances. The innkeeper is a frightened man. I'm beginning to think that there's some threat from the dark on this side of the river. Or maybe there has been in the past. I'd like to get back to Chipenden with the books as soon as possible, but I think we should pay Todmorden another visit in the very near future.'

When Mistress Fresque showed us to the library, there was something a little colder or perhaps more hesitant in her manner. I looked about me and for a moment I grew dizzy. The feeling passed very quickly, but for a moment the shape of the room had appeared to change – along with the atrium. Yesterday I could have sworn it was a perfect circle. Today it looked more like an oval. Was I imagining it? I was probably just tired, I thought – I hadn't slept well.

She gestured at the table. 'You are going to make your final selection from these?' she asked.

'Mostly,' said the Spook, 'but we'll examine the shelves once more just in case we've missed anything.'

'I'm sorry, but there is a book here that I cannot allow to leave the library.' She pointed to the *Doomdryte*, which she had set apart from the rest.

'I'm sorry too,' said my master with a frown. 'But I must have the *Doomdryte* at all costs. It's an extremely dangerous book and one that must not fall into the wrong hands. I would buy it in order to destroy it. If it is the price that bothers you, I am willing to pay a great deal of money to take it away from here. But once again I'd have to stagger my payments.'

Mistress Fresque smiled. 'With reference to that book my hands are tied. In my uncle's will there is a codicil that lists the books which must always remain in this collection. That book is on the list. Every year a lawyer comes to check that they are still present in this library. If they are not, I forfeit the house.' There was a finality about her words that gave my master no room for manoeuvre.

'Is Judd around?' he asked. 'I'd like to have a few words with him.'

'He set off early on business,' she replied, returning the forbidden book to the shelves before leaving us without another word.

We continued our work in silence. I knew that my master was thinking hard, but short of stealing the book there was nothing he could do. John Gregory was an honourable man and certainly no thief.

At last, after another search of the shelves, we narrowed our choice of books down to three hundred and five.

'Right, lad, we're just about finished, so get yourself across the river and find us someone willing to cart these books to Chipenden.'

I nodded and, carrying my staff, set off through the trees towards the bridge. It was late afternoon and the air was still warm and heavy with the drone of insects. I was glad when I emerged from under those leafy branches into the open air. The sky was cloudless and there was just the lightest of breezes from the west.

Crossing the bridge back to the County side of the town, I noticed that, in contrast to the bustle of the previous day, it was almost deserted. It suddenly struck me that the innkeeper was right – hiring a horse and cart would be no easy task. But it proved even harder than I expected. The first two men I approached hurried wordlessly past me, a look of disapproval in their eyes. Strangers just weren't welcome here. Or was it the fact that I was wearing the hood and gown of a spook and carrying a staff? Because spooks dealt with the dark, people were always nervous around us and sometimes even crossed the road to avoid us. But accustomed as I was to such reactions, this seemed more extreme. I felt sure that something was wrong about this place.

In a carpenter's workshop I had my first piece of luck. The man rested his saw long enough to listen to my question. Then he nodded.

'There's no townie here does that kind of work, but old Billy Benson has a horse and cart and he's always short of money. Maybe he'd do it if the price was right.'

'Thanks. Where will I find him?' I asked.

'At Benson's Farm, of course,' the man replied in a

tone that suggested that *everyone* knew that. 'Go north out of the town; it's over the top of the moors. You'll see the track. He runs a few scraggy sheep.'

'How far is it?' I asked.

'You're young and fit. Shake yourself and you could be there and back by nightfall.'

Mumbling thanks for the second time, I left the premises and set off at a jog. What choice did I have? No doubt the Spook would be unhappy that I was taking so long, but we really did need the transport.

It soon became apparent that I was not likely to return to Todmorden by nightfall. It took me well over two hours to reach the end of the meandering track across the moors. As I walked, my thoughts turned once more to Alice and the lies I had told her. My heart felt heavy, and I thought of the future with dread. It seemed we were growing apart. With her increasing use of dark magic, we were following diverging paths.

The farmhouse, when I finally reached it, was a small ramshackle building with slates missing from the roof. When I knocked on the door there was no reply, but I was pleased to see a couple of horses tethered behind the house, and a cart that, although it had clearly seen far better days, at least had four wheels. Mr Benson was no doubt out tending his sheep.

I waited almost an hour, and was just about to give up and go back to Todmorden when a wiry old farmer with a collie at his heels came into view.

'Be off with you!' he cried, waving his stick at me. 'Strangers ain't welcome here! Be off or I'll set my dog on you!'

I stood my ground and waited for him to reach me. The dog didn't look particularly fierce but I held my staff at the ready just in case.

'I've come with an offer of work,' I told him. 'You'll be well paid. We need some books transporting to Chipenden. I was told you had a cart.'

'Aye, that I do, and I certainly need some brass. But books? *Books*, did you say? I've carted some things in my time: coal, manure, mutton, even people, but never books. What is the world coming to! Where are these books?' he asked, looking around as if expecting to see them piled up somewhere.

'They're at the big house at the top of Bent Lane,' I told him.

'Bent Lane? But that's on the other side of the river. You won't get me over that bridge for all the brass in the world!'

'Is it the bridge that worries you? If necessary, we can carry the books over to this side.'

'The bridge is sturdier than it looks, but it's the things on the other side that bother me. I'd never get my horses onto that side of the river anyway. They'd be scared of being eaten.'

'By the bears?' I asked.

'Aye, maybe by the bears – but maybe by *other* things that it's best not to think about – by the foreigners!'

It was a waste of time arguing with a man who held such crazy notions, so I quickly suggested a compromise: 'Will you do the job if we carry the books across the bridge?'

'Aye, that I will, just as long as the sun's high in the sky,' Mr Benson said. 'I'll be there at noon tomorrow. How much will ye pay?'

'That's up to my master, John Gregory, but he said he'll be generous so don't you worry.'

We shook hands on it and I set off back towards Todmorden. It would take several trips for us to get the books to this side of the river, but it was the best deal I could get. And then a word came into my head – *foreigners* – and a chill ran down my spine.

In the County, folk sometimes used the word 'foreigners' when talking about outsiders – even people from a neighbouring county. But I suddenly thought of Mistress Fresque. She came from Romania and was a true foreigner to our shores, like her uncle before her. Was the Spook's instinct correct? Did she pose some kind of threat? Was she the one that people on this bank of the river were scared of?

I suddenly realized that the sun would be setting in less than half an hour. It would be dark before I reached the house! Could my master be in danger? I wondered.

I broke into a run. Surely the Spook wouldn't stay there? No – he'd return to the tavern. But if I got back after dark I'd be locked out . . . or would my master let me in despite the wishes of the innkeeper?

The sun went down well before I began my descent into Todmorden. By the time I reached the tavern it was totally dark. I hammered on the door. The sound echoed along the streets, and I had that strange feeling again – the one I'd had as we'd approached Cosmina's house: as if something dangerous was nearby but invisible; as if the whole world was holding its breath.

Now I felt really scared, and I thumped on the door again, this time with my staff. I kept hammering at it until I got a response. It wasn't the one I'd hoped for. I'd expected my master to come downstairs and let me in. Instead the window directly above the door opened and a voice called down:

'Be off with you! You'll attract trouble making all that noise.'

It was the landlord, but there was no light shining from the open window and his face was in darkness.

'Let me in!' I cried.

'I have told you already: nobody enters here after dark!' he hissed down at me. 'Come back tomorrow morning – if you're still breathing.'

'Please tell my master I'm here, then,' I begged, unnerved by his words. 'Ask him to come and talk to me.'

'You're wasting your time. Your master isn't here. He didn't come back. If he's still at Mistress Fresque's house, you won't be seeing him again. Best thing you can do, boy, is stay on this side of the river until dawn!'

My heart lurched at his words; they confirmed my worst fears. The Spook was in danger.

The landlord slammed the window shut, leaving me alone. My body started to shake, and I suddenly felt a strong urge to take his advice and stay on this side of the bridge. But how could I leave my master? I might already be too late, but I had to try and save him, whatever the cost to myself. What sort of threat did Mistress Fresque pose? Farmer Benson had talked about the 'foreigners' eating his horses. It had seemed a crazy thing to say at the time, but now I considered the implications of his words. Did they eat *people* too? Could they be cannibals?

I crossed the river and set off for Bent Lane, where I stopped and listened. All I could hear was the wind sighing through the trees. Then, somewhere in the distance, an owl hooted twice. A crescent moon hung just above the horizon, but its light could not penetrate the canopy that shrouded the lane. It was a dark tunnel filled with unknown dangers. Gripping my staff tightly, I began to walk up the slope towards the house.

Perhaps the Spook had simply accepted an invitation to spend the night at Mistress Fresque's house. If so, was he simply a guest or in real danger? Was I worrying for nothing – simply letting my imagination get the better of me? Judd would be staying at the house as well, so there were two spooks to deal with any threat. Well, I told myself, I would find out soon enough.

I was about halfway up the lane when I heard something moving to my right. Something big was padding through the trees. I came to a halt, my heart thumping, alert for danger, and held my staff diagonally in front of me.

The noises stopped. When I set off again, they started up too. It sounded like a large animal beside me, almost as if I was being escorted. Was it a bear? If so, at least it wasn't getting any closer.

Suddenly I saw the house through the trees, and whatever had been accompanying me was suddenly gone, as if it had vanished into thin air.

The windows were dark, but I could just make out the outline of the building. I stepped round the tree and walked up to the front door. To my surprise it was wide open, hanging from one hinge. Beyond it I could see nothing. The darkness within was absolute. I rested my staff against the wall, then reached into my breeches pocket and pulled out a candle stub, using my little tinderbox to light it. Holding it up in my right hand, and my staff in my left, I stepped into the hallway.

Immediately I knew that something was badly wrong. There was a strong stench of rot and decay, and I noted a thick coating of dust along the top of the wainscot. It certainly hadn't been there earlier in the day. Not only that, there was paint flaking from the door frame. Previously, everything inside the house had been clean, polished and well-maintained. It didn't make sense.

I went up to the oval door at the end of the passage. I tried the handle, but it was locked. That was no problem because I had in my pocket a special key made by Andrew, the Spook's locksmith brother, which would open most doors. I inserted the key, and within seconds the lock yielded. Returning the key to my pocket, I eased open the door and lifted the candle high to illuminate the lower floor of the library.

But what I saw in front of me was incredible . . . impossible: the shelves were empty of books and many of the bookcases had collapsed. Spiders' webs covered those few that remained intact. I looked down and saw my footprints in a thick coating of dust. It looked as if nobody had entered this room for many long years. Of the table that had held the books we'd selected earlier there was now no sign at all.

How could that be, I wondered, when I had been here with my master this very morning?

I looked up at the other floors of the library. The light from my candle could reach no further than the one directly above, but it appeared to be in the same state of disrepair and neglect.

Suddenly a chill ran the length of my spine – the warning that a seventh son of a seventh son often receives when something from the dark is approaching – and, out of nowhere, a strong wind blew up. The candle flame flickered and went out, plunging me into darkness.

CHAPTER 10
COWARDLY PANIC

For a moment the darkness seemed absolute. The moon could not penetrate the trees that shrouded the house, and no light was coming in through either door or window.

My heart thudded and quickened. I took a deep breath to calm myself and realized that I was mistaken – there *was* a faint source of light in the room, coming from one of the dilapidated bookcases beside the oval door. On it a single book was glowing with a lurid red light.

I took a step closer. The book was propped up against the back of the shelf, its title clearly visible. It was the *Doomdryte,* the dangerous grimoire that my master had wanted to destroy.

I heard a deep growl to my right and spun round. What I saw made me take an involuntary step backwards. Terrifying, malevolent eyes stared at me out of a bestial face. The creature's head was completely bald and its ears were large and pointed and covered in long fine hair. Long curved fangs curled down over its bottom lip. Orange light radiated from the whole body, which was human in shape and stood about six feet tall. It wore heavy boots and filthy ragged clothes that were caked in mud. Its hands were twice the size of mine, each digit ending in a long sharp talon.

It growled again and took a step towards me. I retreated, holding my staff across me defensively. I couldn't remember seeing anything like this before. Had I ever glimpsed an image of this creature in the Spook's Bestiary? A sketch he'd made from someone else's description? I vaguely remembered something. What was it . . . ?

With a click I released my staff's retractable blade – made of a silver alloy and effective against most creatures of the dark. I was ready to repel any attack, but this did me no good at all. The creature was incredibly fast. One minute it was glaring at me with its menacing eyes; the next it had surged past me in a blur, snatching the staff out of my hands. I lost my balance, fell to my knees and saw it standing on the other side of the room, examining my staff. Suddenly it snapped it in two and threw the pieces down.

'The weapon was puny and no threat to me at all,' it growled. 'You are young. You will taste better than your master!'

At those words I shuddered. *Taste?* Had the creature killed and eaten the Spook? Was that what it meant? Was I too late? I felt a moment of anguish, then pushed my feelings aside and forced myself to concentrate as my master had taught me.

I suddenly wondered about Mistress Fresque. The house and library looked very different now. Was the girl in her true form? Was she a shape-shifter? I wondered. Or was this something else?

The creature slowly took a step towards me; it might attack at any moment.

So I moved first, reaching inside my gown with my left hand.

I drew the Destiny Blade.

Immediately there was a third source of light in the room to add to that of the *Doomdryte* and the fanged creature that threatened me. It came from the sword.

I glanced down at it. The ruby eyes of the skelt were glowing, and from them beads of blood were dripping onto the floor. The blade was hungry.

I readied the sword as the bestial creature stared at me, eyes glowing. Suddenly a blur of orange light streaked towards me. I slashed at it horizontally, striking more by instinct than skill. Maybe I got lucky – but whatever happened, I felt an impact and the sword was almost torn from my hands. Somehow I held onto it and gripped it tighter. Blood was still dripping from the ruby eyes, but now there was also a fresh stain on the blade.

The creature reappeared in front of me, its back to the dilapidated shelving. It was crouching, head bowed forward, holding its shoulder, from where blood was spreading in a large stain. I'd cut it, but had I hurt it badly enough to give me an advantage?

'Where is my master?' I demanded.

Its reply was a low growl. The time for words was past. One of us was going to die here.

I took a cautious step towards it, and then another. It might still be able to move faster than I could react; it could rip out my throat before I moved to defend myself.

So I called upon one of my gifts – the special ability that I'd inherited from my mother. I could slow time . . . make it stop. It was very difficult, but I'd been trained to use the blade by Grimalkin, the witch assassin, and she'd made me practise this skill under combat conditions.

Concentrate! Squeeze time! Make it stop!

The creature attacked again, but my heart was steady and my focus on the task was increasing. The blur of orange light moving towards me resolved itself into a shape. Its intent was clear, for its mouth was open, revealing two sets of teeth. The upper ones were long fangs; the lower ones were smaller and thin, like needles. The beast's arms were held wide, ready to embrace me in a hug of death.

Concentrate! Squeeze time! Make it stop!

It was working. I was beginning to control time. Every step the creature took towards me was slower. Its whole body was rippling with urgency but now it was hardly moving. Now *I* was running towards it. I hefted the sword, putting into the blow all the strength that I could muster – along with the fury and anguish I felt at the news about my master.

The blade sliced into the creature's neck, cutting the head clean off. It hit the floor hard and rolled away into the dust under the bookshelves. The body tottered and took another step towards me, black blood spraying out of the severed neck. Then it collapsed at my feet, the blood forming a widening pool around it.

I'd felt a strange satisfaction on striking that blow. It was almost as if the blade had moved with me; we'd combined to deliver the perfect killing stroke. Grimalkin had trained me in its use, but I'd moved on from that. It truly was the Destiny Blade; our futures were now bound together.

I stepped back to avoid the blood, but I didn't sheathe the sword. Some creatures of the dark had incredible powers of regeneration, so I had to stay on my guard. But this one did something else.

The orange light that had illuminated the creature from within suddenly floated up to form a helix, a slowly twisting spiral that hovered just above the body, then shot off, passing through the wall to my left and disappearing from sight.

Immediately a nauseating stench of rot filled the room. The body at my feet was just visible in the glow of the ruby eyes in the sword hilt. It began to bubble, an acrid steam rising from it. I stepped back, placing one hand in front of my mouth. It was decomposing rapidly. What had left it? I wondered. Its soul? What kind of creature was I dealing with?

With a heavy heart I remembered what it had said about the Spook. Could he *really* be dead? It was hard to accept. A lump came into my throat. I couldn't just leave the house without being sure one way or the other. I needed to search for him.

I lit the candle stub again and approached the other door; the one that Mistress Fresque had used. I had assumed that it led to her living quarters, but to my surprise I found myself in a very small room with stone steps going down into the darkness.

What was below – a cellar? Is that where she'd gone each time she'd left us? Did the bell ring somewhere down there?

I began to descend the steps, the sword in my right

hand, the candle held aloft in my left. I had switched them because the staircase curved away widdershins, in an anti-clockwise direction, and this way I had more room to deploy the blade. I was counting the steps, and realized that the cellar must be very deep. My count had already reached forty when they straightened out, and I saw below me what looked like the cellar floor. After two more steps I came to a halt. In the small pool of yellow light cast by the candle I could see bones scattered across the floor. One glance told me that they were human; some were covered in blood. I could see a skull and part of a forearm amongst the other fragments. This was the lair of creatures who fed on the blood and flesh of humans. I wondered if any of these bones belonged to my master.

I suddenly realized that there could well be another creature like the one I'd slain. Perhaps Mistress Fresque was waiting down here in the darkness, ready to leap on me.

Then I heard a noise, and a cold gust of wind blew out the candle again. I waited, hardly breathing, and put the stub in my breeches pocket. Then I gripped my sword with both hands and went into a crouch, ready to defend myself. The blade began to glow once more, and as my eyes adjusted to the darkness I saw red points of light moving towards me. There were a dozen or more. I heard a low growl to my right; another directly ahead. I began to tremble, and the ruby-red light from the sword quickly faded. There were eyes – too many eyes! How many of the creatures were there?

In a panic, I turned and ran up the steps, away from the threat. I blundered across the library, crashing into shelves, feeling rotten wood crunching beneath my boots. My terror intensified when I couldn't find the door, but the light from the sword flared briefly, showing me the way. I hurried along the passage and out of the house.

Once on the path, I started running. Once again I heard noises, as if some large creature was keeping pace with me. That made me run even faster, and soon I'd left Bent Lane behind and was sprinting through the deserted streets.

I didn't stop until I'd crossed the bridge. Even then I didn't feel safe, and after I'd got my breath back I walked on until I'd left Todmorden behind. And as I walked I thought of Judd. What was his part in all this? He had visited Chipenden to hasten our visit to Todmorden. Surely he must have known what he was leading us into. I felt bitter and angry. Was he another of the Spook's apprentices who had gone to the dark?

Then, on the edge of the moors, I sheathed the sword, crawled under a hawthorn hedge and, completely exhausted, fell into a deep dreamless sleep.

I awoke to find that the sun was already high in the sky. My mouth was dry and my limbs ached, but the worst thing was my sense of shame. I had run from the threat in the cellar. No – not just run: I had fled in a cowardly panic. I'd been a spook's apprentice for more than three years now, but I couldn't recall another occasion when I'd behaved so shamefully. I'd faced terrible things from the dark and somehow found the courage to stand and fight. So what had been different this time? All I could think of was that the years of fear, fighting the dark and being in continual danger had finally taken its toll. What if I'd lost my courage? How then could I function as a spook?

And there was something even worse to face. What

if my master was still alive? I'd abandoned him. He deserved better than that – much better. I got to my feet and began to walk slowly back towards Todmorden. This time I would stand and fight.

CHAPTER 11

THE CURSE OF THE PENDLE WITCHES

It was almost noon, but there were no hawkers or market stalls; few people were about on the west side of the town. As I walked through the narrow streets, I counted no more than half a dozen, and the last of these, the old gentleman with the stick we'd spoken to before, hobbled across to the other side of the street to avoid me. Then, as I approached the river, I saw Mr Benson sitting on his cart amongst the trees, some distance from the bridge.

'Where are these books of yours?' he demanded. 'I haven't got all day. They should be piled up here, ready to load onto the cart. My horses are getting nervous.'

For a moment I considered asking him to wait in case my master was hurt and needed a ride, but I saw that it was a waste of time. The two horses were rolling their eyes and sweating excessively. I had to do this alone.

'I'm sorry,' I told him, 'but there won't be any books to carry today – here's something for your trouble.'

I reached into my breeches pocket, pulled out a few coins and held them up to him.

'Is that all?' he asked angrily, snatching them from my hand. 'It's hardly worth getting out of bed for that!' He whipped the horses twice, brought the cart round and headed off without so much as a backward glance.

I headed for the river, but when I came to the dilapidated wooden bridge, a tremor of fear ran through me. On the other side, the servants of the dark lay in wait for me, and judging by the glowing eyes in the cellar there were a lot of them – far too many for me to face alone. But it had to be done. I had to find out what had happened to my master or I wouldn't be able to live with myself.

I took one step, and then another. I kept putting one foot in front of the other until I was standing on the eastern bank of the river. It was daylight, I told myself, and the sun was shining. My enemies would have to take refuge in darkness, somewhere underground. I would be safe unless I left behind the light of the sun. But wasn't that exactly what I would have to do? I needed to find the Spook. At some point I would have to search the cellar.

I began to climb up Bent Lane towards the house of Mistress Fresque. As I walked, I remembered something else – another failure, a further dereliction of duty. When I fled the house I should have taken the *Doomdryte* with me and destroyed it. It was something that my master would certainly have done. I could imagine him now, telling me off for making that mistake. Would I ever hear his voice again? I wondered.

It was gloomy beneath the trees, but this time I could hear nothing following me. When I saw the house, I realized that the door was no longer hanging open. I stepped round the tree, drew the Destiny Blade and rapped upon it with the hilt.

Almost immediately I heard footsteps approaching. The door opened and Mistress Fresque stood there, pointing at my sword with a frown on her face.

'Put that away!' she commanded. 'You will not need that while I am at your side.'

When I hesitated, a smile came to her lips but her eyes were hard. She was still young and pretty, but now there was an imperiousness to her manner – something she had hidden previously. 'Trust me,' she said, her voice softening a little. 'I bid you enter. This time when you enter freely across the threshold of my home you will be under my protection.'

What was I to do? Although she was an attractive young woman, I knew that she must be allied with dark forces. One part of me wanted to push her aside and force myself into her house; the other thought it more prudent to accept her offer of safe conduct. By so doing, I might find answers to the questions that were spinning around inside my head.

When I had sheathed my sword, the smile spread to her eyes. 'Enter freely and be safe!' She stepped aside to allow me to cross the threshold. 'Follow me,' she said, leading me down the passage towards the library. The wainscot was now clean and shining and the house smelled sweet and wholesome. The library was once again as I had first seen it with the Spook, the shelves orderly and filled with books. And our selection of volumes lay on the table once more. Some type of extremely powerful dark magic was at work here.

But there was one change to the room that made me halt just inside the doorway. In the middle of the floor lay a skeleton. The bones were yellow-brown and old and the head was missing. I glanced to my right and saw a skull lying beside the bookcase to my right. My broken staff was beside it. These must be the remains of the creature I had slain.

'That was my partner,' said Mistress Fresque, gesturing towards the skeleton. 'We lived together happily for many years until you encountered him last night!'

'I'm sorry that you lost him,' I said, keeping my voice even. 'But it was him or me. And I think he killed my master, John Gregory.'

'He would indeed have killed you, but you are wrong to think that he is no more. I did not lose *him* – merely the body that he had inhabited for many years. He will soon find another host – I hope it is to my taste!' she said with a smile. 'Then, in revenge for what you did, he will come looking for you, wanting to take *your* head.'

'What kind of creatures are you?' I asked.

'I am a strigoica,' she replied, 'the female of our kind. My partner is a strigoi. We are from the Romanian province of Transylvania, which means, "The land beyond the forest". We are daemons.'

'Where is Judd Brinscall?' I asked. 'What part has he played in all this? When did he start to serve the dark?'

'Do not concern yourself with him. He is close to death now. His life can be measured in nights or maybe even hours.'

'Is that his reward for betraying us?'

Mistress Fresque frowned and tightened her lips. It was clear that she would not answer. So, despite my anxiety about the Spook, I remained calm and asked another question, determined to learn all I could, gathering knowledge just as my master would have done.

'Why did you come here?' I demanded.

'There are many reasons for that, but we have kept ourselves to ourselves and lived here in happiness for some time, causing as little disruption as possible. Then I was ordered to lure you and your master to this place.'

'Ordered? Who told you to do that?'

'I cannot say. There are many from Romania who now dwell here. Most have arrived very recently. Some are very powerful and I have no choice but to obey them. They can call upon a terrible being that could obliterate me in an instant.'

'Why were we tricked into coming here? So you could kill us? You've killed my master and now it's my turn!' I cried, reaching for my sword.

'Draw that blade and you will no longer be under my protection!' snapped Mistress Fresque. 'Your master is not dead but in desperate need of your help. Calm yourself and I'll take you to see him.'

I relinquished the hilt of my sword and nodded. The strigoica pointed to the door that led to the cellar steps. 'He's down there,' she said, walking towards it.

She opened the door and, very cautiously, I followed her into the small room. A lot had changed since the previous night. The steps were clean and the walls were painted green and free of cobwebs. There were torches in brackets set at frequent intervals so our descent was well-lit. Had the Spook been down here last night, trapped in the darkness and surrounded by creatures from the dark? I wondered. I could have stayed and helped him, but instead I had panicked and run. I was ashamed of my behaviour and found it hard to explain. A lump came to my throat as I remembered the curse of the Pendle witches, which had once been used against the Spook: *You will die in a dark place far underground, with no friend at your side!*

We reached the stone flags of the cellar. The only piece of furniture I could see was a wooden table, upon which stood a large black box with a hinged lid. Embossed in silver upon that lid was the image of a creature that I immediately recognized. I grew cold at the sight of it.

It was a skelt. But why was its head depicted on the box? It made me think of the *Doomdryte*'s cover, and the hilt of my sword.

I shuddered. There was something ominous about it, and my heart began to bang in my chest. Mistress Fresque walked straight up to it and lifted the lid.

'Here is your master,' she said.

Within the box lay the head of the Spook.

CHAPTER 12
WORSE THAN DEATH

My heart sank into my boots and a flood of grief washed over me. I was too shocked to reply. I felt numb, unable to accept what I was seeing. The strigoica had lied. They had killed my master.

'He can still speak,' she said, 'but he is in agony and no doubt constantly prays for release. Why don't you ask him?'

No sooner had she said this than the Spook's eyelids twitched and he stared up at me. His mouth opened and he tried to speak, but he could only croak, and a dribble of blood ran down his chin. An expression of pain flickered across his face and he closed his eyes again.

'This has been done in revenge for what you and your allies did to the Fiend,' Mistress Fresque said. 'Your master will have no peace until you do what we require. To free his soul his head must be burned. I am willing to give it to you – but first you must bring me the head of the Fiend.'

The Spook groaned and opened his eyes again. He murmured something unintelligible, so I bent forward so that my right ear was close to his lips.

He seemed to choke, his eyes rolling in his head, then cleared his throat and struggled to speak again. 'Help me, lad!' he croaked. 'Get me free of this. This is unbearable – worse than death. I'm in pain. I'm in terrible pain. Please set me free!'

The world spun about me. Overwhelmed by grief, I almost fell.

'Can you bear to allow your master to remain in this pitiful state for a moment longer than is necessary?' Mistress Fresque demanded. 'We know of the witch who carries the Fiend's head. Her name is Grimalkin. Summon her. Lure her to this place and, in exchange, you will be permitted to release your master from his torment.'

I felt sick to my stomach at what I was being asked to do. In order to destroy the Fiend I was being asked to sacrifice Alice; now his supporters wanted me to bring about the death of Grimalkin, another of my allies. But betraying Grimalkin was only the first of the consequences of returning the Fiend's head to his servants. They would take it back to Ireland and reunite it with the body, freeing him from the pit at Kenmare. He would come for me and Alice, and snatch us away into the dark, dead or alive. The prospect terrified me, but my duty was clear in any case: it was owed to the people of the County. I could not allow the Fiend to return to the earth – which would soon become a darker and more desperate place. No, I could not do it. But I could seize my master's head by force and give him peace.

I drew the sword.

Instantly a freezing wind gusted into the cellar and all the torches were extinguished. Out of the darkness I saw eyes staring at me. Each pair glowed red, as they had the previous night – but this time there were even more, and I heard threatening growls and noises that sounded like claws on the flags. I spun round, ready to defend myself, but saw that I was surrounded. Where had they come from? I wondered.

I was afraid. There were too many of them. What chance did I have against such odds?

'It is not too late!' Mistress Fresque hissed at me from the darkness. 'Put away the sword immediately and you will be under my protection once more.'

With trembling hands I tried to sheathe the Destiny Blade. It took me three attempts to return it to its scabbard, but when I had done so, the red eyes faded, the scratching ceased, and the torches flared and filled the cellar with yellow light once more.

'Another second and it would have been too late,' Mistress Fresque told me, closing the lid of the box and turning to leave. 'Follow me. Now that you have drawn your sword it isn't safe for you to spend too much time below ground. My protection is limited.'

She led the way back up the steps and into the library. 'Do not delay in summoning the witch assassin,' she warned me. 'We offer to release your master's head in exchange for that of the Fiend, but it must be done soon. Every day you delay his torment will be increased. We can inflict unimaginable pain upon him.'

'Where is the remainder of him?' I asked, feeling cold inside at the thought of what had been done to my master. 'I would like to bury his body.'

I knew I'd have to burn the head to release his sprit from the dark magic used, but burying the rest of him would make me feel better. The Church wouldn't allow a spook to be put to rest in hallowed ground, but I might find a sympathetic priest to say a few words and allow my master to be buried close to a graveyard. But even that hope was quickly dashed.

'That is not possible,' Mistress Fresque said coldly. 'The rest of his body was not needed for our purposes so we fed it to a moroi. They are extremely hungry elemental spirits which have to be appeased.'

Disgusted and angry, I turned on my heel and left the house without another word. I headed for the riverbank, crossed the bridge and sat down under the trees to think things through and consider my options.

The thought of my master suffering like that was unbearable – he was enduring such terrible pain. However, my duty was clear: I had to leave him for now. How could I possibly deceive Grimalkin and lure her here, allowing the Fiend's head to fall into the hands of the strigoica and her allies? It must be kept away from them; I had to use the time to find a way to destroy him for ever.

I don't know how long I sat there, pondering my limited options, but at one point I wept for the Spook, who had served the County well and suffered much to protect it. He had also been more than a master to me; he had become my friend. He deserved a better end to his life. I'd hoped that as I completed my apprenticeship, he would start to reduce his own workload while I took a greater part of the burden until he finally retired. Now our future together had been snatched away. I was alone, and it was both a sad and a scary feeling.

Eventually I came to a decision and walked back to the tavern. I went up to my room and from the Spook's bag I took a small piece of cheese and enough money to pay the landlord. I left both bags in my room, locked it and went downstairs.

He scowled when I approached, but soon brightened when I dropped a silver coin into his palm.

'That's for two more nights,' I told him.

'Did you find your master?' he asked.

I didn't reply, but as I walked away he called after me, 'If he's not back by now he must be dead, boy. You'll end up the same way if you don't go home!'

I headed back to the bridge, nibbled at the cheese and washed it down with a few mouthfuls of cold river water. I thought about Mistress Fresque's house. How could it be clean and orderly during the day, with its library full of books, but a dilapidated ruin at night? Some type of powerful dark magic was being used here – a spell of illusion.

So what was the truth about that house – its day-time and night-time condition? Spooks had to develop and trust their instincts, and mine told me that its ruinous condition at night was its true state.

What would my master advise me to do? I asked myself. Instantly I knew. He would advise me to be bold and act like a spook! I would put my fears behind me. I could take back my master's head by force and thus give him the peace he deserved. I had the Destiny Blade, and I was determined to use it. I would clean out that vile cellar and kill all the creatures of the dark within it. And I would attack at night when things were as they seemed.

It was time to stop being afraid. Now *I* would become the hunter.

CHAPTER 13
I WON'T SEE DAWN

Soon after dark I began to climb Bent Lane once more. As I walked, I pondered on what I was facing. The Spook's Bestiary was back at Chipenden – it would be the first book to be placed in the new library – so I could not use it as a reference source. Desperately I dredged my mind for what I had read about Romanian creatures of the dark.

Strigoii and strigoica were daemons, male and female respectively. They worked and lived in pairs. The male possessed the body of a dead person and had to spend the daylight hours hidden from sunlight, which could destroy him. The other, the female, possessed the body of a living person and was on guard during the day. No doubt Mistress Fresque had once been a nice ordinary young woman, but now her body had been taken over by a malevolent creature of the dark. I had decapitated her partner, but she'd said that wasn't the end of him. Normally slaying a daemon with a silver-alloy blade would bring about its destruction, but these Romanians seemed very powerful. I had seen the strigoi leave its dead host; now it would be searching for another. Once it had found one, it would seek me out. How could I put a permanent end to it? I wondered. There were far too many unknowns here.

There was something else that was even more worrying. Mistress Fresque had said that she had been ordered to lure us to this place – commanded by others who could summon a being so powerful that it could 'obliterate her in an instant'. What could that be? Had there been anything about such an entity in the Spook's Bestiary? I could not recall anything. Romania had seemed so far away, and I could not believe that its denizens of the dark posed much of a threat. Consequently I had read the entries fast – skimming the information rather than absorbing it properly for future use. I shook my head, annoyed with myself. From now on I must become more thorough, and think and act like a spook rather than an apprentice.

Now I was approaching the dark tunnel of trees once more. I hadn't taken more than a dozen paces along the path when I heard those disturbing noises to my right.

I stopped, and whatever it was stopped too, but I could still hear slow heavy breathing. I had a choice: either I could continue along the path until I reached the front door of the strigoica's residence, or I could stop and deal with this creature once and for all.

Without delay, I drew my sword. Instantly the ruby eyes of the Destiny Blade began to glow red, illuminating what I faced. A huge bear was lumbering towards me on all fours. All at once it stood up on its hind legs, towering over me, and for the first time I saw its claws clearly. They resembled long curved daggers and looked razor-sharp, capable of tearing human flesh to shreds. The bear was immensely powerful and could no doubt crush the life out of me in seconds. It opened its mouth wide and roared, saliva dripping from its teeth, the stench of its hot breath washing over me. I raised the sword, ready to meet its advance.

Then, suddenly, I had another idea.

I retreated three steps, until I was standing on the path once more. Instantly the bear dropped back onto all fours. It regarded me intently but did not attack. I remembered the warning I'd been given – not to stray from the path because of bears. So was I safe if I remained on the path? I wondered.

I sheathed the sword and began to walk towards the house again. The bear followed but made no move to attack me. It must be some sort of guardian, patrolling the grounds of the house for Mistress Fresque, just as the Spook's boggart had once guarded his garden at Chipenden. And then a word dropped into my head: *moroi!*

Mistress Fresque had told me that they'd fed the Spook's body to a moroi. I vaguely remembered reading about them in my master's Bestiary. They were vampiric elemental spirits that sometimes lived inside hollow trees. But they could possess animals – bears being their favourite host. They hunted humans and crushed them to death before dragging them back to their lair. Direct sunlight could destroy them, so they weren't seen abroad during daylight hours. Then I remembered something else: a moroi was often controlled by a strigoi and strigoica. So my guess had been correct. Mistress Fresque was using the elemental as a guard.

But why didn't it attack those who used the path? The answer came to me in a flash of insight. It was because the path itself didn't need guarding. Anyone using the path would be instantly known to those within the house. And it provided a safe route for anyone who was welcome there.

I realized that there was no need to fight the moroi. I had numerous other enemies waiting for me inside the house. I'd be safe as long as I stuck to the path, so I might as well save my strength. I hurried on, and as I neared the house I heard the bear move off into the trees.

The door was open so I drew my sword and stepped inside. I didn't bother with my tinderbox and candle this time – I was ready to face my enemies. My courage was high, and that was enough to cause the ruby eyes of the Destiny Blade to flicker into life, then cast a red beam to illuminate the passage.

I passed through the second doorway, expecting to see the dilapidated library empty of books and curtained with cobwebs. Instead, dozens of red orbs gleamed in the darkness.

For a second I thought they were pairs of eyes – creatures of the dark preparing to attack. But then I realized that I was staring at reflections of myself – or rather, of the ruby eyes of the sword hilt. Gone was the library; I was in a hall of mirrors, each set within an ornate iron frame and at least three times my size.

I took a careful step into the chamber, and then another. The mirrors all faced me, set one behind the other like a pack of cards spread out against the walls on either side. At first they all reflected my image in the same way. I was looking at a young man wearing the hooded gown of a spook's apprentice, but instead of holding the customary staff, crouching down with a sword held in both hands, ready to attack.

Then, as I watched, the surfaces of the mirrors flickered and the images began to change. Now cruel, hostile faces peered out at me as if about to leap out and devour me on the spot. Some seemed to be chanting; others opened their mouths as if uttering bestial growls. But they were merely images and the atrium was absolutely silent. Then I *did* hear a noise, and I whirled round, expecting to see some dangerous creature, but it was just a mouse that twitched its tail and scurried off into the darkness.

I turned back to face the mirrors, took a deep breath and studied the images. There were fierce women, their hair tangled with thorns; grim, cadaverous faces; things that had surely crawled straight out of the tomb. Were they strigoica? If so, why had they not chosen younger hosts like Mistress Fresque? All had one thing in common – their lips were red with blood. I wondered if they were some other type of dark creature. They reminded me of witches.

One thing I was sure of: I was no longer afraid. I was angry! Fearsome eyes had peered at me from mirrors before. I only wished that the ones here had substance so that I could strike them down with my blade. I did the next best thing – it achieved little but gave vent to my fury and made me feel better.

I laid about me with my sword, stepping forward and twisting left, right, and left again, to smash each mirror as I passed. There was the crash and a tinkle of breaking glass, shards of it exploding upwards to fall like silver at my feet; each glittering image was replaced by darkness. Soon the last mirror was shattered, and still the ruby eyes of the Destiny Blade glowed red. But when I stepped beyond the dark empty frame of that final mirror, I was filled with dismay.

Instead of the door that opened onto the cellar steps there was just a blank wall. I had been prepared to fight my way down there to release my master from his torment. If necessary, I would have given my life to do so.

But I had been wrong about the house. I had assumed that its true condition was revealed during the hours of darkness. I knew now that the magic employed was more complicated than that. The house could change and change again. My master's remains were now hidden; I had no way of freeing him.

Baffled and angry, I turned and retraced my steps. I left the shape-shifting house and followed the path down through the trees. This time the bear possessed by the moroi did not approach me. I wandered through the streets but did not cross the river, instead sitting amongst the trees by the bridge.

A sword or staff could be used to fight enemies once they were before you, but such weapons were useless to me at the moment. I needed to use my brain. I needed to think.

However, this had become impossible. Emotions were churning within me at the thought of the terrible state my master had been reduced to. I couldn't dispel the image of his severed head. Every time I closed my eyes it returned to haunt me. My chest felt tight, and I struggled to hold back the tears. John Gregory didn't deserve to end his life in this way. I *had* to help. I *had* to do something to save him from that.

Restless, I came to my feet. I'd been up on the moors to the west of Todmorden but not on this side. It might help to find a vantage point above this part of the town. Was there another approach to the house – perhaps another entrance? I wondered. Or maybe another building I hadn't seen where my master was being kept now?

I walked back through the narrow streets and then found a track that led straight up the hill. Soon I was walking beneath trees; at last I came to a five-barred gate. I climbed over and continued up through pasture land, heading north, until I found myself at a point high on the moor's edge.

I had chosen an excellent spot. The sky was clear and the stars were out so there was just enough light to see by. Far below, I could see the lane that led up to Mistress Fresque's house, which was hidden beneath the trees – I could learn nothing more of that from here. There was no other path to the house; just dense foliage crowding in on it from every side.

I searched lower. Nothing moved; the streets were empty, the dwellings huddled together as if for protection – but then I noticed other large houses on the hillside, each surrounded by trees.

Were these the dwellings of other strigoii and strigoica? I counted them carefully – there were at least thirty, with others perhaps hidden beneath the trees. I waited and watched. At one point an owl hooted, to be answered by the roar of a bear somewhere in the forest. The wind was getting up, a ridge of cloud blowing in from the west, obscuring the stars one by one. It was growing darker; now the houses were barely visible. But suddenly I noticed a thin column of yellow light extending up from the ground high into the sky. As I watched, the light grew brighter and changed colour, becoming first purple, then a dark red.

What was its source? It was emanating from a dense clump of trees some way from the nearest of the buildings. It was then that I saw the first yellow orb of light soar upwards from the house east of there. It was immediately followed by a second, then a third glowing sphere. Each made its first appearance directly above one of the large houses. I counted quickly. There were nine in total, gathering together to form a group of dancing orbs that circled the column of dark red light. They moved like summer midges; hovering, then darting around to exchange places.

Suddenly it felt as if something had reached into my mind and tugged hard. It happened again, and with that strange tug I felt an overwhelming compulsion to walk towards the glowing orbs. I gave a gasp of fear and lurched to my feet in terror. I had seen such entities before – I knew what they were and the terrible danger that they represented.

They were Romanian witches, who lived isolated lives, and in human form did not usually form covens like other types of witch. These were their souls, projected from their bodies using animism magic; it was only in this way that they ever gathered together. According to my master's Bestiary, unlike the other dark Romanian entities, they didn't drink human blood; but if they encountered a human when in the form of orbs, they could drain his animus, his life force, in seconds. It was a quick and certain death. I could feel their power. They knew that I had travelled to Todmorden with my master and was still somewhere in the vicinity. However, they didn't know my precise whereabouts and were trying to summon me, using dark magic.

At first it was like strange powerful music inside my head – it reminded me of the sirens off the coast of Greece, who had used their melodious cries to lure our ship onto the rocks. I had managed to resist them: a seventh son of a seventh son possesses some immunity against witches and other entities of the dark. Now I did the same, until the music inside my head eventually faded and ceased altogether.

Maybe they sensed my increasing strength, because next the lure became visual. The spheres of light moved more rapidly, pulsing and changing colour in an ever more complex dance, and I felt my will slipping away, my mind like a moth drawn towards the candle flame that would consume it.

I crouched down on all fours and fought hard against the compulsion; rivulets of sweat ran down my forehead. Gradually the urge to go towards them lessened then faded away. But still I was in danger – if they noticed me, then I was doomed.

After about ten minutes of dancing together high above, darting in and out of the red light, the nine orbs combined to form one large glowing sphere, which then sped northwards and vanished.

Where had they gone? Were they hunting some chosen victim? It struck me that they would try to avoid killing too close to their homes, which would attract attention. Todmorden would rapidly become depopulated and terror would spread westwards through the County.

The wind, which had been blowing fiercely, first lessened to a breeze then died away altogether. A deep silence settled upon the river valley. The few sounds were greatly magnified. I heard the eerie screech of a corpsefowl, and soon afterwards the call of an owl. In the distance beyond the river, a baby cried; then someone coughed and swore. After a few moments the child was quiet – no doubt its mother was feeding it. These were all natural sounds of the night – but then I heard something else.

First there was a deep groan, followed by a shrill scream that made the hairs on the back of my neck stand up. The sounds came from two different directions. Next, from somewhere directly below me, a voice began to beg:

'Leave me tonight, please! Not again, not so soon. I won't see the dawn if you do that again! Please, please, leave me be!'

Drawn by this cry for help, I was on my feet in an instant and began to scramble down the slope. Soon I had climbed over a wooden fence and was under the trees. The sounds were closer and much louder now.

'Oh no, please don't. That's enough. Don't take too much. Please don't carry on or my heart will fail! Don't stop my heart, please! I don't want to die . . .'

I was running now, and I drew the sword. Instantly the ruby eyes cast their red light in my path, and I saw the horror before me. It was a strigoi which could have been the twin of the one I'd fought at the Fresque house; it glowed with a lurid orange light, and its head was bald, with the same large pointed ears.

The strigoi was crouching over a man dressed in a ragged gown; it had half pulled him out of a dark hole in the ground, beside which lay a large stone. Its teeth were fastened onto its victim's neck and it was sucking his blood.

Chapter 14

They'll Expand Westwards

The strigoi turned, saw me coming, and cast its victim aside on the grass. It spun round to face me, then attacked, mouth wide, fangs ready to bite me, talons extended to rend my flesh. I hardly broke my stride. I was in a rage, all the pent-up emotion of the past twenty-four hours released in a violent fury.

I lunged at the daemon, but it quickly retreated, and the tip of my blade missed it by less than an inch. I swung at it again, but it evaded that blow too. It snarled at me and took a step forward, preparing to attack. I remembered the speed of the strigoi that had attacked me in the library, and immediately started to focus on slowing time.

Suddenly I felt the sword move in my hand, and blood began to drip from the ruby eyes in the hilt. I became one with the blade. Gripping it with both hands, I took one step to the left, two to the right, and then, with all my strength, brought the blade down vertically upon the head of the strigoi. It sliced clean through its skull, cleaving it to the jaw, and the creature fell at my feet. I tugged the blade free, feeling a tremendous sense of satisfaction.

As I had expected, an orange helical light spiralled up from the daemon, spun there for a couple of seconds, and then shot up into the sky, disappearing over the treetops. I had killed the body, but its soul was still free. Would it now, like the partner of Mistress Fresque, go in search of another host?

Still shaking with anger, I returned the Destiny Blade to its sheath and turned to look at the man, who had crawled onto his knees. He stared up at me, his eyes wide with astonishment. But he couldn't have been more surprised than me – it was Judd Brinscall.

'You betrayed us!' I shouted. 'You led us into the clutches of those daemons!'

He tried to speak, opening his mouth, but no words came out. I leaned down, put my hand on his shoulder and dragged him to his feet. He felt like a dead weight leaning against me, and his whole body was trembling. He stank of blood and the earth he'd been entombed in. I thought of what had been done to my master, and I had half a mind to put him back in the pit and cover it with the stone. No doubt another strigoi would find him and finish him off. It was no more than he deserved!

I started to push him towards the pit but suddenly thought of Dad and how he'd taught me right from wrong. And no matter what Judd Brinscall had done, it was wrong to give him back to the strigoi. And I wondered about his situation: was his reward for betraying us to be drained of blood? It didn't make sense. Not only that . . . I'd run like a coward myself. Who was I to judge him?

But it was something to worry about later – we had to make our escape before something else found us.

'We must get away from here,' I told him. 'We need to cross the river.'

Very slowly we began our descent. I was nervous, expecting to be attacked at any time – maybe by a strigoica, the partner of the creature I'd just encountered. Or maybe the witches would return – nine orbs that would fall upon us and suck away our lives without spilling a drop of blood. I had no defences against such an attack.

Judd groaned from time to time, as if in pain, and I had to keep stopping to rest because it was hard work; I was almost carrying him. At last we reached the river, but something told me we had to cross. It was safer on the other bank. Maybe the creatures couldn't cross running water – though it would be no barrier to witches in the form of orbs; they could soar across without being affected.

By now I was exhausted, but at last I dragged Judd across the bridge and we collapsed together on the far bank. Instantly he fell into a deep sleep.

I started to think things through and tried to decide on my next move. I needed to contact Alice and let her know what had happened. It was also vital to warn Grimalkin of the threat. She had to keep the Fiend's head away from this cursed place at all costs. But I needed a mirror to do that. It would have to wait until daylight, when I could return to my room.

I must have fallen asleep, because when I opened my eyes, the sun was just above the eastern moors. I rose to my feet and yawned, stretching to relieve the stiffness in my limbs.

I stared down angrily at Judd, who lay at my feet; his gown was torn and stained with blood where the strigoi had bitten him. There were livid purple puncture marks on his neck.

He suddenly opened his eyes and sat up, then groaned and held his head in his hands for a while, his whole body shuddering as he drew in deep breaths of air. At last he looked up at me. 'Where's your master?' he cried.

'He's dead,' I told him bluntly, feeling my throat tighten with emotion. 'No – it's worse than that. They've cut his head from his body but it still talks. They've used powerful dark magic, and his soul is a prisoner inside that head – and in terrible pain. I have to free him. I have to bring him peace. And it's all thanks to you. Why didn't you warn us? Why did you lead us into a trap? You claimed to know Mistress

Fresque. Surely you realized that she was a daemon?'

He just stared at me without replying.

'It was all very convenient, the way you had to go off to deal with that supposed boggart, leaving us to visit her house alone. You knew what was going to happen, didn't you?'

'Yes, I knew. It's a long story but I had little choice. Believe me – I didn't want to do it. I'm sorry for what happened.'

'Sorry!' I exclaimed. 'That's easy to say but it means nothing.'

He looked at me for a few moments without speaking before turning away. Then he reached towards me with his left hand. 'Help me up, Tom!'

Once on his feet, he swayed as if about to fall. I didn't try to steady him. At that moment he could have fallen onto his face and smashed his teeth in for all I cared.

'I need food. I'm weak – he took so much blood from me,' he muttered.

Could I trust him? I wondered. He certainly wasn't in league with the daemons now. I had to take a chance.

'I have rooms at the tavern over there,' I said,

pointing. 'I have money as well. I can buy us breakfast.'

Judd nodded. 'I'd be grateful for that, but go slowly. I'm as weak as a new-born kitten.'

There were fewer people about today, and I led the way through the near-empty streets towards the inn. I had to rap on the door a long time before the innkeeper finally opened it. He bent forward and scowled into my face as if trying to intimidate me.

'I'm surprised to see you again, boy! You must have more lives than a cat.'

'Mr Brinscall here will be using my master's room,' I told him as we went inside. 'But first we need a very big breakfast—'

'Aye, and make it thick slices of ham, eggs, sausage and lots of bread and butter. Oh, and a big pot of tea and a bowl of sugar,' Judd interrupted.

'Let's see the colour of your money first!' the innkeeper snapped angrily, noting his dirty ragged gown.

'I'll pay the bill, and in silver,' I told him.

'Then pay me before you cross that bridge again!' he sneered; then, without another word, went off to fry our breakfast.

'We've a lot to say to each other, Tom, a lot to explain, but I'm weary to my very bones. What do you say we eat first and talk later?' Judd suggested.

I nodded. I could hardly bear to look at him, and we ate in silence. Judd put three large spoonfuls of sugar into his tea. He sipped it slowly and smiled. 'I've always had a sweet tooth, Tom, but I really need that now!'

I didn't return his smile; I didn't even like to hear him using my name. The sugar didn't seem to help: soon he started nodding off at the table, so I tapped him on the shoulder and suggested that he went up to his room to sleep for a while.

While he did so, I put the time to good use. First I attempted to contact Alice using the small mirror in my room. After almost an hour I'd had no success. Deciding to try again later, I took my notebook out of my bag, crossed the bridge and walked back up onto the eastern moor.

I felt relatively safe with the sun shining, so once there I drew a rough map of Todmorden, concentrating on the positions of the big houses set back in the trees on this side of the river. I put crosses by the ones

I thought the orbs had emerged from. I was pretty sure about four of them, but the remaining five were in doubt. I also tried to pinpoint the place where I'd seen that strange column of red light. It was difficult to locate exactly, but I marked the general area. Whatever it was, it had certainly been of interest to the disembodied witches.

Then I went back to my room and tried once more to contact Alice, again without success. What could be wrong? I wondered. She usually responded much more quickly than this. I dozed on my bed, thinking through all that had happened. It was noon before Judd knocked on my door. We left the inn and walked into the trees near the riverbank. What we had to say wasn't for the ears of the innkeeper or anyone else.

We settled ourselves down, staring at the water, and I waited for him to speak.

'I have to begin by thanking you for my life, Tom. I would have died last night. At first they used to take only a little of my blood every seventh night – my body could just about cope with that. But that was the third time they'd fed since I last saw you.'

'You mean they'd kept you in the pit *before* they sent you to Chipenden?'

'They let me out so I could bring you here,' Judd explained.

'How long were you in the pit?' I asked him.

'A couple of months, give or take a few days. Strange, isn't it? We spooks put witches in pits. I never thought I'd end up in one myself!'

'How did you survive? What did you eat?'

'Luckily it wasn't the dead of winter or I'd have frozen to death,' Judd went on. 'But they fed me all right. They had to keep me alive in order to get the blood they needed. Each pair – each strigoi and strigoica – keep one or more prisoners whom they feed on. They'd really prefer to hunt and kill their prey in the surrounding countryside, but that would draw attention, and the military might be called in. As for food, they drop it into the pit raw. I've been living off raw mutton – sometimes offal.'

I pulled a face at the thought of eating raw offal.

'What would you do, Tom?' he asked, seeing my expression of disgust. 'I had little choice – eat that or die. Without food to replace what I lost when they bled me, I'd have been dead within a couple of weeks.'

I nodded. 'It's true,' I agreed. 'We do what's necessary in order to survive. I'd have done exactly the same.'

I knew that I was certainly not guiltless myself. Over the course of my three years as a spook's apprentice, the morals and standards taught me by my dad and mam had gradually been compromised. I'd been less than honest with my master, using dark magic to keep the Fiend at bay.

'Aye, it's a long twisting road that brings you to such a situation,' Judd murmured bitterly. 'As I said, my travels eventually took me to Romania, where I learned all about Transylvanian creatures of the dark and how best to combat them. Fat lot of good it did me in the end!

'They work together in that country, you see – elementals, daemons and witches plot and actively set out to destroy spooks. It wasn't long before I became their next target. They watch and wait, working out the best way to hurt or destroy you. I was easy meat. I was in love, you see. Spooks in the County don't usually take a wife, but in Romania the custom is different. I'd asked for a young woman's hand in marriage and had been accepted. We were in love and looking forward to the wedding. But it was not to be.

'A strigoica claimed her – they prefer living to dead bodies. You've met the daemon – she possesses the body of Cosmina Fresque.'

'Mistress Fresque is the woman you love? And she's host to the daemon?' I said, thinking how pretty Cosmina was and understanding why Judd had fallen in love with her. 'Isn't there anything we can do? Can't we drive the strigoica out of her body?'

'I only wish that were so, but possession by a Romanian daemon doesn't work like that – it's not the same as in the County. It can't be reversed. The soul is driven out and is unable to return.' Judd shook his head sadly. 'So consider her dead – I certainly do, and must learn to live with my grief. She's gone off into Limbo. I just hope she can find her way to the light. I've lost her, and have had a long time to think of my folly and how I was so easily duped.'

'So how did you end up here, back in the County?' I asked him.

'At first I was devastated by what had happened,' he

replied. 'For almost a year I wandered like a man insane, unable to do my job. They could have killed me then – and would have, but for the Romanian spook who'd trained me. I didn't even know he was there, but wherever I went, he followed close behind to defend me from the servants of the dark who wanted my life. Eventually I came to my senses, but then my mind was fixed only on vengeance. I wanted to kill that strigoica, or at least drive her from the body of my beloved Cosmina. I searched and searched but could find no trace of her – until at last I discovered that she had gone abroad with her strigoi partner. So I followed.

'They had been warned by witches – I told you that they work together – and were ready for me. Like a fool, I walked straight into their trap and ended up in the pit – food for the strigoi. After a week or so they passed me on to their neighbours further up the valley. They swap victims in some sort of trade. I think the flavour of blood varies – they like a change every now and then.'

'So did they promise you your freedom in exchange for luring me and the Spook here?' I wondered.

'That and something much more precious to me,'

Judd told me. 'You see, I'm half Romanian and, as I told you, still have family back in that country – my mother and her kin. If I didn't do as they said, they threatened to take their blood – to kill every last one of them. Of course they'd no intention of letting me go. After I left you I headed north, trying to put as much distance as possible between me and this cursed place. It hadn't been dark for more than an hour when they caught me and dragged me back to that pit. I just hope my family are all right.'

I understood the pressure he'd been under and sympathized, but I was still far from happy. There had been times when I'd be threatened by the dark in a similar way. But the Spook had instilled in me a strong sense of duty and I'd resisted. How could I ever forget that Judd Brinscall's betrayal had resulted in my master's death?

It was quite a while before I broke the uneasy silence that had fallen between us. 'Why are there so many Romanian servants of the dark here in Todmorden?' I asked.

'They came here to find space and fresh victims,' Judd told me. 'Romania has so many of their kind that whole areas, especially in the province of Transylvania, are under their control. They've been building up their numbers on the County border for years, but lying low so as not to draw too much attention to themselves. When there are enough of them here and they grow stronger, they will no longer be content to exist on the blood of victims confined in pits – they'll expand westwards into the County, killing wantonly.'

CHAPTER 15
THE VAMPIRE GOD

Our visit to Todmorden had cost my master his life, but he had not died in vain. Now that I knew of the increasing danger, and of the threat to the County, I could perhaps do something about it. Otherwise it might have developed and grown unchecked for many years. But first I had to retrieve the Spook's head and burn it in order to free his soul. Perhaps Judd Brinscall's knowledge of Romanian dark entities might help me to do that.

'How do you destroy a strigoica?' I asked him. 'I mean permanently, so that it can't go off and possess another body. How do you do that? I've killed two strigoi hosts already but it hasn't achieved anything in the long term. And Mistress Fresque told me that the first strigoi I drove from its body would quickly find a new one and be back to hunt me down.'

'Two? You've killed two? Which was the first one?'

'It was the partner of your enemy.'

'Well done, Tom,' Judd said with a grim smile. 'Then Cosmina is half avenged already. There are many ways of dealing with strigoii and strigoica, but few are permanent: even decapitation or a stake through the left eye can only drive them out of their host. Garlic or roses can be used as a defence, and while salt can't do them any great damage, a moat filled with salty water keeps them away.'

'That's the same method we used against water witches . . .' I realized.

'That it is, Tom. No doubt you spent a tough six months getting thick ears from Bill Arkwright. I'd had enough of it and ran back to Chipenden before my stay was half over,' Judd told me.

I nodded sadly. 'Bill's dead. He was killed in Greece fighting the dark.'

'Well, I can't say I liked the man,' he said, 'but I'm

sorry to hear that he's dead. The northern area of the County will be a more dangerous place now. What became of Tooth and Claw? They were good working dogs but Tooth didn't take to me much: he was well-named. He bit a piece out of my leg one night and the scar is still here to this day!'

'Tooth is dead, killed by water witches. But Claw is still alive and has two pups, Blood and Bone. We left them back at Chipenden with the local blacksmith,' I explained.

'Pity, that. They'd be more use here helping us with these witches,' Judd replied. 'But to return to what we were discussing: the way to put a permanent end to the strigoica who possess living bodies is to burn the body while they are still within it. With the strigoii who possess the dead, the only sure way is to expose them to sunlight. I know a lot about dealing with such creatures. We need to work together now – I want to make up for what I did and there's a lot that I can teach you. But one thing I can tell you: there's little to fear from the strigoi coming back to kill you. Oh, it'll find itself another host eventually, but once it's been driven out of a body its memory starts to disintegrate. With a different host it'll start a new stage of its existence and forget all about Todmorden and its former strigoica partner. She was just trying to frighten you, Tom, that's all.'

'I saw your book in the daemon's library – the one about the moroii,' I said.

'I wrote that in happier days. The daemons took it from me to make the library seem more convincing. You see, each strigoi and strigoica dwelling is a place of deceit, a house of illusions. They use a grimoire as the source of those illusions. That and my own book were probably the only real books in there. Now, explain why they wanted you and John Gregory here. They never bothered to tell me.'

I explained about our struggle against the Fiend and how we had bound him temporarily. Then I told him that Grimalkin was on the run with the Fiend's head, trying to keep it out of the hands of our enemies.

'Because you were guiding us here, we put most of our suspicions aside. It was only after they'd murdered my master that the strigoica explained what they wanted,' I explained. 'She had been put under pressure to lure us to Todmorden. You told me that they all worked together – well, they are certainly doing that now, and for a special purpose. They killed my master and bound his soul within his head just so they could put pressure on me. They want me to summon Grimalkin so that they may kill her and take back the Fiend's head in exchange. That's something I'm certainly not going to do. I need to find my master's head and burn it. They must have hidden it somewhere. We must search the hillside and check the house of every one of those daemons.'

'I'm sorry, Tom, but if we attempt that, they would know what we were up to before we reached the first house. Day or night, one of each pair is always awake and alert to any threats. They'd sense us almost immediately and summon the witches to defend them. Romanian witches use *animism magic.* Unlike Pendle witches, who generally use blood, bone or familiar magic, they draw the life force out of their victims without even touching them. Their orbs would be there in the blinking of an eye. Within seconds we'd be dead, our animas drained. Later they'd use what they'd taken from us in rituals and incantations, and gather further power from the dark.'

'So what *can* we do?' I demanded, frustrated by Judd's explanation. I already knew most of what he'd just told me, but that knowledge wouldn't deter me. I *had* to release my master's spirit. I was determined to do *something*.

'We'd have to deal with the witches first,' Judd continued, 'picking them off one by one. That might give us half a chance. Unlike female daemons, witches sleep during the day so that's the time to strike. They don't have a partner to watch over them.'

'Are the witches more powerful than the daemons?' I asked.

'Yes, without a doubt – the moroii are the weakest of the hierarchy. So we try to kill the witches first – take them unawares while they are sleeping.'

'Well, I know where at least four of their houses are,' I told Judd. 'While you were sleeping, I went up onto the moor again and marked them on a map. Here they are . . .' I reached into my breeches pocket, pulled out my sketch and handed it to him.

He studied it for a few moments and then gave me a searching glance. 'What's that?' he asked, pointing to a mark I'd made.

'There was a strange beam of light, coloured an unusual dark shade of red. It came out of the ground beneath the trees and shone high into the sky. I've never seen anything like it before. The witches came in the form of orbs and circled it in a sort of dance, flitting in and out of the beam. After a while they soared off. It wasn't long afterwards that the strigoi started to feed from you and I came down the hill to see if I could help.'

Judd shook his head and stared at the ground for a long time without speaking. What I'd just said had clearly affected him. Then I noticed his hands – they were shaking.

'What's wrong?' I asked.

'This is going from bad to worse. From what you've just told me, the witches are attempting to summon Siscoi, the greatest and most powerful of the Old Gods in Romania. Their spooks have many successful methods for dealing with ordinary vampiric entities such as witches, elementals and daemons, but the vampire god is truly dangerous – we are utterly powerless against him.'

The name sounded familiar. Again, I was annoyed at

myself for not reading the Spook's Bestiary more carefully. I was sure it had made some reference to Siscoi. 'Is it easy to summon him?' I asked. 'Some of the Old Gods are difficult to bring to our world.'

'That they are, Tom, and they can turn on those who summon them,' Judd replied. 'Some welcome the chance to destroy those who dabble in the dark. But unfortunately for us, Siscoi is different. He loves being worshipped and looks kindly upon those who bring him through a portal into this world. Romanian witches are able to summon him at midnight, but he can stay here only until dawn. That's the good news. The bad news is that even from his domain in the dark, he can temporarily send out his spirit to reanimate the dead or possess the living. So you might think you're dealing with a strigoi, and then, too late, you realize that the silver blade on the end of your staff is having no effect because it's Siscoi. And that's the end of you. There's nothing to be done.'

'What about this?' I asked, drawing the Destiny Blade.

Judd whistled through his teeth and his face lit up in admiration. 'Can I examine it?' he asked.

I nodded and handed him the weapon.

'So this is the sword you used to kill two strigoi hosts,' he said, studying the hilt closely. 'The skelt has been skilfully wrought, and those rubies that form its eyes are priceless. How did such a weapon come into your possession?'

'It was given to me in the Hollow Hills by Cuchulain, one of the ancient heroes of Ireland. It was forged by the Old God Hephaestus. He made only three swords, and this is supposed to be the best of them.'

'Well, Tom, you certainly mix in exalted circles. Made by one of the Old Gods, you say! I wonder if it has the power to slay one of their number?' Judd asked.

'I used it against the Morrigan – it didn't destroy her, but it slowed her down and gave me a chance to escape,' I explained.

'You fought the Morrigan?'

'It was in the Hollow Hills, just after Cuchulain gave me the blade.'

'You've certainly had an eventful apprenticeship. I never ventured out of the County. No wonder I got the urge to travel and ended up in this mess,' Judd said, handing me the blade. 'But even if it could damage

Siscoi, you'd never get near him. Vampiric entities can be fast, but nothing compared to him. You'd be dead before you knew it.'

My ability to slow time would give me a fighting chance of wounding Siscoi with the sword, but it didn't mean I could put an end to him. The Old Gods had great powers of regeneration. Using the blade against the Morrigan had just bought me sufficient time to make my escape. However, I didn't bother to correct Judd – it wasn't wise to tell him too much. I didn't tell him about Bone Cutter either. If the daemons put pressure on him in the future, he might tell them what he knew about me. So instead I asked him a question.

'So what was that light shining out of the ground? How do the witches raise Siscoi?'

'They create an *offal pit,*' Judd replied. 'First they search for a deep fissure in the ground. It has to be in a special location where dark magic is particularly potent. Over a period of weeks, they drop blood and offal down into it – mainly slices of raw liver. When combined with rituals and dark spells, this generates tremendous power within the pit – the beam is just a fraction of this escaping into the air. Siscoi grows himself a body by feeding on the offal and blood. When he is ready, the witches come at midnight to complete the final ritual. Then he climbs out of the pit within his flesh host, existing in the same manner as the Fiend. From what you've described, it seems that the witches' rituals have reached the point where he is almost ready to emerge. It could happen at any time – maybe even at midnight tonight.'

'What could be their purpose for summoning him right now?' I asked.

'They might just want to worship him. In return, he'll give them power. But they've already tried to pressure you into bringing Grimalkin here. They want the Fiend's head badly. Siscoi is fast, and once in the flesh can cover great distances rapidly. He might go after Grimalkin himself. After that you might be second on his list.'

CHAPTER 16
THE OFFAL PIT

'So we need to find a way to stop Siscoi,' I said.

Judd gave me a humourless grin. 'There's nothing I'd like better. At this time of year it's about four and a half hours from midnight to dawn. He could do a lot of damage in that time. But all my training in Romania doesn't give me the slightest inkling of how it could be done. And even if we had the means, the witches would be there within seconds.'

'Not if we do it during daylight hours. They'll be sleeping then. If warned, could they still project their souls from their bodies when the sun is shining?'

'I've never heard of such a thing – though it *might* be possible. I assume you're thinking of attacking Siscoi while he's still forming in the pit. What have you in mind, Tom?'

'I'd like to try one of the oldest tricks in a spook's repertoire – salt and iron,' I said.

Judd shook his head. 'We'd most likely be wasting our time. Salt and iron don't work against Romanian witches, elementals or daemons.'

'They don't usually work against the Old Gods, either. But that's when they are fully awake and ready to rend the flesh from your bones. Siscoi is still growing his body from the blood and offal in the pit. I'm sure salt could burn that vulnerable half-formed body, and iron might bleed away its strength. They might not stop him, but they could slow him down and give us a chance to search for my master. What do you say? Isn't it worth a try? Let's do it now while the sun's still shining! We can tip salt and iron into the offal pit and then deal with the sleeping witches one by one.'

'But there's one other danger to consider, Tom,' Judd warned me. 'The strigoica will be awake now, guarding their partners. Even if the witch orbs don't threaten us, *they* certainly will. And they are as fast and dangerous as the strigoii.'

'I have speed too. And I have the sword,' I pointed out.

Judd frowned. 'If I'm to be any help at all, I need a weapon of my own.'

Tucked into my belt beneath my cloak hung Bone Cutter, the dagger I'd been given by Slake. But I wasn't going to lend it to Judd – it was one of the three sacred objects, and I couldn't risk losing it. So I kept quiet about it. I wasn't sure if we'd find a blacksmith to help in Todmorden. Judging from what we'd experienced so far I didn't expect much cooperation. Then I remembered the village. I glanced up at the sun. 'We've about seven hours of daylight left,' I told him. 'Remember the village we passed through on our way here. It had a blacksmith and a grocer's and it's less than an hour away. We could get large bags of salt from the shop – we'll need more than just pocketfuls – and all the iron filings we need from the smith. Maybe even a weapon of some sort for you.'

Judd got to his feet. 'Very well – let's get moving.'

We walked fast through the empty streets. Why was

the town so quiet? I wondered. I noticed that a few curtains twitched as we passed by, but no one was abroad.

We climbed the hill up onto the western moors and reached the smithy within three-quarters of an hour. A large bag of iron filings proved no problem, but acquiring a weapon for Judd was more difficult. The blacksmith's routine tasks consisted of shoeing horses, mending ploughs and forging domestic ironmongery. He had never crafted a blade in his life. But he did have a number of axes used by farmers to clear their land of trees and scrub. They weren't the double-bladed war-axes used in battle, nor did they have silver-alloy blades, but they could do considerable damage if wielded correctly.

Judd tried a few of these but did not choose the largest. Of course, we didn't discuss our requirements in front of the smith, but I noticed that he selected one that was light and sharp and easy to wield.

Next we visited the village grocer and bought up most of his supply of salt. Soon, carrying our sacks of salt and iron, with Judd resting the axe across his left shoulder, we were retracing our steps towards

Todmorden. As we crossed the river, I felt the bridge shudder and glanced down at it in alarm. It looked more dilapidated than ever and ready to fall into the river. I hoped we wouldn't have to cross it too many more times.

The sun was still shining from a clear sky and I estimated that we still had just over five hours of day-light remaining – ample time to deal with Siscoi and kill as many witches as possible, I told myself, trying to bolster my confidence.

I didn't dwell on the details of what was involved. What we were attempting was extremely risky. Our enemies cooperated and worked together, and an attack on one would constitute an attack on them all. If they gathered together quickly, we would be hope-lessly outnumbered. But I put that thought out of my head, driven by my sense of duty to the County and the hope of somehow freeing my master's spirit.

We climbed up onto the edge of the eastern moor, and once again crouched down in the scrub.

'Look, over there,' I told Judd. 'That's where I saw the beam of light shining up through the trees.'

He nodded. 'Which are the witches' houses?'

I got out the map again and pointed to the four houses I had marked.

'Think they're the right ones?' he asked. 'We need to be sure.'

'Yes, I definitely saw the orbs leave them. There are other possible witch houses, but I've only marked those I'm certain of.'

'Once we've done our best with these,' Judd said, pointing to the sacks at our feet, 'we'll deal with those four witches, then hurry back across the river and try to survive the night.'

I nodded in agreement, and we picked up the sacks and made our way down the slope, heading for the clump of trees that shrouded the offal pit. No sooner had I moved into the gloom of the forest than it hit me – the cold feeling that warns a seventh son of a seventh son that some evil entity from the dark is close.

Judd glanced at me sideways. 'I feel it too,' he remarked. 'But what is it – Siscoi growing himself a body? Or is something else on guard, lying in wait for intruders?'

'We'll soon find out,' I said, moving forward.

I found out even sooner than I expected. There was no warning growl. The attack came so quickly that, taken by surprise, I only had time to drop my sack and reach for my sword. A large bear was coming directly towards us on all fours, its teeth bared. It rose up before us, immense on its hind legs, all muscle, fur and furious eyes, ready to rip us apart. Before I could get my blade clear of its scabbard, Judd pushed past me and swung the axe in a fast arc.

There was a sickening, crunching thud as it made contact. The first blow landed high up on the bear's shoulder. The wounded creature gave a roar of anger and pain. When the second swing drove the axe into its neck, it screamed – a shrill sound that could have come from a human throat. Judd got in three more blows before the bear fell sideways like a huge tree toppled by a woodsman's axe.

Judd stepped back from his kill. 'Fast?' he said, glancing at my half-drawn sword with a grin. 'I was faster! You'll need to do better than that when the first strigoica comes after you!'

'Don't worry, I will,' I said, sheathing my sword again. 'A moroi, wasn't it?' I gestured down at the dead bear. 'It was guarding the approach to the Fresque house last time I saw it.'

'Maybe it was, but there'll likely be more than one, Tom,' Judd told me. 'This one was set to patrol and guard the area around the pit. It's gloomy and sheltered, but they don't usually come out in daylight, so powerful magic has been used to bring it here.

'I've been thinking, and I realize that there's a much easier way to deal with moroii: they are creatures governed by compulsions. If you cast nuts, seeds, berries, twigs or even blades of grass in front of them, they immediately drop down on all fours as if in a trance. They are compelled to count and retrieve every last one and until that's accomplished they can do nothing else. And one count is never enough. They have to repeat the procedure to check that the total is the same. They can spend hours counting and re-counting. This means that we could either escape or deal it a killing blow!'

I nodded and smiled. That was worth knowing for future reference. It made me realize how much I still had to learn. Now that my master was gone, my apprenticeship had come to a premature end: I had to learn whenever the opportunity presented itself – even from Judd. I couldn't afford to let my feelings get in the way of that need. I had to update the Bestiary whenever I could, and even write books of my own. My master's work had to continue.

Judd and I moved forward cautiously, searching for the entrance to the offal pit. Our noses found it well before our eyes. The stench was overpowering: the stink of offal, rotting meat and the sharp metallic odour of blood. Close to the root of a large oak was a large, irregular-shaped flattish stone. There was an oval hole near its centre, and its edges were still wet with blood. We stepped forward together and peered down into the darkness. I shuddered with fear and took a deep breath to calm myself. But I had good reason to be afraid. Unless we found a permanent way to stop him, soon the Old God, Siscoi, would climb up and emerge from the pit.

'I can't see a thing,' I told Judd, stating the obvious.

'Trust me, Tom, neither of us wants to see what's forming down there – but listen carefully and we might hear it.'

We listened. From deep within the fissure came faint,

sinister noises. I held my breath so as to hear them better. Then I almost wished I hadn't. Far below, mercifully hidden by darkness, something was breathing. The rhythm was slow and steady, and suggested a very large entity.

'The host is down there, all right,' Judd said. 'But don't you worry. There's no way he'll be able to climb up until Siscoi takes possession of his flesh. It can only happen at midnight, with the help of witches performing spells and rituals.'

'How many witches do we have to deal with to stop that?' I asked.

'Hard to say – even three survivors might constitute a coven. But one thing's certain. The fewer there are, the harder they'll find it.'

Without further debate we carefully tipped out the bags of salt and iron to form mounds beside the opening. Then, working quickly, we mixed the two substances together with our hands.

'Ready?' Judd asked.

I nodded, ready to push the mixture down into the darkness.

'Well, we're about to find out if you were right,' he

said. 'On the count of three, we do it! One, two, *three*!'

Working together, we sent the salt and iron cascading down into the pit. For a moment nothing happened, then suddenly there was a scream of agony from below, followed by low groans.

Judd grinned at me. 'Well done, Tom! Sometimes the tried and trusted methods *do* work best. Siscoi will be none too pleased when he finds his host damaged. Now for the first of the witches – but first I'd better tell you a bit more about them,' he said, rising to his feet. 'They collect the life force of humans to achieve certain ends, one of which is to accumulate wealth. They like to live in big houses and lord it over the local humans.'

'So that's why the people here avoid spooks and seem so uncooperative. They're scared. They know what they are dealing with,' I realized.

'That's right, Tom. No doubt the whole town is terrified,' Judd replied.

'I know about the orbs and their use of animism magic, but what about when their souls are back in their bodies? Are they similar to Pendle witches or lamias?' I asked.

'Like many witches, they try to scry the future in order

to destroy their enemies. But the summoning of their vampire god Siscoi is the icing on the cake – he gives them power and makes them even more formidable.

'They do have one thing in common with lamias – they are shape-shifters. But whereas lamia witches change from the domestic to the feral form over a period of weeks or months, Romanian witches do it in the blinking of an eye. One moment you're looking at a woman dressed in her finery. The next it's in tatters on her back and she's all claws and teeth. And here's where John Gregory's Bestiary needs updating: it's true that they don't use blood magic, but that doesn't stop them eating flesh and taking blood. Most victims have fallen to the ground before they can even react to the danger. Moments later they're ripped to pieces.'

I frowned, my mind reeling with all the information I'd just been given.

'Let's go and deal with the first one . . .' Judd suggested.

We left the trees and headed across a sunny meadow towards the nearest of the big houses I'd seen an orb emerge from. As far as I could tell, apart from a buzzard hovering to the west, there was nothing moving on the hillside, but I could hear the distant sounds of human activity from the County side of the river.

We climbed over a stile and continued downwards. Each large house was surrounded by its own protective clump of trees and, as we approached our target, the sunlight was blocked out again. Judd signalled a halt, put a finger to his lips and leaned close, whispering into my ear.

'There should be no illusions to bother us here – witch houses don't shift their shape – but there could be traps set to warn her. As soon as we enter the premises she'll wake up. So it's no good creeping in – stealth won't work. We go in fast. I'll take the lead; you cover my back – all right, Tom?'

I nodded. 'You're the expert here,' I conceded in a low voice. I had to be pragmatic and force myself to trust Judd. We had to work together.

The house was big and there would be lots of rooms to search. Judd wasted no time. He went straight up to the front door and kicked it open. I drew my sword and followed him inside. We found ourselves in a small entrance hall with three doors leading off it. He chose the central one. Despite the fact that there was no obvious lock, he used his left boot again and went in fast. We found ourselves in a large drawing room. I looked around, surprised: County witches usually lived in hovels, with unwashed pots and dishes, cobwebbed ceilings and filthy floors, a pile of bones – some of them human – lying in a corner. But this room had been meticulously cleaned and was expensively furnished. I saw paintings of strange landscapes – possibly in Romania: one showed a castle on a high hill rising above green forests. There were two comfortable chairs and a settee placed close to a fire, where the ashes still glowed in the grate. On the mantelpiece above stood three candlesticks; the candles were of best quality beeswax rather than the black ones favoured by the Pendle witches (who used the blood of their victims mixed with cheap tallow from animal fat).

But the inhabitants of this house were witches all right – creatures of the dark – and the familiar cold warning moved down my spine.

There was a door to the right at the far end of the room. Judd went over and kicked that open too. There wasn't much light, but over his shoulder I could just make out a large bed draped with a purple silken cover.

Somebody lay sleeping there. Judd raised his axe and prepared to bring it down hard and fast.

Suddenly I sensed that something was wrong.

The witch wasn't in the bed; she was *under* it.

She was upon us in an instant, all teeth and claws.

CHAPTER 17 THE PACT

Her claws were just inches from Judd's left leg when I stabbed downwards with the sword, transfixing her through the heart and pinning her, face down, to the floorboards.

The witch struggled desperately to free herself, growling deep in her throat, spitting blood, and shaking her long matted hair from side to side. Her long-taloned hands clenched and unclenched, and she twisted her head to look up at me, ill-wishing me with her venomous eyes.

I had seen hideous water witches and shuddered at the ugliest of the Pendle hags, but this was a terrifying sight indeed. The witch's skin was coarse, with clusters of hairy warts sprouting like fungi all over her face, and when she opened her mouth in a growl, I saw that her canines were two black tusks protruding down over her bottom lip.

Then she reached round to her back, gripping the blade, cutting her fingers to the bone as she desperately tried to pull it out of her body. But the growls turned to gurgling, choking noises, and blood began to spurt from her mouth to splatter on the floor. I held fast to the sword, pushing it harder into the wood. Judd put the matter beyond doubt when he brought down the axe to sever her head from her body.

'Good man!' he cried. 'You were fast enough that time. Oldest trick in the book!' He drew back the bed-cover to show the two pillows artfully arranged to suggest the contours of a body. 'She must have been awake even before I kicked down the first door.'

I pulled the sword free and wiped it on the bedcover, then returned it to its scabbard. Judd had used an axe and I a sword – and the thought came to me that it was unusual to have two spooks fighting without staffs. But we had to adapt to the circumstances.

'We need to make sure she doesn't come back from the dead,' I said. 'Do the usual methods work for Romanian witches?'

Judd shook his head. 'Eating the heart is useless with this lot, but burning works. However, it's usually at least a month before they can reanimate their bodies. If we kill them all, we can burn them in their own houses long before then.'

Suddenly the room became even gloomier and we looked towards the window. Judd dashed across and drew back the curtain. When we'd entered the house the sky had been blue, but now rain clouds were racing across the sky, which was growing darker by the second.

We hurried out of the witch's bedroom and stopped just outside the front door. A flash of lightning lit the sky to the north, to be answered by a deep rumble of thunder a couple of seconds later.

'This isn't a natural storm,' Judd said. 'They must all be awake and alert by now. When they work together, Romanian witches can raise the wind and darken the skies. They probably know what we've done.'

The next moment a fork of lightning split the sky; the

thunder was deafening and almost instantaneous. In the eerie silence that followed, we both heard the noises. Twigs cracked, footsteps shuffled through the grass; unseen things were approaching through the trees from more than one direction.

'Run, Tom – this way!' Judd cried, sprinting down the hill towards the river. I obeyed without question, hot on his heels. I could sense our enemies closing in on all sides. My greatest fear was that the other witches would project themselves after us in the form of orbs. It wasn't night-time, but it might be gloomy enough for them to venture forth.

However, we were soon running through the narrow streets, the rain beginning to drum on the cobbles. There were other noises coming from the direction of the bridge. When we reached the trees, we saw half a dozen men with axes on the far bank, attacking the bridge supports.

'Stop that!' Judd cried. 'Stop now!'

The men simply ignored him and continued with their work. We ran faster, but before we reached the bank, with a groan and a crash, the bridge fell into the river. For a moment the wreckage remained attached to our side, but then the whole rotten structure collapsed into the water, where it was instantly broken into pieces and swept downstream.

The men on the far bank waved their axes at us threateningly. 'Stay on that side!' one shouted. 'You're a danger to us all. You're not wanted here. Cross at your peril!'

Why had they cut down the bridge now? Was it to trap us on the eastern bank so that the witches and daemons could seize us more easily? Were they were trying to appease them? I wondered.

Judd spoke into my ear, keeping his voice low. 'They'll soon get fed up and clear off – we just need to be patient. There's no need for anybody to get hurt. They're scared, that's all.'

He was right. If we forced our way across the river, the men looked desperate enough to put up a fight. So we sat down on a log, each lost in his thoughts, while they glared at us from the far bank.

We'd escaped for now, but I felt dejected. I had done nothing to help my master, and now we had alerted the witches. They would be ready for us next time.

After a while Judd's prediction proved correct. The

men shouted a few curses at us, then headed off through the trees towards the huddle of houses. We gave it another five minutes, then scrambled down the muddy bank and found a place to cross; years ago, no doubt, it had been a ford. Then, our breeches soaked to the knee, we made our way directly towards the inn, ready for trouble. I doubted we'd seen the last of the townsfolk.

'Grab some sleep before supper, Tom,' Judd said. 'Once it's dark, anything can happen. We may not even be safe on this side of the river.'

I tried to sleep but just dozed intermittently. My mind was whirling with all that had happened during the past few days. I couldn't see any way to salvage our situation.

It was then that I suddenly started to think about Alice again. I wondered if she'd managed to find Grimalkin. I just hoped she'd kept her promise and hadn't gone off into the dark without talking to me first. But one part of me was glad she hadn't come to Todmorden with us: she would be in terrible danger here. The other part was desperate for her help and company. She'd got me out of tight situations before and had saved my life more than once.

I decided to use the mirror on the bedside table to try and contact her again, but no sooner had the thought crossed my mind than it suddenly lit up. I realized why thoughts of Alice had come into my mind. She was trying to contact me. A moment later her face was smiling at me from the mirror, but then she looked concerned and began to write quickly with her finger. The text appeared backwards, but we'd used this method of communication many times and I was well practised at reading it.

Is something wrong, Tom?
I expected you back long before now.

She had guessed that I was in trouble because our return to Chipenden was long overdue. We should have been back two days ago. Suddenly my need overcame my reluctance to draw her into danger, so I knelt in front of the bedside table, breathed on the mirror, and wrote with my forefinger. I did it very slowly, doing my best to make it legible. And I chose my words carefully. I didn't say that my master was dead because I wanted to break that news to her face to face. There would be time for explanations later.

A daemon took my master . . .

Then, to save time, I wiped the mirror with the back of my hand, put my face close to it and started to mouth words. I did it in an exaggerated way to make it easier to understand:

'The daemon is powerful and has many allies. We are in great danger. Help me if you can. Get here as soon as you can or it may be too late . . .'

I hated the thought of bringing Alice into danger, but I knew that she could make all the difference. However, I also thought about her use of dark magic. On our journey back across Ireland she had experienced pain every time we crossed a bridge over running water, and it had been hard to hide the fact from my master. I'd complained when she'd given Agnes Sowerbutts strength – so asking her to help now made me feel like a hypocrite, and I knew that it would have upset my master. But sometimes, in order to survive, we'd had to use the powers of the dark in order to overcome it.

Before Alice could reply, the mirror suddenly went

dark. I waited, expecting her to re-establish contact – but in vain. Suddenly a terrifying thought came into my head. What if Alice had already found Grimalkin and was bringing the witch assassin with her? The Romanian forces wanted the Fiend's head. If the sack was here, their task would be made far easier. I should have remembered that and warned Alice, but I'd expected our conversation to be longer than this. I held the mirror and called Alice's name, but there was no response.

After a while I gave up and went to knock on Judd's door. He came out yawning and rubbing his eyes. 'Time for supper?' he asked.

I frowned. 'Can't say that I'm very hungry.'

'Neither am I, Tom,' Judd said, 'but we need to keep up our strength. It could be a long, dangerous night.'

'My master never ate much when facing the dark,' I pointed out.

Judd nodded and gave me a wry smile. 'I remember it well – a few nibbles of County cheese was all he allowed us. Some nights I was so hungry, my belly thought my throat had been cut.'

We went downstairs to be served supper by the fire

by the surly innkeeper. It was tough cold mutton and stale bread, and I found it difficult to swallow. I was nervous about what might happen when night fell. Judd had no appetite either. After a while the landlord came back to collect our plates.

'How long have you lived in Todmorden?' I asked, trying to draw him into conversation and learn more about the town.

He shrugged. 'More years than I care to remember. I was born here, and no doubt I'll die here. But I mind my own business – and so should you. I'm off to bed now,' he told us with a scowl.

We weren't going to get any information from him, and I was glad to see the back of him. As soon as he'd clumped upstairs, Judd and I were able to talk more freely. I began to tell him about Alice – and some of the things she'd done in the past.

'I'll bet John Gregory found most of that difficult to stomach – even worse than our supper!' he joked. 'I find it hard to believe that he'd ally himself with the dark. I've never known any other man with such strong principles.'

'He had little choice,' I explained. 'It was a question

of survival – but he found it difficult all right. Alice might just be able to find what we're looking for, though. She could sniff my master out – lead us straight to the place where they're keeping his head.'

'That's certainly true. They'll be ready for us, but if we know precisely where to go, we can get in and out quickly,' he agreed.

The hours passed and there was no sign of the anticipated attack. But just before dawn we heard a sudden loud hammering at the front door of the inn.

Judd rose to his feet and readied his axe. I drew my sword, wondering what to do for the best. We had no intention of opening the door, and I was sure that the innkeeper would not do so before the sun came up. Was it better to wait for them to break it down or take the fight to them outside? Then I heard a sash window being raised upstairs.

'You have two within your walls who have committed crimes against my people!' a woman's voice cried out. 'Surrender them to us so they may be punished!'

I saw a look of pain flicker across Judd's face, and suddenly recognized the voice calling up to the window. It was Mistress Fresque. I could see that Judd was determined to leave the inn and confront the daemon who was using her body.

'No!' I said, grabbing his arm to restrain him. 'There may be other strigoica concealed nearby.'

He nodded and relaxed a little. Then the innkeeper called out: 'It will be done before nightfall. We will keep to the pact, don't you worry.'

'A *pact*?' Judd said, raising his eyebrows. 'I wonder what that's all about ... I think that surly fellow upstairs has a few questions to answer!'

We heard the innkeeper slam the window shut, and sat by the embers of the fire, waiting for him to come downstairs.

When he appeared, he was dressed in a jacket and scarf. He seemed surprised to see us sitting by the hearth. No doubt he'd thought we were fast asleep in bed.

'I have to go out,' he blustered. 'I'll be back within the hour to attend to your breakfasts.'

But before he could reach the door, Judd had intercepted him, laying a firm hand on his arm and leading him towards the fireplace. 'I don't think you'll be going out until later. We have a few questions to put to you!' he said, pushing him down into a chair.

The innkeeper looked up at Judd with frightened eyes.

'We heard you talking to the daemon!' Judd accused him.

'Daemon? I don't know what you're talking about.'

'Do you deny that you were talking to Mistress Fresque? We heard every word. So tell us – what's this "pact" you have with her?'

The innkeeper stared up at him but didn't reply.

Judd raised the axe as if he meant to bring it down on the man's head. 'Talk or die!' he commanded. 'I'm a desperate man, and the way things are at the moment, I don't expect to live much longer. If necessary, I'll take you with me. What's the pact?'

'It's an agreement we have with the foreigners on the other side of the river. It's what keeps us safe and stops them from eating us . . .'

'Go on – tell me more,' Judd commanded when the man hesitated. 'What's your side of the bargain?'

'Every week we supply them with three cartloads of offal and animal blood from the surrounding farms. We leave it in sacks and barrels on this side of the river, and they come across after dark to collect it.'

So this was where they got their supplies for the offal pit. They no doubt fed themselves and their prisoners from the same source. The pact also probably explained why the orbs of the witches hadn't pursued us over the bridge.

'So in return they leave you alone?' I asked.

'Yes, they don't kill humans on this side of the river. But we must stay indoors after dark – they sometimes pass through our streets to journey elsewhere. They're making maps of the County to the west of here.'

'Maps!' Judd exclaimed. 'You fool! Don't you see what's happening? They're charting the County to decide how best to seek out more victims! Can't you see what you're doing? You're selling the lives of your fellows so that you may live. And now you plan to hand us over for the same selfish purpose. Don't deny it because we heard every word! You're not going anywhere. You can stay here and cook us some breakfast instead – and we want something better than what you served up last night.'

'But if we do nothing before night falls, the pact will

be at an end. They'll slaughter us all!' the landlord cried.

'Let us worry about that,' Judd replied. 'Some of the townsfolk have destroyed the bridge – so isn't the pact over already? If so, it's time to fight for your lives.'

'The bridge can be replaced. Once they have you, things will return to normal – they've promised us.'

'*Normal!* You call that "normal", you fool!' Judd shouted. 'Just get out of my sight! Breakfast – that's what you need to concern yourself with. Make it quick.'

The innkeeper scurried off with a fearful backward glance at Judd, who immediately spoke quietly into my ear so that he couldn't be overheard: 'When do you reckon the girl will get here?'

'Well before sunset,' I replied. 'She'll have been travelling through the night.'

'Then I see it this way, Tom. As soon as she arrives, we can get her to sniff out what's left of your poor master. We'll collect his remains and head straight back to Chipenden, where we can muster help as best we can. We might even have to enlist the services of the military.'

What Judd was saying made sense. We were

hopelessly outnumbered. We *did* need the military. But would they listen and intervene? I wondered.

The innkeeper had just starting frying our breakfast when there was another thumping on the door. We went to the window and saw about two dozen of the townsfolk outside. They looked desperate and angry; some were armed with clubs. No doubt Mistress Fresque had told them of the situation. Either that or they'd heard what she'd shouted up at the window.

'Open up!' they shouted. 'Do it now or we'll break down the door.'

We didn't bother to reply. There was no point in trying to reason with a terrified mob. After a while they withdrew down the street, but then I saw them approaching the inn again. This time they were carrying a heavy battering ram – a stout cylindrical log with brass ends. I didn't think the door would stand up to that, and I was quickly proved correct.

'One! Two! Three!' someone shouted – and on 'three' there was a tremendous thud as the battering ram struck the door. It buckled under the force of the blow, and the crash brought the innkeeper running in from the kitchen. It wouldn't be long before the lock gave way. What then? It was one thing to use my sword against dark entities; quite another to attack terrified men who were no doubt fathers, brothers and sons.

The innkeeper ran forward as if to open the door and let the men in, but Judd seized him by the collar and held him in an arm-lock.

I was at war with myself, not sure what to do for the best. I drew my sword anyway. If taken prisoner, we would end up in the pits, food for the strigoii.

The second blow to the door was louder than the first. It groaned, and a shower of plaster fell down from the ceiling.

'Don't have much respect for your property, do they?' Judd commented, but the innkeeper remained tight-lipped.

In the intervals between each blow the air was filled with curses and shouts. The men sounded desperate, and it was only a matter of time before the door gave way.

At the fifth attempt, it crashed inwards and we stood facing our attackers. We stared at them in silence, but then I heard the sudden barking of dogs in the distance. There was something familiar about the sound that caught my attention; something I recognized. It was the distinctive hunting calls of Claw, Blood and Bone.

It must be Alice. She had brought the dogs with her!

The men turned nervously, and suddenly scattered. I knew that the three wolfhounds were a fearsome sight, but the men seemed terrified beyond reason. We stepped out onto the cobbled street, and moments later I realized why.

Alice was accompanied by someone else – Grimalkin, the witch assassin. She was running towards us, black mouth agape to reveal sharp filed teeth. Blades hung from the leather straps that criss-crossed her lithe body, and she clutched a dagger in each hand. It was fortunate that the townsfolk had fled. She looked ready to kill.

I would normally have welcomed her as a formidable ally, but she was carrying the Fiend's head in the leather sack over her shoulder. She had come to the one place that should have been avoided at all costs.

This was exactly where the Romanian dark entities wanted her.

This was a trap.

CHAPTER 18

THE MOST DANGEROUS PLACE

We stood aside to let the pair in, followed by the dogs, then closed the door as best we could and sat around the largest of the inn's tables.

The innkeeper kept glancing at Grimalkin, clearly terrified, but he served us a hot breakfast, heaping our plates with ham, eggs and fried bread until we could eat no more.

'What about the dogs?' I said to him. 'They've travelled a long way and need feeding too.'

For a moment he hesitated, but then Grimalkin glared at him, opening her mouth to show her sharp pointy teeth. His hands began to tremble and he hurried away, returning with scraps of meat for the dogs.

While we ate, I made the introductions and explained the situation in Todmorden, relating everything that had happened since I left Chipenden with my master and Judd.

When I came to the condition of my master, the words stuck in my throat and I couldn't go on. Alice reached across the table and put her hand on my arm in sympathy. I felt a surge of warmth for her. Despite our recent differences I had really missed her.

At that point Judd Brinscall interrupted. 'Please, before Tom goes any further, I have to tell you my part in this. It won't make for good listening – I'm truly sorry and ashamed of what I did.'

I was relieved – it saved me from having to tell everybody about his betrayal. So, with a tremor in his voice, Judd told his story, making no attempt to justify his actions, other than to explain the threats that had been made against his mother and her kin, and the possession of Cosmina Fresque's body by the daemon. When he'd finished, he bowed his head and stared down at the table.

Nobody offered him any sympathy. I still found it impossible to forgive him. Grimalkin glared at him with death in her eyes.

But then my conscience forced me to confess my own failings. 'I've nothing to be proud of, either,' I admitted. 'At one point I was down in the cellar, trying to find my master. Suddenly I was faced with daemons. It was dark and there were lots of them. I fled in a panic . . . I ran away.'

There was another silence until Alice spoke relieving the tension in the room. Her words were addressed to me. 'What did you see down in that cellar the second time, Tom? What exactly did the strigoica show you?'

A lump came into my throat, and for a few seconds I was unable to speak. In my mind's eye I saw her lifting the lid of the box to reveal the horror within.

'They had my master's head in a box. By means of dark magic, it still lived. She said they'd fed the rest of his body to a moroi. He talked to me and said he was in terrible pain. He begged me to release him from his torment.'

Judd lifted his head and stared at me, then stood up

and gripped me by the shoulders. 'Where were you when you saw the head?'

'The Fresque house.'

Judd slapped his hand hard against his head three times and his eyes widened. 'Now I see!' he cried. 'How many times have you been in that house, Tom?' he demanded.

'Four . . . no, five times,' I answered.

'And am I right in thinking that its appearance changed each time you entered?'

'Yes – on the last occasion I was there, the door to the cellar was gone. There was just a blank wall.'

'Listen to me, Tom. Nothing in there ever remains the same for long. Remember what I told you about the houses of strigoii and strigoica? They draw power from a grimoire to maintain their illusions. I don't want to raise your hopes too much . . . but you know what I'm getting at, don't you?'

My heart soared, and despite his warning I was filled with new hope. 'I saw their grimoire. They were using the *Doomdryte*, one of the most powerful and dangerous of all. So you mean the head in that box might have been an illusion . . . that my master isn't really dead? Could that really be possible?'

'As I said, don't get your hopes too high, but yes, it is a possibility. He could well still be alive. They could be keeping him in one of the pits scattered across the hillside. He's strong for his age, but he won't last long if they feed from him frequently. He could be dead already, but I'll tell you one thing: I know of no Romanian daemon or witch magic that can keep a soul living on in a severed head.'

'Why didn't you tell me this before?' I asked, suddenly angry.

'I wasn't thinking straight, Tom. I'm sorry. There were a lot of things whirling around in my mind at the time.'

'What about the Fiend?' I nodded towards the leather sack at Grimalkin's side. 'We decapitated him but his head still talks.'

'That's different, Tom. The power comes from within him – it's part of his being. To do that to John Gregory would be almost impossible.'

'Almost?'

'Who knows what can be achieved when the resources of the dark combine – they must indeed be desperate to restore the Fiend to his former state. But we may hope . . .' Judd trailed off, frowning.

I continued my account, shaking my head bitterly at the end. I turned to Grimalkin, who was sitting next to Alice opposite Judd and me. 'This is exactly what they wanted,' I told her. 'For me to lure you here so that they could seize the Fiend's head. This is the most dangerous place you could possibly be.'

'We sensed that you were in trouble and were on our way here anyway, so don't blame yourself,' she replied. 'I have been in danger many times since I last saw you, child, but each time I have prevailed – sometimes with the help of others.' She nodded at Alice. 'But I agree that the most important thing is that this' – she tapped the leather sack – 'should not fall into our enemies' hands. From what you've told me, the Old God, Siscoi, constitutes the greatest threat, so we should not stay in this place longer than necessary.'

'I can't leave without trying to save my master,' I told her, 'or at least ensuring that he really is dead and at peace. Alice, will you try to find him for me? I wouldn't ask this of you, but there's no other way.'

'Of course I will, Tom,' she replied. 'That ain't no trouble at all. I can do it now . . .'

Alice closed her eyes, took a deep breath and started to mutter under her breath. Her actions took me completely by surprise. I had expected her to go up onto the hillside with me and sniff out his whereabouts. But here she was, almost casually resorting to some sort of dark magic; such actions seemed almost second nature to her now.

She opened her eyes and stared at me. When she spoke, her voice was matter-of-fact. 'They have him in a pit high to the northeast.'

I had to force the words out: 'Is it just his head or the whole of him?'

'I can't say, Tom. I can sense his spirit, that's all. It could be either. Whatever the situation, it's best we go and get him now before it's too late.'

But Grimalkin shook her head. 'No, Alice, I will go with Tom. You take this and defend it with your magic if need be.' She rose to her feet and handed the sack to Alice. Then she turned to Judd. 'You go with her. Both of you wait at the top of the western moor. We'll join you as soon as we can.'

Judd agreed without question. The fearsome Grimalkin had taken command and it seemed natural to obey her.

'There's a farmer up there,' I said. 'His name is Benson and he has horses and a cart. He was going to take our books to Chipenden – he was angry when they weren't waiting for him and seemed far from happy with the compensation. But pay him well enough and we could use the cart to get my master away safely. Wait for us on the edge of the moor.'

It was quickly agreed, and I went upstairs and brought down the Spook's bag and my own. I gave one to Alice and one to Judd for safe-keeping.

'What about the innkeeper?' I asked.

Grimalkin gave me an evil grin. 'He's as scared as the rest of them in this town, and no threat at all. The danger is up on that hill.'

So, without further ado, Alice and Judd set off west while Grimalkin and I started to walk towards the river.

The town was deserted and all was quiet, but hiding behind locked doors wouldn't help the folk who lived here. If they had any sense they'd leave.

'No doubt they'll see us coming,' Grimalkin told me. 'Your actions will have made them vigilant. To attack by night would be better, but the threat to your master's life gives us no choice. We must simply be bold and fast. As soon as we cross the river, start to run – remember to draw your sword first!'

By now we were under the trees and had almost reached the ford. I was hoping against hope that we'd find my master alive. I could hardly bear to think about what awaited us in the pit. What if it was just his head, still conscious, and I had to burn it to give his spirit peace? It was a terrible prospect.

'Once we're near the place Alice indicated, I'll sniff out his precise location,' Grimalkin said. 'Our enemies could arrive very quickly. When we are attacked, stand behind me and keep out of my way. Your job is to guard my back. Understand?'

I nodded. Seconds later, we'd crossed the river and Grimalkin set off at a furious pace. I ran at her heels, struggling to keep up. Soon the cobbled streets were behind us and we were climbing. Even now she hardly slowed, despite the steepness of the incline.

The weather, which had been bright and sunny when

we crossed the ford, now began to change. Once more the creatures of the dark were using it against us. But this time, instead of a storm, tendrils of mist began to snake up the hill towards us.

When we were nearing our destination, Grimalkin paused and sniffed three times while I waited at her back, sword drawn, panting for breath. She pointed at a group of trees surrounding one of the large houses and immediately began to sprint towards it. They proved to be hawthorns – an overgrown hedge that had once marked the boundary of a field – and beside them was a deep ditch. By now the mist had reached us. It soon began to thicken and the light grew dim.

That was no impediment to the witch assassin's skills. Grimalkin ran on to the furthest of the trees – the one closest to the house – and immediately found the pit. It was sealed with a heavy stone, but she grasped it firmly and wrenched it off to reveal the dark fetid hole beneath. My eyes are pretty good in the dark but I couldn't see a thing.

'Can you stand, John Gregory?' she called down into the darkness. 'If so, extend your arms upwards as far as you can. It's me, Grimalkin – and your apprentice, Tom, is by my side.'

Could she see him with her witchy eyes? I wondered. Was he whole? Or was she just calling down to find out if he was there?

A series of coughs issued from below; it was the sound of an old man struggling to clear his chest and get air into his lungs, but I remembered the head coughing and spluttering inside its box. In a moment we would learn the truth. But now I could hear other noises from the direction of the house: a woman's voice called out angrily in a language I did not recognize – it had to be Romanian.

'Quickly, there is little time!' Grimalkin hissed into the pit.

Again there was a fit of coughing from below, but this time my master spoke. I was glad that he was alive, but his words were not the ones I'd hoped to hear.

'Leave me be, witch!' he cried in a quavering voice. 'My time has come. I would rather die here.'

It was awful to hear him sounding so old and frail. I peered down into the pit, my eyes slowly adjusting to the dark. Now that I could finally see him, a wave of relief washed over me. My master was leaning back against the side of the shaft, staring up at us. He looked terrified and defeated, but his head was still attached to his body.

'Your work isn't over yet!' Grimalkin said. 'Hold up your arms. The enemy are approaching – every second you delay endangers all our lives!'

'Please, master!' I called. 'The whole County is in great danger. The murderous daemons and witches plan to move westwards. They're trying to raise Siscoi too. We need your help. We can't do it alone. Don't let us down. Don't let it end like this.'

For a moment there was silence. Then I heard Mr Gregory let out a long weary sigh and he stretched his arms upwards. The next moment Grimalkin reached down into the pit and drew him up so that he was standing beside us.

I had never seen him look so weak and old. He was trembling from head to foot, barely able to stand. His gown was stained with what I assumed was his own blood, and there were deep bite marks on his neck. In his eyes I saw such an expression of weariness and anguish that my heart lurched with pain.

Without a word Grimalkin hoisted him over her shoulder, his arms and head hanging down her back.

All at once I heard feet pounding towards us through the thickening mist, but the speed of the attack took me completely by surprise. A strigoica had been lurking in the ditch we'd passed, and suddenly I saw her taloned fingers lunging towards my face.

I swung my sword at her hastily, losing my balance and slipping forward onto my knees on the damp grass. For a second I thought my time had come, but now it was the daemon's turn to fall: a blade was deeply embedded in her left eye and blood ran down her cheek. After her first throw, Grimalkin already had another blade at the ready. She turned again, gripping the Spook's legs, and set off down the hill. I quickly got to my feet and followed in her wake.

When I had fled with Judd, nothing had stood in our way; on this occasion daemons were waiting for us in the thick fog. We broke through the first line, Grimalkin cutting down a shadowy figure as we did so. I glimpsed something huge to my right, and slashed at it, feeling a momentary shock as my blade made contact. The creature fell back, giving a cry of pain – another bear possessed by a moroi.

Then we were in serious trouble. Our enemies were all around, and claws and teeth lunged for us out of the mist. There were both strigoii and strigoica; the heavy fog conjured by dark magic was allowing the former to attack even during daylight hours.

'My back!' Grimalkin shouted. 'Remember what I said. Guard my back and I'll do the rest!'

She began to fight in earnest, all fluidity and grace, each blow spilling the blood of our enemies. But guarding her back proved difficult because she never remained facing in one direction for long. At first I slashed wildly with my sword, struggling to keep my footing on the slippery hillside while keeping our attackers at bay. Just in time, I drew the dagger and was able to stab a fanged strigoi who had ducked beneath the Destiny Blade. The creature put up its right hand to shield its face. That cost it three of its fingers. Not for nothing was the dagger named Bone Cutter.

Even though she was carrying the Spook across her shoulders, which meant that she could fight with only one blade at a time, Grimalkin was constantly whirling and spinning round, each blow bringing forth a cry of pain. I continued to try and shield her back, using both blades. At one point I attempted to slow time, but so fast and furious was the fight that I was unable to summon the necessary concentration.

Finally I was no longer able to keep up with Grimalkin: I was hard pressed on all sides, struggling to keep my enemies at bay. My arms grew heavy; I was exhausted. But then Grimalkin was at my side again. 'That way!' she ordered. 'Follow me!'

The witch assassin had cut an escape route through those who stood in our way, and soon we were running down the hill, our enemies left somewhere behind us in the mist.

We encountered no more dark entities, and somehow we managed to cross the ford. But I knew that we were no longer safe on this side of the river. The pact was over.

The streets were empty and utterly silent as we climbed the slope of the western moors. Had the inhabitants locked and barred their doors even though it was still daylight? Or had they fled westwards?

'Put me down,' the Spook cried feebly. 'I don't want to be a burden. Let me walk.'

Grimalkin didn't bother to reply; simply increased her pace. As we left the houses behind and followed the track up onto the moor, the fog began to thin and soon we emerged into bright sunshine. I glanced back, but the town and the river were still shrouded from our view. There was no sign of Alice and Judd. I was just starting to worry when they appeared in the far distance, walking alongside a cart.

When they drew closer, I saw Benson's eyes widen with fear at the sight of Grimalkin. However, he had been paid well, and once the Spook had been carefully lifted up onto the cart, he urged his horses off at full tilt. Quickly Alice handed the leather sack to Grimalkin who hoisted it onto her shoulder. Then we ran after the cart.

We were retreating now, but it was only temporary. It was our duty to return to Todmorden to deal with the threat.

For the first half-hour Grimalkin, Alice, Judd and I sprinted beside the cart, alert for danger, but then Benson turned towards us.

'It'll kill the horses to keep up this pace!' he shouted, shaking his head.

The beasts were sweating, and at a nod from Grimalkin he flicked the reins and slowed them to a trot. After dark we rested for a few hours, taking it in turn to keep watch. Soon we were moving again. The anticipated attack never came, and as the hours passed, Chipenden drew steadily closer.

Normally this would have quelled my anxiety, but the combined power of the Romanian entities could reach us even there. Nowhere was safe.

[illegible] to keep up the pace" he shouted, shaking his head.

[illegible]

[illegible]

CHAPTER 19

THE TERMS OF THE CONTRACT

The first night back in Chipenden passed without incident, but we felt certain that our enemies would attack soon, so we remained vigilant. My master was having a difficult time of it – about an hour before dawn I heard him cry out in anguish.

As yet there were no beds, so we'd made the Spook as comfortable as possible on the kitchen floor. He was wrapped in blankets, lying on a pallet of straw to insulate him from the chill of the flags. I rushed over to find him groaning in his sleep. No doubt he was having a nightmare, reliving the horrors of his incarceration and the draining of his blood. I considered waking him, but after a few moments he quietened down and his breathing became steadier.

I found it difficult to get back to sleep. Soon after first light I went outside to stretch my legs and inspect the work on the house. The new roof was now up and the doors and windows had been replaced so at least we were sheltered from the elements.

Inside, much remained to be done. Upstairs, the bedrooms could not be used because the floorboards had either been burned away entirely or were clearly unsafe. This was the carpenter's next job. However, he had already reconstructed the library floor, as that was high on my master's list of priorities.

Later, when I went to check on the Spook again before breakfast, he was sitting with his back against the wall, facing towards the fireplace. On one side of him was half a bowl of chicken soup. On the other, close at hand, was his Bestiary.

Logs were burning in the grate and, although sparsely furnished, the kitchen was cheerful and warm; but my master's face looked sad and anxious, and despite the fire, he was shivering.

'Are you feeling any better?' I asked.

'Better than I was, lad,' he told me, his voice weak and tremulous. 'But I've not much appetite and I hardly managed a wink of shut-eye last night . . . When I did doze off, it was straight into the same terrible nightmare. I wonder if I'll ever get a good night's sleep again.'

'At least you're safe now,' I told him. 'I really thought you were dead.'

It was the first time we'd had a chance to talk properly since I left him in the library at Mistress Fresque's house, and I quickly related all that had happened – including my conversation with what I thought was his head.

'I thought the same, lad – that it had really happened. I felt terrible pain as they cut off my head, and then I was confined in that box. I was choking, fighting for breath. It was just about the worst experience I can remember in all my long years of fighting the dark.

'Then I was in the pit, and I realized I still had my head on my shoulders. I should have been relieved, but having my blood taken was almost as bad. After the initial bite there wasn't much pain, but it was terrible to be in the grip of that hideous creature and feel so utterly powerless and weak – to feel the labouring of my heart as the life was drained from my body.'

The Spook closed his eyes for a moment and took a deep breath before continuing. 'I thought that by binding the Fiend we'd seriously weakened the dark, but it seems resilient. It's as strong as ever – maybe more so. On the Isle of Mona we put an end to Bony Lizzie, then, in Ireland, stopped the goat mages raising Pan, as well as cutting off the Fiend's head. But there's always something else to take the place of those we defeat. And now it's the Romanian entities threatening the County.

'Still, it seems to me that you've acquitted yourself well, lad. I'm proud of you. You've proved yourself to be the best apprentice I've ever had – though I'd better not let Judd Brinscall hear me saying that,' he said with a smile.

By now I was smiling from ear to ear: it was a rare thing to receive praise from my master.

In response to my delight, he frowned. 'Don't let my words go to your head, lad – you still have a long way to go. Now listen carefully – we can do a few things to increase our chances of survival!'

I wiped the grin off my face and nodded.

'An attack by daemons and witches will almost certainly come at night – we have the daylight hours before the first threat appears. Go down into the village, lad, and get the blacksmith to make up three staffs with retractable silver-alloy blades – one for you, one for me and one for Judd. Tell him it's urgent and you'll collect them before nightfall. If I'm going to die, I want to go down fighting! Then you can pay a visit to the grocer, the baker and the butcher and bring back our usual food order.

'And there's one other thing you can do. It's a long shot, but it's worth attempting. Remember the boggart? Track it down, and then try to persuade it to come back. Make a new pact with it.'

When still a young man, my master had made a bargain with the boggart that Judd and I had talked about on our journey to Todmorden; the pact had endured only so long as the house had a roof. So the fire had freed it.

'How will I find it?' I asked.

'With difficulty, lad, but it won't have gone far. You need to check down the ley-lines. My hunch tells me that it will have taken the one that runs north to south. No one has asked me to deal with a boggart, so my guess is that it's holed up in some abandoned building south of here – or maybe somewhere people tolerate it. Who knows, lad – it could be making breakfast for somebody else by now! Follow the line and find out. It might even have gone back to the old wood-mill where I first encountered it. Boggarts are creatures of habit and often return to where they were once comfortable.'

Leys were invisible lines of power along which boggarts moved from one place to another. The Spook could well be right. He said 'guess', but his instincts were often correct.

'Do you think you can follow the line without a map?' he asked me. 'Or would you like me to sketch it out for you?'

The Spook's maps had been destroyed in the fire, but I'd walked that ley with my master twice before. 'I can remember the route,' I told him.

'Did you ever read the account in my Bestiary about how I made the pact with the boggart?'

'I skimmed it once but didn't read it carefully,' I admitted.

'You do too much skimming and not enough careful reading, lad. It's one of your faults! Well, read it now. It might help,' he said, handing the book to me.

I quickly turned to the section on boggarts. There are four stages in dealing with a boggart: negotiation, intimidation, binding and slaying, and the first of these had eventually proved successful with this boggart. After a few early difficulties, with my master receiving a tremendous blow to the head and scratches to his cheek, he had finally come to an agreement with it. I read the terms of the contract very carefully:

The following night I entered the kitchen with some trepidation and spoke to the invisible boggart.

'Your reward shall be my garden!' I called out. 'In addition to cooking, washing, cleaning and tidying you will also guard the house and garden, keeping at bay all threats and dangers.'

The boggart growled at that, angered that I'd demanded more work from it by extending its duties to the garden. Quickly I continued explaining what its reward would be.

'But in return for that, the garden shall also be your domain. With the exception of things bound within pits or chains, or my future apprentices, the blood of any creature found there after dark is yours to claim. But if the intruder is human you must first give three warning howls. This is a pact between us which will endure as long as this house has a roof!'

'If I can find the boggart, do you think it's likely to accept the same contract?' I asked.

The Spook scratched at his beard. 'With boggarts, the more you give 'em, the more they expect, so you need to think of something extra. Negotiating is always the first sensible step when dealing with a boggart. But if we could get it to guard the house and garden again, it could certainly take care of some of the strigoii and strigoica, should they come here. Unlike some of the daemons I've encountered, once they've entered a human body, they are bound there, and that makes them more vulnerable.'

'What about the witches?' I wondered.

'If the witches approach in the form of orbs, that could prove more difficult – and then of course there's Siscoi: the boggart wouldn't stand much of a chance against one of the Old Gods.'

Three years earlier the boggart had defended the garden against an evil entity called the Bane. It had been wounded in the process, but had prevailed. At the time, the Bane had been steadily growing in power, but its strength wouldn't have matched that of the Old Gods.

'It's still worth it,' my master went on. 'We need all the help we can get.'

'I'll go down into the village and get the smith started on our new staffs straight after breakfast,' I told him. 'Then I'll go hunting for the boggart.'

The Spook shook his head. 'Sorry, lad, but you'll soon be facing the dark. Take a bit of County cheese with you – that'll have to suffice for now.'

My stomach was already rumbling with hunger and I groaned silently.

'You know, lad, I had a lot of time to think while I was trapped in that pit praying for death to release me. Although in the past I've blamed you for getting close to the dark, I've been no better. I've always been suspicious of young Alice and warned you against her, but that was because I'd failed in my own duty by associating with Meg . . .'

My master fell silent. Meg was a lamia witch – the love of his life. He'd lived with her for many years but now she'd returned to Greece.

'I closed my mind to much of that,' he continued, 'but I have to admit that my dealings with the dark began earlier than that. The pact I made with the boggart was the start. It was my first ally from the other side, the first step that eventually led to my alliance with Grimalkin.'

I was confused. What was he saying? 'Then you don't want me to search for the boggart after all? You've changed your mind?'

'Nay, lad, it's vital that you find it and make another pact. Using the dark is one way to beat the dark – so that's what we must do. I'm not happy about it, that's all. The old standards I tried to live my life by – we've had to let them go in order to survive. It's a sad, bad business. Anyway, off you go – but whatever happens make sure that you're back long before dark.'

Suddenly his expression became serious. 'I've forgiven Judd for what he did, and I hope that you can do the same, lad. Nobody is perfect and he went through a lot. I've been in one of those strigoi pits, so I should know – not to mention the threats to his family . . . So, let bygones be bygones, eh?'

I nodded. I knew that what had happened belonged to the past. I was doing my best to forgive Judd, though I was finding it hard.

'After breakfast Judd is setting off for the barracks at Burnley to tell the military about the threat to Todmorden,' the Spook continued. 'With a bit of luck they might listen to what he has to say and send a force up there to investigate. We have to do something while we are gathering our strength. It might at least make our enemies lie low for a while and save a few lives.'

Grimalkin, Judd and Alice were in the garden, finishing off bacon and eggs that they'd cooked over a fire. I looked at it longingly. The dogs came bounding across, pleased to see me, and after I'd patted them, I sat down by the fire and told them what I'd been asked to do.

'It's worth a try,' Judd said. 'I miss that boggart – it's one of my strongest memories of my apprenticeship here at Chipenden. It belongs here – it certainly will make our defences stronger.'

'I'll come with you, Tom,' Alice offered.

'Yes, the two of you will be safer together,' said Grimalkin, rising to her feet and lifting the sack up onto her shoulder. 'Later I'll search the area in case there is any sign of an impending attack. They could have sent out an advance party to see where we are based.'

'That means I'd best get back from Burnley as soon as I can to keep an eye on John Gregory,' said Judd. 'I'll see if one of the local farmers will lend me a horse. But it's agreed that you'll all return here at least a couple of hours before the sun goes down? If I don't make it back on time, can I rely on that?'

We gave him our promise, and I walked down into the village with Alice. I'd have liked to take the dogs with us, but that wasn't wise – dogs and boggarts don't mix and their lives would have been in danger.

Usually I was comfortable with Alice even when we just walked and said little. I'd never felt the need to fill the silences. But now I was ill at ease. Time was running out – it was less than five months till the ritual to destroy the Fiend had to take place. The thought of her going into the dark pained me, but even worse was the truth I'd withheld: that the sacred object she sought there – the third hero sword, the dagger called Dolorous – was intended to take her life.

Alice was giving me some strange glances. Had she somehow found out that she had to be sacrificed to destroy the Fiend? I wondered. Who knew what she could now achieve with her magic. I felt relieved when we reached the village.

During the war Chipenden had been visited by an enemy patrol. Houses had been burned and people killed, and the remainder of the villagers had fled. It was good to see that a lot of reconstruction had already taken place and that many houses were occupied once more. I visited the blacksmith and he promised to have the three staffs ready for collection by the afternoon. Then I popped into the grocer's, baker's and butcher's shops in turn, told them that things were getting back to normal up at the Spook's house, and to please have our usual orders ready by the end of the day.

Once that was accomplished, we turned our attention to the Spook's next instruction. I had to find the boggart, and somehow persuade it to come and guard the Chipenden house and garden once more.

CHAPTER 20
JUST LIKE OLD TIMES

Trusting the Spook's intuition that we would find the boggart somewhere along the ley-line he'd indicated, Alice and I started east of Chipenden and headed directly south of the Spook's house.

It was a sunny spring morning, and the walk was pleasant, though I still felt a degree of discomfort in Alice's company. We crossed the small meandering river twice, splashing across the fords, and approached the first likely location of the boggart: an old barn which still had a roof, even though it was sagging ominously.

'Ain't been used for some time, that,' said Alice.

'Looks promising to me. It's a likely enough place for a boggart to have made its home.'

'Then let's take a closer look,' I suggested.

We strolled around the building and then went inside. There were birds nesting under the eaves, but apart from their chirping all was silent. I had no sense that something from the dark was nearby.

We continued south and eventually came to a small cottage, which I remembered from my last walk down the ley. It had been occupied by a farm labourer, his wife and child, but since then the war had intervened. The doors and windows had gone and the cottage was a shell, the roof likely to collapse inwards the next time a storm blew in from the west.

I led the way inside, glancing up nervously at the blackened beams. Again I had no intimation that the boggart had made its home here – but I found something else. There was a faint shimmer in the corner, and the ghost of a child appeared, a girl of no more than five. She was wearing a white dress, but it was splattered with blood. Tears streaming down her cheeks, she held out her arms and called piteously for her mam and dad.

It could be that her parents had died in the fire or been murdered by the soldiers. But she had come back to the place where she'd been happy, searching for the mam and dad who had cherished and protected her until that terrible day when war had come to this little cottage.

'Oh! Help her, Tom. Help her – please!' Alice cried, gripping my hand tightly, tears running down her own cheeks. Alice might be using her witch powers more and more, but her heart was certainly in the right place. It seemed to me at that moment that she was a long, long way from becoming a malevolent witch.

I approached the ghost, knelt down and brought my face level with hers. 'Listen to me,' I said gently. 'Please stop your crying and listen carefully. I'm here to help you. It'll be all right, it really will.'

She just carried on crying bitterly, so I tried again.

'Wouldn't you like to be with your mam and dad again?' I asked. 'Wouldn't you like to be with them for ever and ever? I can tell you what to do. It's easy.'

The ghostly child rubbed her eyes with the back of her hand. 'How?' she asked; her bottom lip still wobbled but new hope now lit up her face.

'All you have to do is think of some happy memory from the past.'

'Which one? Which one? There were so many. We were happy before the soldiers came,' she replied. 'Happy, happy, happy – we were happy all the time.'

'There's got to be a really special one. Think hard. Isn't there a very special memory, better than all the rest?' I insisted.

The child nodded. 'It was when Mam gave me a white dress for my birthday. Dad carried me on his shoulders!'

'Is that the dress?' I asked. 'Is it the one you're wearing now?'

'Yes! Yes! Mam said I looked pretty, like a princess, and Dad laughed and spun me round and round until I grew dizzy.'

As the child laughed at the memory, the bloodstains faded and the dress became so white that my eyes hurt.

'Can you see your mam and dad?' I asked gently. 'Look into the light!'

Tears rolled down her cheeks again, but she was smiling – they were tears of happiness. I knew that her parents were there waiting for her, holding out their arms and beckoning her forward.

The little girl turned her back on me and began to walk away. Soon she had faded and disappeared.

Alice and I strolled on without speaking. I felt happy, and the tension between us seemed to have evaporated. Sometimes it was really good to be a spook's apprentice – I felt a real sense of achievement.

Ten minutes later we reached the wood-mill. As the Spook had commented, boggarts were indeed creatures of habit. It had once been comfortable here, and there was a good chance that it had returned.

The main door of the mill had fallen off its hinges and the workshop was deserted. There were no signs of violence or wanton destruction. The mill had simply been abandoned – probably when news came of the approach of the enemy patrol that had eventually attacked Chipenden. And the workers hadn't returned. The County was still a long way from getting back to normal.

As I approached the long workbench, a sudden chill ran the length of my spine – I knew that something from the dark was approaching. The next moment I heard purring, a noise so loud that it made the wood files and chisels vibrate in their racks. It was the cat boggart, and the fact that it was purring had got us off to a good start. Clearly it remembered me. So, wasting no time, calling out in a clear firm voice, I began to negotiate.

'My master, John Gregory, asks that you return to Chipenden. The house is being repaired and it already has a new roof. We thank you for your work in the past and hope that our association can continue into the future on the same terms as before.'

There was a long silence, but then I heard the *scritch-scratching* of the cat boggart. It was using its invisible claws to mark its reply on a huge piece of timber propped up against the wall. When the sounds ceased, I stepped forward and read its answer.

Gregory is old and weary. The future belongs to you. We make the pact.

I didn't know how my master would feel about that and I hesitated.

'Agree to it, Tom!' Alice insisted. 'You *are* the future:

soon you'll be the spook at Chipenden. Ain't no doubt about it – the boggart is talking sense!'

In response to her words the purring began again. I shrugged. The important thing was to get the boggart back to Chipenden to help fight off the imminent attack.

'I agree!' I called out. 'The pact will be between you and me.'

Again there came the *scritch-scratch* of the invisible claws on the wood. When I read what it had written, I was filled with dismay.

My price is higher this time. You must give me more.

The Spook had been right. The boggart was no longer satisfied with the terms of the previous pact. I thought quickly. What more could I offer? Suddenly I had a moment of inspiration. The boggart could travel down ley-lines, and plenty of them ran through the house; they led off in most directions.

'In addition to killing dark things that try to enter the garden,' I told it, 'I have another task for you.

Sometimes when I hunt out creatures of the dark I find myself in extreme danger; then I will summon you to fight by my side. You will be able to slay my enemies and drink their blood! What is your name? I must know your name so that I can call you!'

It was a long time before the boggart's claws scratched on the wood again. Perhaps it was reluctant to tell its name to anyone? But at last it was revealed:

Kratch!

'When I am in danger, I will call your name three times!' I said.

Again I heard the deep purring. But then I realized there was another condition I had to impose. 'In addition to what is already protected within the garden, there are three wolfhounds. They must not be touched. They are our allies. Nor must you harm guests that I invite into the garden. Is it agreed?'

The purring deepened, and again came the scratching on the timber:

How long will the pact endure?

The answer came straight into my head. I didn't even have to think. It was as if someone else was speaking for me.

'The pact will endure until three days after my death. During that time you must protect my allies and drink the blood of my enemies. After that you will be free to go!'

Suddenly the boggart appeared before us in the gloom, taking on the appearance of a big ginger tom-cat. There was a vertical scar across one blind eye – the wound it had suffered fighting off the attack of the Bane, I assumed. It moved forward and rubbed itself against my leg, purring all the while – then suddenly disappeared.

'You've done it, Tom!' Alice cried.

I smiled at her, feeling pleased with myself. 'Well, Alice, we can't be sure until we get back to the house, but I'm certainly hopeful!'

'Would you really summon the boggart to help you, Tom?' Alice asked. 'That would leave the house unprotected.'

'That's right,' I agreed. 'I'd only do so if my life was in great danger. And I certainly wouldn't summon it to face Siscoi.'

We set off for the village right away, and collected the staffs from the blacksmith. As usual, he'd done an excellent job and I paid him on the spot. Then I visited the three shops to collect our provisions – a good supply of vegetables, bacon, ham and eggs, not to mention bread fresh from the oven. I carried the heavy hessian sack full of food and Alice carried the three staffs.

I should have felt safe close to Chipenden but I was uneasy. We would surely have been followed from Todmorden; the Fiend's servants must be getting nearer.

As we walked up the lane that led to the house, we spotted a figure up ahead and my heart lurched. But then I saw that it was a tall woman carrying a sack. Grimalkin! The witch assassin was leaning on the gate. Over her shoulder was the leather sack containing the Fiend's head – she never let it out of her sight. She smiled, showing her pointy teeth.

'You have succeeded,' she said. 'I went off sniffing for our enemies, but on my return I heard a warning growl as soon as I set foot in the garden. The boggart is back and hungry for blood! I don't think I'm very welcome.'

We climbed over the farm gate and walked up the hill until we reached the perimeter of the garden. There we paused and I called out into the trees: 'By my side is my guest, Grimalkin. Allow her to cross the threshold safely and grant her the same courtesies as you would me!'

I paused, and then cautiously led the way into the garden. There was no warning growl. The boggart was keeping to the terms of our pact. There was no need to speak on behalf of Alice – the Spook had already done so some time ago. And Judd was safe too – ex-apprentices who completed their training to the Spook's satisfaction could usually enter the garden with impunity.

'Did you see any sign of our enemies?' I asked Grimalkin as we approached the house.

She shook her head. 'Neither hide nor hair. I ventured southeast, almost to the edge of Accrington, but there was nothing. Unless the witches come in the form of orbs, there is little chance of an attack much before dawn.'

In the kitchen I found that the Spook had taken delivery of a new table and six chairs, which stood opposite the fire. He was on his feet now, one hand resting on the back of a chair, a little smile on his face.

'Are you starting to feel better?' I asked him.

'That I am, lad,' he replied. 'You did well to get the boggart back. And you've brought our provisions too,' he said, nodding at the sack I'd set down on the flags. 'Hopefully it'll cook us breakfast tomorrow morning. It'll be just like old times!'

Judd Brinscall returned about an hour before dark. His mission to the barracks at Burnley had been successful. It seemed that reports of strange deaths over the past few months had already reached the ears of the commander, and with a spook's report to add to that, he quickly made up his mind. A sizeable force was to be despatched to Todmorden – though there would be a delay of a day or so. It seemed that all their available troops were busy clearing out gangs of robbers, who in the aftermath of the war were now occupying Clitheroe. They would no doubt soon restore law and order there, but they had no experience of dealing with dark entities. I had some misgivings about how they would cope with what awaited them in Todmorden, but I kept them to myself. It would help if one of us contacted the soldiers with advice – but first we had to survive the night.

We spent it out in the garden. It was certainly no hardship – the weather was just about as warm as it gets in the County after dark. Although still weak, the Spook was able to walk around now, and he congratulated me again on getting the boggart back. I didn't have the heart to tell him that it had insisted on making the pact with me. It wouldn't make much difference to what happened and there was no need for him to know.

We took turns to keep watch, but the Spook, Judd and I slept with our staffs by our sides. I got the first watch and spent my time patrolling the inner boundary of the garden where the rough grass met the trees. To pass the time I checked the eastern garden to see if the dead witches were still safely bound in their graves; I also checked the bound boggarts. All was well.

I felt calm, confident that the boggart would take care of any encroaching strigoii. My greatest fear was that Siscoi might have already been brought into our world by the witches and come for the Fiend's head. I hoped that pouring salt and iron into the offal pit had delayed him.

Grimalkin took the second watch and I tried to sleep. I kept drifting off but waking up again with a sudden jerk. I was vaguely aware that the watch had changed once more when a terrible howl brought me up onto my knees.

Something had invaded the garden and was being challenged by the boggart.

CHAPTER 21
EMPTY EYE-SOCKETS

An instant later I was on my feet, staff in hand; beside me, my master was struggling to rise. I grabbed him under his arm and supported his weight until he was standing. Someone was running off into the trees. I recognized the gait – it was Grimalkin, sprinting towards the source of the danger as the boggart's warning growl erupted for a second time.

Alice was standing beside me, but there was no sign of Judd Brinscall. He had been on watch and could be anywhere in the garden.

'I'll go and see if Judd is all right,' I said.

'Nay, lad, stay here. If he's in trouble, the boggart's

on the spot and the witch will be there in a few moments to help.'

'That's right, Tom,' Alice said, agreeing with the Spook for once. 'Best wait here.'

Suddenly there was a third roar from the boggart – followed almost immediately by a high thin scream, which was suddenly cut off. Moments later someone came running towards us. I readied my staff and so did the Spook. We relaxed when it proved to be Judd.

'I was in the western garden,' he said. 'It's all clear there. I thought it best to leave things to the boggart.'

'Aye, that's the most sensible course of action,' said the Spook. 'I trained you well – though the witch couldn't wait to get involved. This attack's come from the south. We'll know what's what in a few moments.'

Everything was silent, and even the breeze died down. We stood there, alert and ready for danger. After about five minutes Grimalkin emerged from the trees.

'It was a strigoi,' she confirmed. 'The boggart dealt with it before I got anywhere near. It didn't seem happy with what it had caught and was busy tearing it to pieces.'

We settled down before the embers of the fire but

none of us felt like sleeping now. I suppose we sensed that another attack was likely.

It happened within the hour. Alice suddenly sniffed twice very loudly. 'The witches – they're almost here!' she cried, leaping to her feet and pointing to the east.

We all stood and searched the sky in the direction she had indicated. It was a clear night, the heavens liberally sprinkled with stars. Now some of the points of light were moving. I counted eight speeding towards us. Soon they had become distinct orbs, which paused above the trees of the eastern garden and began their dance, circling and weaving and exchanging places.

Both the Spook and Judd looked grim. They held their staffs in the diagonal position – though such weapons would offer no defence against the animism magic of Romanian witches, who would soon move in close and try to suck the life force from our bodies.

Grimalkin was whispering into Alice's ear; she nodded as if in agreement. I suspected that they were going to use magic against our enemies. Back in Ireland I had witnessed the terrible power that Alice had at her disposal. She was reluctant to use it, for it signalled yet another stage in her journey to becoming a malevolent witch. And it would hardly be welcomed by the Spook.

The orbs ceased their dance and swooped towards us, but there was a sudden roar of anger from the boggart – a terrible howl to challenge the witches. Something red streaked up towards them, and they scattered before re-forming and attacking again. Once more the challenge was roared out, and the boggart soared upwards for a second time. This time there were several shrill screams, followed by flashes of light. The orbs gathered over the trees again, but now there were only five – which now dispersed again, each in a different direction.

'That seemed almost too easy,' observed the Spook. 'No doubt they were taken by surprise. The boggart dealt with several of them, but we need to remain on our guard. The rest could try again at any time. No doubt they'll eventually conjure up some means of fighting it off.'

Once again we settled down uneasily by the fire, but the attack never came, and soon the pre-dawn light began to colour the eastern sky. The five of us headed into the southern garden to investigate the aftermath of the intrusion. The remains of the strigoi host were scattered over a wide area: we found the skull up in a tree, impaled on a thin branch, twigs sprouting from the empty eye-sockets. Of course, the daemon itself would eventually find another host.

'We need to gather as many of the bones as possible and bury them,' my master said. 'These are the remains of an innocent person, after all.'

We did as he asked, and I went back to the house and managed to find a spade that had survived the fire. It was badly singed but still intact, and I used it to dig a shallow grave beneath the trees. In it we laid the bones we had managed to find, then I covered it with earth. When I'd finished, we all stared down at the freshly turned soil and, very softly, the Spook said, 'Rest in peace.' That was just about the nearest he'd ever come to offering up a prayer.

'No doubt the boggart dismembered it because it felt cheated,' he observed. 'Any blood inside the strigoi would have been second-hand, taken from a victim. My boggart likes its blood fresh! Let's hope it's in a good enough mood to serve us breakfast!'

When we entered the kitchen, five steaming plates of ham and eggs were waiting on the table, and a central dish was piled high with thick slices of buttered bread. We settled ourselves down without delay. The bacon was slightly overcooked, but we were all very hungry and we tucked in.

At last the Spook pushed his plate away and looked at each of us in turn, his eyes finally settling on me again. 'It's time to talk,' he said. 'We need to discuss what needs to be done.' Then he turned to Alice. 'I asked you once before, girl, and now I must repeat my question. Are you prepared to go into the dark and bring back what we need?'

'There's got to be another way!' I cried out, before Alice could reply. 'I won't allow it.'

'I don't blame you, lad, for trying to protect her. But we know what needs to be done. Just how far are we prepared to go to achieve our aims?'

'We must do what is necessary. How long must I continue to carry this?' Grimalkin asked, rising to her feet and patting the leather sack. 'Come with me, Alice. I need to speak to you alone.'

Alice followed the witch assassin out into the garden, leaving the Spook, Judd and me to stare at our empty plates.

'We have our present problem to deal with before we consider the Fiend,' said the Spook. 'And it's urgent. We may be relatively safe within the boundaries of this garden, but what about the poor folk outside it? Those to the east near Todmorden may already be losing their lives. We have to help them. It's our duty.'

'You mean return to Todmorden?' Judd asked. 'I knew we'd have to go back – but surely not right away!'

'It'll be weeks before I'm strong enough to make the journey, let alone be effective once I get there,' said the Spook, shaking his head. 'It hurts me to have to ask others to do the work but I have no other option. By now those soldiers from Burnley will be setting off to investigate Todmorden, but they fight wars against human foes and have no knowledge of dealing with the dark. We need to send expert help. Would you go, Judd, and take the lad with you? I don't expect you to cross the river, but you could certainly help those on the County side. Our enemies will likely prey on isolated dwellings beyond the town to begin with. Those are the ones who will need you.'

'Of course,' Judd said. 'The townsfolk won't

welcome us, though. They'll be concerned about their own survival. Still, it must be done. We'll set off immediately.'

I nodded in agreement. It was better to be out there doing something than just waiting for whatever our enemies decided to dish out.

After that we fell silent again. I was just wondering where Alice and Grimalkin had gone and what they were saying to each other, when suddenly I heard a distant bell.

Someone was at the withy trees crossroads, ringing the bell to summon the spook. Usually I went to find out what the problem was. It could be anything, from a rogue boggart to a graveside-lingerer. Sometimes people were just scared and under no real threat; at other times a whole family was in danger, and my master would set off to sort things out immediately.

'Sounds like someone's in trouble,' the Spook said. 'You'd best go and see what's up, lad.'

'Then I'll keep him company,' said Judd. 'It could be a ruse to lure one of us out of the garden.'

'Aye, you're right. It'll be safer with two of you,' my master agreed.

Soon we'd crossed the garden and were heading for the crossroads. 'It's just like old times!' Judd joked. 'When I came down here as young apprentice, I was usually shaking with nerves: I knew it meant setting off on spook's business within the hour.'

'Me too,' I said. We'd crossed the meadow and had entered the trees again. Now we were nearly at the crossroads, and heavy rain clouds were blustering in from the west. It seemed to be growing darker with every step we took. Suddenly the bell rang out again.

'At least they're still there,' said Judd. 'Sometimes they used to lose their nerve and head off back the way they came.'

'Some of them are more scared of the Spook than a boggart!' I agreed.

We both laughed, then stifled our laughter simultaneously. Because, despite the gloom, we could now see who was ringing the bell.

It was a pretty young woman and I remembered her well – the one who had lured us to Todmorden with the promise of books for the Spook's new library.

It was Mistress Cosmina Fresque. Or, to be precise, the daemon clothed in her flesh.

'I bring you a message – the chance of life!' she cried, letting go of the rope. The bell continued to dance in the wind, pealing several more times before falling silent.

We approached her warily, holding our staffs diagonally across our bodies. There were two clicks as we released the retractable blades.

'Just give us what we want! Give us the head of our master, the Fiend!' the daemon told us. 'Do that and we will return to our own land, and your homes will be safe and your people may live out their little lives in peace.'

'And what if we don't give it to you?' Judd said. We were still walking towards the figure – now she was no more than ten paces away. She was standing beneath the bell rope, her back to the tree. I glanced sideways at Judd and saw the tears running down his cheeks. Daemon she might be, but the face and body were that of a girl – the girl he had loved.

'Then this will become a land of the undead: we will rule here and take blood wherever we choose.'

'This is our answer!' cried Judd, and he drove the blade of his staff towards the daemon. She stepped sideways to evade the thrust, but he then went straight into the classic manoeuvre taught by the Spook. He flicked the staff from his left hand to his right, and drove it straight through the heart of the daemon, pinning her to the tree trunk.

She let out a tremendous shriek, and blood spurted from her mouth and dripped onto her shoes. Then her eyes rolled up into their sockets and she gave a great shudder and slumped backwards. She would have fallen to the ground, but the blade held her fast against the tree. The silver alloy must have penetrated her heart: almost immediately a glowing orange helix rose up from the body, hovered for a moment, gained elevation, then shot off eastwards.

We both stood staring at the body of Cosmina. Finally Judd turned to me, tears still streaming from his eyes. 'Do me a favour, Tom,' he said. 'Go back to the house and bring me a spade. I need to lay her remains to rest.'

I ran back, briefly told the Spook what had happened, then collected the blackened spade from under the new lean-to at the side of the house. When I reached the crossroads again, Judd was kneeling down, holding the corpse's hand.

'I'll dig it if you like,' I offered.

Judd came slowly to his feet and shook his head. 'No, Tom, that's my job. Thanks for bringing the spade. You go back to the house. I'll be there as soon as I've finished.'

But I didn't return immediately. There was a chance that the daemon hadn't come back to the crossroads alone, so I headed into the trees and watched Judd from a distance. He dug the grave beneath the tree and lowered Cosmina's body into it. Suddenly he gave a terrible cry of anguish and struck hard down into the grave with his staff.

He had cut off the head of the corpse. It was one way to ensure that no daemon or other entity could possess her again. I could hear him sobbing as he filled in the grave and collected some stones to lay on the soil to ensure that no dog or wild animal could dig up the body. Only then, when he knelt with bowed head and stared down at what he'd done, did I set off back to the house.

His task had been a painful one. How would I fare if I had to sacrifice Alice? It didn't bear thinking about.

Time was running out. I had to find another way to destroy the Fiend that did not involve her death. But Mam was powerful and had struggled to find the method she'd presented to me. How could I hope to do better?

CHAPTER 22
LET THEM COME TO US!

The following day, just after noon, we prepared to carry out the Spook's wishes. Leaving him behind with the dogs and the boggart, Grimalkin, Alice, Judd and I set off for Todmorden once more.

As we left the garden, Alice came up alongside me. She was carrying a book. 'Here,' she said. 'This is for Old Gregory. I wrote it myself.'

With a smile, I took it and read the title: *The Secrets of the Pendle Covens*.

'It's about some of the darkest secrets than nobody but a witch knows – not even a spook. It should be really useful. Your master won't accept it from me, but if you pass it on he might put it in his new library.'

'Thanks, Alice. I'll give it to him when we get back,' I said, putting it in my bag. 'I'll give him my notebooks too. Everything helps. But I've a question for you. What did you talk about when you went off with Grimalkin yesterday?'

'It was women's talk, Tom. Nothing to concern you.'

I stared at her, annoyed, but hurt too.

'Ain't happy, are you? Don't like me keeping secrets from you. But do you tell *me* everything?'

I opened my mouth in shock. Had she somehow found out about the sacrifice that was required?

But before I could reply, Alice strode on, leaving me to walk with Grimalkin. Our conversation had saddened me, but I thought it best to ask no further questions.

The sky was grey and a light drizzle was drifting in from the west but the air was mild. It was what passed for summer in the County.

I glanced round at Judd, who was clearly still upset. After a while he came alongside me and clapped me on the back. 'Cosmina's body has been laid to rest now, something I've been hoping to do for a long time. I feel as if I've turned the corner at last.'

'What will you do afterwards? Will you go back to Romania?' I asked him.

'No, Tom. I've had my fill of travelling for a while. Maybe I should take over poor Bill Arkwright's patch north of Caster.'

'That's a great idea!' I exclaimed. 'You'll certainly have plenty on your plate with all those water witches. As far as I know, no spook has been working in the region for well over a year. The Spook told me that Bill left the mill – to be used by future spooks. So you'd have a roof over your head.'

While we talked, Alice and Grimalkin were deep in conversation ahead of us. Clearly they were hatching some sort of plan and I was shut out of it. Then, as we continued southeast, skirting Accrington, they dropped back to walk alongside us.

'Grimalkin needs to speak to you alone, Tom,' Alice told me.

I glanced at the witch assassin, who nodded and pointed towards a copse on our left. She began to walk towards it and I followed.

'We'll wait here for you!' Alice called out.

I wondered why Grimalkin couldn't speak in front of Alice and Judd. No doubt he was the problem. Maybe she didn't trust him after his betrayal of the Spook . . . I'd find out soon enough.

The witch assassin came to a stop amongst the trees and turned to face me. She eased the leather sack off her shoulder and placed it on the ground between us. 'The Fiend has asked to speak to you,' she said, 'but you must choose whether to allow this or not. No doubt he wishes to intimidate you or make threats. But I believe that we can learn from whatever he says.'

'Do *you* speak to him?' I asked.

Grimalkin nodded. 'From time to time we have exchanged a few words, but recently no amount of goading has made him speak. However, he said he was willing to talk to you.'

'Then let's hear what he has to say!'

We sat down on the grass, and Grimalkin undid the leather sack and pulled out the Fiend's head by its horns, placing it on the ground so that it was facing me. I was shocked by its appearance. It looked smaller than when it had first been cut from his body, and the face was crusted with dried blood. One eye was gone –

there was just a red-rimmed, pus-filled socket, and the lids of the other eye were stitched together. The mouth seemed to be stuffed with nettles and twigs.

'What happened to the eye?' I asked.

'It took it in revenge for the deaths of my comrades,' Grimalkin replied. 'He may keep the other one for a little while.'

She reached forward and pulled the nettles and twigs out of the mouth. Immediately the head, which had previously seemed still and dead, became animated. The stitched eyelid twitched, and the jaw and lips began to move, showing the stumps of yellow teeth.

'It could have been so different, Thomas Ward,' the Fiend said, his voice hardly more than a croak. 'We could have worked together, but you rejected me and reduced me to this. Now you will pay a terrible price.'

'You are my enemy,' I told him. 'I was born so that I might put an end to you.'

'Of course,' said the Fiend, his voice becoming stronger, 'that is your "destiny" – or so you have been told. But believe me, a very different future awaits you. You think I am helpless? Well, you are wrong. Do you think that taking one eye and stitching the other makes me blind? My spirit can see all it wishes. I see exactly where you are most vulnerable. I see those you love and the means by which they can be hurt. Do you think that sealing my mouth renders me dumb? I speak to my servants all the time, and they are as numerous as the stars. They are eager to act for me. Defeat one, and another will rise up to do battle with you. You will meet your match eventually – and far sooner than you think!'

'This is just empty talk,' hissed Grimalkin, seizing the head by the horns.

'We will see!' cried the Fiend. 'You are a seventh son and have six brothers. This day, one of them will die at the hands of my servants. And he will be only the *first* to suffer thus. Soon you will be the last of your mother's sons!'

As I got to my feet, my head spinning at the thought of what might happen to my brothers, Grimalkin stopped the mouth again and returned the head to the leather sack.

'Take no notice,' she said to me. 'I was wrong to subject you to that. And we have learned nothing new.

He could have sent his servants against your family at any time. He is making threats to unsettle you and divert your focus from what needs to be done.'

I nodded. On returning from Ireland two weeks earlier I had sent a letter to the farm enquiring about the health of my eldest brother Jack, his wife, Ellie, and their child; I'd also asked about my brother James, who had been staying with them to help out with the farm work and build up his business as a blacksmith. The reply had been reassuring. All was well, and apart from the loss of a few animals, the war had left them unscathed.

We were a long way from the farm now, though. As for my other brothers, they were scattered across the County. I could do nothing to help them – I just had to put my concerns aside.

We returned to join Alice and Judd. I told them what the Fiend had said and the threat he had made. Judd nodded sympathetically and Alice squeezed my hand. For now, there was nothing that any of us could do.

'Where did you plan to make your base?' Grimalkin asked Judd.

'We could stay to the west of Todmorden, well clear

of the village,' Judd said. 'That way we can start to work the area without drawing too much attention to ourselves.'

'But that's exactly what we do want to do – we want to attract their notice!' the witch assassin exclaimed, her eyes flashing. 'We should stay at the inn. Let them come to us. Once we've depleted their numbers we'll move on to the attack. It'll be like clearing out a nest of rats!'

'Isn't that risky?' Judd asked. 'By keeping our distance we could do some good before they even notice we're there.'

'You might help a few people, yes,' Grimalkin replied. 'But it would reach a crisis soon enough anyway. It would be a matter of hours before you were detected. This way we decide the killing ground. They will abandon the quest for other victims and come for this!' She held up the leather sack. 'They will come for it and die. Our struggle against these Romanian entities is just one in a series of battles we have waged against the servants of the Fiend. I want to put an end to it quickly so that we can get down to the real business – his final destruction.

So what about you, Tom Ward? Are you in agreement?'

I looked at Judd and shrugged. 'Sorry, but I have to agree with Grimalkin,' I told him.

'Me too,' said Alice.

Judd smiled. 'It seems that I must bow to the will of the majority. Let battle commence!'

We continued on our way for another couple of hours. By now the cloud had cleared and it promised to be a fine night. As the sun sank towards the horizon, we set up camp for the night beside the track. Alice caught three rabbits, and soon they were turning on spits over the fire, the aroma making my mouth water.

Suddenly, in the distance, I heard the steady beating of a drum. It was getting closer, and soon we could hear a penny whistle too. It was music to march to. The soldiers from Burnley were on their way.

Realizing that they were coming along the track and would pass quite close by, Alice and Grimalkin retreated into the trees. There had been clashes in the past between the Pendle witches and the military, and they would certainly recognize Grimalkin again.

'I've never understood why they wear jackets that colour!' Judd exclaimed. 'I was taught to wear a gown like this to camouflage me in the forest. They seem to be doing their best to be seen!'

I had to agree. The soldiers' jackets of vivid County red made them clearly visible through the trees. We strolled over to the path.

There were about thirty men, all but one on foot. An officer on horseback led the column, and as they drew nearer I realized that he looked familiar. He had a ruddy complexion and was stoutly built. Then the small, neat black moustache confirmed it – this was Captain Horrocks, the officer who had led the group of soldiers laying siege to Malkin Tower. I had been imprisoned, falsely accused of murdering Father Stocks. Would the captain remember me? I wondered. The war had intervened, and after my escape I would surely have been forgotten. I was older and taller now, in any case.

As he came abreast of us, the captain raised his arm to bring his column of men to a halt. The penny whistle and drum fell silent. All that could be heard was the breathing of the horse. I looked down, avoiding his eyes.

'I know you . . .' he said quietly.

My heart missed a beat. Should I run for it? The witch, Wurmalde, had killed the priest, but she was dead now and I had no evidence to prove my innocence. I could still hang for a murder I hadn't committed.

'Aye, I'm Judd Brinscall. I brought your commanding officer warning of what's afoot in Todmorden.'

When Judd spoke, I realized my mistake and breathed a sigh of relief.

'What you've done is brought us out here on a wild-goose chase,' the captain said, his voice caustic. 'You spooks take money from gullible people for fighting the supposed dark, but you don't fool me. Witches are nothing more than beggars and scoundrels. And as for your latest tale' – he laughed contemptuously – 'it is quite beyond belief. I'm following orders and have to investigate, but if I find the slightest evidence that you've brought us here under false pretences, then I'll take you back to Burnley in chains! Do I make myself clear?'

'People have been murdered, Captain,' Judd said quietly, 'and you'll find the killers mostly ensconced on the other side of the river, as I explained. But if you'll take my advice, make camp for the night and cross at dawn. Our enemies are at their strongest in darkness.'

'So you'd have us believe. I don't deny that there have been deaths, and if we find the perpetrators, justice will be swift. But you don't scare me with your foolish tales. I've just fought a war and seen lots of deaths – scenes of carnage that I'll carry with me to my dying day. After that, what we'll encounter in Todmorden is nothing! Do I make myself clear?'

Judd didn't reply, and with a scornful shake of his head Captain Horrocks led his men onwards. Some of the foot soldiers were smiling but others looked scared, especially the poor little drummer boy marching at the rear. After a few moments the drum and penny whistle started up again. We watched the column disappear into the trees and went back to our supper.

We were up soon after dawn and did without breakfast, pressing on towards Todmorden.

As we crossed the western moor above the town, people began to pass us, heading in the opposite direction – mostly individuals, but occasionally whole families carrying their possessions tied up in bundles.

They were refugees fleeing the County side of the town. None of them looked very happy to see us. Some might have been from Todmorden itself and were perhaps aware of our part in triggering the crisis; others simply saw the spook's garb and reacted as most folk did.

Everyone we tried to stop brushed past us angrily.

'How bad is it?' Judd asked, finally waylaying one old man who was struggling up the muddy path with the aid of a walking stick.

'They're murdering children!' he exclaimed. 'What could be worse than that? And they killed armed soldiers too. Who's going to protect us now?'

I exchanged glances with Judd. No doubt, like me, he was hoping that they'd just picked off a few of the men from Burnley – maybe ambushed a small reconnaissance patrol that the captain had sent out. But it was worse than that – far worse.

The soldiers had camped on the top of the western moor within sight of Todmorden. Now they were all dead. Captain Horrocks had been decapitated. He lay on his back with his head between his boots. The embers of their fires were still smoking and they lay where they had been slaughtered, their throats ripped out. Some were on their backs, murdered as they awoke. Others had tried to run. None had got very far. Their corpses were covered in flies and the stench of blood made me retch.

We passed by without comment. I exchanged grim looks with Alice and Judd, but Grimalkin simply stared fixedly ahead, her face resolute. She had seen death many times and was no doubt hardened to it. There was in any case nothing to be done and too many for us to bury. The army would have to come and claim its own, but that might not be for many days.

When we got our first clear view of the west bank of the river, the town looked deserted. Soon we were walking through the cobbled streets towards the inn. We arrived just as the landlord was about to lock the front door. It had been mended since we were last here.

'You're going nowhere!' Judd said, pushing him back into the inn.

'You've a nerve coming back here!' he said. 'Because of what *you* did, the pact is over. By keeping to the agreement we've managed to live here safely for many years. We're all food now!'

'And which of the townsfolk made the pact?' asked Judd. 'Were you one of them?'

The man nodded. 'There were three of us. The mayor, the grocer and me – the three wealthiest citizens – and when we did it, just over two years ago, things were very different. I didn't realize how quickly things would go into decline and folk would leave. We did it for everybody – to save lives. Most people were scared to go anywhere near the foreigners, but we crossed the river and signed in our own blood. It was the best thing to do in the circumstances. Provided we gave them what they needed, they left us alone. But now the pact's over and they're out for revenge. I've got to get away from here. Once it's dark I'm as good as dead! Mistress Fresque said I'm next on their list!'

Judd looked at us in turn and raised his eyebrows. We all nodded. There was no point in holding the terrified innkeeper here. He was thrust outside and his bundle of belongings thrown after him. Then we barred all the doors and waited for the first attack.

Outside, the breeze had died away almost to nothing and the night was warm. So we didn't make a fire but settled down in the small dining room close to the bar.

We didn't even light a candle, allowing our eyes to adjust to the dark as best they could.

After about an hour we heard noises outside: a faint sniffing and scratching at the door, like a pet seeking entry. We kept perfectly still. Next we heard a growl, as if the creature had lost patience and wanted to get in immediately.

Suddenly the door bulged inwards, creaking and groaning on its hinges. Our attacker was almost certainly one of the moroi using the body of a bear. This was the means by which our enemies would force entry.

Grimalkin eased a throwing blade from its sheath. Once the head of the bear became visible, it was as good as dead. Her blade would find one of its eyes. But as soon as the door crashed open the bear dropped onto all fours and bounded away, giving her no clear shot. I heard her whistle through her pointy teeth in frustration.

All was silent again, but now we had a view of the cobbled street through the open doorway. In the middle distance, figures moved into view. There seemed to be three. Two were wearing capes and looked female; the nearer one was carrying a torch, and in its flickering light I could see her savage mouth and taloned hands. They were witches, without doubt. But the third figure was a man whom I recognized: the innkeeper. He hadn't managed to escape the town, after all. Now he was their prisoner and his hands were bound behind his back. It was like watching a tableau, a play put on for our benefit. But it soon became clear that this was no play but a matter of life and death.

'Now you will see what happens to those who defy us!' cried the witch holding the torch.

I found it hard to make sense of what happened next. Something seemed to float down from the sky and land directly in front of the innkeeper. But how was that possible? Witches couldn't fly. The idea that they rode broomsticks was just a silly superstition. The figure moved closer to its victim.

'No! It wasn't my fault!' the innkeeper shouted, his voice shrill with terror. 'Spare me, please. Don't take my life, Lord! I always did what you asked. I was generous. I gave—'

There was suddenly a thin, high-pitched scream – it sounded like one of the pigs being slaughtered by

Snout, the pig butcher back on the farm. The noise hung in the air, growing fainter and fainter. The innkeeper slumped to his knees and then fell forward onto his face.

Grimalkin drew a throwing blade and stepped forward as if to attack the witches. We prepared to follow her, but before we could do so our enemies took the initiative.

One of the figures – the one that had somehow dropped down from the sky – started to move towards us. There was something odd about its gait. It seemed to be gliding rather than walking. Nearer and nearer it came, until it filled the whole of the open doorway and started to drift into the room.

To my right Alice lifted a candle stub and muttered a spell under her breath, igniting the wick. In my time as the Spook's apprentice I had seen many horrors, but there before me, lit by that flickering yellow flame, was something that outdid them all. The effect on me was bad enough – I began to tremble and my heart tried to thump its way out of my chest – but Judd must have been truly horrified at what manifested itself before us.

Floating before us was a woman. We seemed to be

looking at her naked body, but something was terribly wrong. Her form was translucent – the candle flame showed what lay within. It was not inflated to its full taut shape; the bones and flesh were missing, and it was filled – *bloated* is maybe a better word – with blood. The skin was whole but there were just two blemishes: a horizontal scar around the neck where the head had been reattached to the body, and an area of puckered stitching over the heart.

It was the skin of Cosmina.

The mouth moved and spoke in a deep masculine growl: *'I am Siscoi, the Lord of Blood, the Drinker of Souls! Obey me now or you will suffer as few have suffered. Give to us what we seek and I will be merciful! I will kill you quickly. There will be little pain.'*

Grimalkin hurled a dagger straight at the throat of the grotesque figure but the blade skittered away harmlessly as if deflected by some invisible shield.

CHAPTER 23
MIDNIGHT UNTIL DAWN

If this was indeed Siscoi, he wasn't at all what I'd expected. He wasn't using a host grown from the blood and offal in the pit. This seemed to be some bizarre form of possession – yet the skin was filled with blood, and given that the innkeeper had just died, some of it was probably his. The god could probably take our blood too – we were all in danger.

I lifted my staff and prepared to attack. I started to concentrate. I would use my most powerful gift – the ability to slow time. I'd employed it successfully when we'd bound the Fiend, and he was more powerful than any of the Old Gods, so I was confident that it would work here. But I'd hardly begun the process when Grimalkin snapped out a command:

'You deal with it, Alice!'

In response, Alice lifted her left hand and began to mutter a spell; then, taking us all by surprise, Judd raced past us and, with a blood-curdling yell, drove the blade of his staff into the body – at the very point where he'd previously impaled Cosmina's heart. I expected his blade to be deflected, but to my surprise it pierced the skin.

There was an explosion of blood. It went everywhere, and I was blinded for a few moments. When I'd wiped it out of my eyes, through the blood dripping from the ceiling I saw that Judd was kneeling on the floor, sobbing. He was gazing down at something – the ribbon of bloody skin that had once been Cosmina.

The two witches who'd accompanied Siscoi fled immediately, and there were no further attacks – the remainder of the night was quiet.

At dawn we found some lamp oil and used it to burn the skin. It sizzled on the wet cobbles, giving off a terrible smell, but it had to be done. Judd wasn't prepared to bury Cosmina's remains again.

We crouched there in silence until it was over. Drizzle came down out of a grey sky, washing the blood from our faces and hair.

'Do you feel like talking about it?' I asked at last. 'Was that really Siscoi? Was it some form of possession?'

Judd nodded. 'Yes, it was possession of a kind. Siscoi can animate the skin of a newly buried corpse. But first his servants remove the bones and cut the skin away from the muscle. Then the god may visit the close relatives of the dead, enjoying their anguish. At first the skin he inhabits is just filled with air. Then, as he begins to feed, it turns red, filling up with the blood of his victim. The process involves powerful dark magic. But whether I'd dealt with him or not, he couldn't have stayed in that form for very long. That type of possession lasts only a few minutes.'

It made me sick to think of what had been done. After Judd had buried the body of Cosmina it had been dug up again, almost certainly that very night, and the process he'd described carried out.

'How was it that your blade proved successful while mine failed?' Grimalkin asked.

'Close kin and those who love the deceased have the power to end the possession with a blade; even knitting needles have been used by outraged and grief-stricken widows. Of course, the victims don't usually fight back. Siscoi simply takes their blood and they die.'

'Did you harm him with your blade?' Alice asked. 'Will he be less powerful now?'

Judd shook his head. 'No doubt he felt some sort of pain, but that will only make him angrier and more determined. He can briefly possess both the living and the dead without using a portal or the magic of witches. But he is most dangerous when he animates a host grown with the help of witches. He'll have from midnight until dawn to wreak havoc. I don't want to be anywhere nearby when that happens.'

'Then I think you should go back to Chipenden,' said Grimalkin.

Judd looked at her in astonishment and then his expression hardened. 'Look! I'm not a coward!' he exclaimed angrily. 'I'm just stating the facts, that's all. I want to stay here and play my part, but I'm sure we're all going to die.'

Grimalkin smiled at him without showing her teeth. 'Nobody doubts your bravery, despite your betrayal of John Gregory. You have been through things that would have broken most men. But you have suffered enough. Go back and help John Gregory for a while. The house and garden may yet come under attack.'

Judd opened his mouth to protest again, but suddenly fell silent. Out of the corner of my eye I saw Alice muttering to herself.

'Yes, you're right,' he said, coming to his feet, a bewildered expression on his face. 'Mr Gregory will need help. He could be in danger as we speak. I might as well get started right away – I need to get back as soon as possible.'

I was annoyed: Alice had used dark magic to make him change his mind. But when I opened my mouth to speak, she laid a finger against her lips and smiled sweetly. One part of me wanted to protest – I thought Judd would be more useful here. But I knew that Alice must have a good reason for what she'd done. So I kept quiet. And within five minutes, Judd Brinscall had gathered his things, said a brief farewell and set off for Chipenden.

'Why?' I asked once we were back inside the inn. 'We need all the help we can get.'

'We three alone have the speed, skill and power to do what must be done,' said Grimalkin. 'You have the Destiny Blade and Bone Cutter – in addition to the talents inherited from your mother. Alice wields powerful magic, and I am Grimalkin. To send him away is a kindness – a quality that I show only rarely. But despite his past failings, Judd is a competent spook and a strong enemy of the Fiend – we need all the allies we can get. He must live to serve our cause again should it prove necessary; if he stays with us, he will surely die. Tonight we must attack our enemies and prevent Siscoi from entering the world.'

'Tonight? I thought we were going to allow them to attack us and deplete their strength first?' I exclaimed.

'They have a new host growing in the offal pit, Tom,' Alice said. 'And this very night the surviving witches will combine their strength to open the portal, allowing Siscoi to animate it.'

'How can you know that?' I asked.

'Alice scryed it,' Grimalkin replied.

'You can scry?'

Alice nodded, her face serious.

'That's just one of the talents that Alice has hidden for so long,' said Grimalkin. 'Scrying is never totally certain: there are variables – things that constantly change and affect outcomes – but I have faith in Alice's information. These witches rarely meet in the flesh. They much prefer to appear as orbs of light above the trees. But tonight is different: to open the portal they need to be together, and Alice has discovered the place where they plan to gather. We will kill them all.'

'They're going to use the house where Mistress Fresque and her strigoi partner lived,' Alice told me.

That made sense. Thanks to Judd, I knew that Romanian witches were very private and didn't like any other witches seeing into their homes.

'That's the house that shifts its shape,' I said. 'That could be a problem. You can't be certain of *anything* in there.'

'We'll take care of that,' said Grimalkin. 'We're about to find out who has the stronger magic – those from Romania or those from Pendle.'

Alice said nothing, but a little smile turned up the corners of her mouth.

* * *

We spent the remainder of the day preparing for our attack. The town was deserted, and we took up temporary residence at the smithy. There Grimalkin sharpened her blades and forged three more to replace those she had been unable to retrieve.

I had no need to sharpen the Destiny Blade – its edge was always ready for blood – but I cleaned it carefully, and the ruby eyes set into the hilt glowed as I did so. Nor did the dagger require sharpening, but I did attend to the silver-alloy blade of my new staff.

I showed Bone Cutter to Grimalkin; she turned it over and over in her hands, inspecting it carefully. 'It's a formidable weapon,' she said, 'a smaller version of the sword. I wonder if the dagger that lies within the dark is a replica of this.'

As Grimalkin spoke those words, I looked across at Alice, my heart lurching at the thought that she was supposed to retrieve it. But Alice wasn't listening. For most of the afternoon she had been sitting cross-legged on the stone floor, oblivious to the clash and clang from the forge, her eyes closed. When I had tried to speak to her, she made no response. It seemed to me that while her body was present, her mind, and perhaps her soul, was far away. In some mysterious way she was focusing her power for the struggle that lay ahead.

At last it started to grow dark and we were ready to leave for the sinister house on Bent Lane.

'Alice, could you hide the sack for me?' Grimalkin asked. 'If the worst comes to the worst and we do not return, I would like to make its discovery as difficult as possible for our enemies. Your magic is stronger than mine.'

That was praise indeed from the witch assassin. In addition to her formidable combat skills, Grimalkin had strong magic of her own. But I had seen with my own eyes what Alice was capable of. I wondered just how powerful she really was. It hurt to know that, although we had been close friends for years, she had hidden so much from me.

Alice nodded and reached for the leather sack. As she did so, we heard the sound of coarse laughter. But the sound seemed to come from the ground beneath our feet. The very flags were vibrating.

'Let's see what the old fool finds so amusing!' Grimalkin said.

She undid the cord that bound the head, lifted it out by the horns and placed it on the anvil. It was a terrible sight – even worse than last time. One eye was still stitched shut, the other a gaping ruin. Skin was flaking from the forehead, boils forming all over the face, as if the evil within was forcing its way to the surface.

Grimalkin tugged out the nettles and twigs so that the Fiend could speak. This time the laughter issued from the mouth, not the ground. It went on for a long time. Grimalkin waited patiently. I looked at the stumps of the teeth that she had shattered with her hammer when we'd bound him back in Kenmare, and at the crusted dried blood on his face. His situation was dire – what could he find so amusing?

'You seem to be in good spirits, but in truth you have never been lower or closer to final defeat!' Grimalkin said when the laughter finally ceased.

'You are proud and arrogant, witch!' growled the Fiend. 'With your two eyes you see less than I do. Siscoi is the greatest of my present servants – soon he will free me from captivity and take all your blood. How reckless you are, witch, to bring me so close to him! You could not have made his task easier!'

'You have already lost many servants, fool,' Grimalkin retorted. 'Prepare to lose another! They have died or been defeated by those who face you now. We are the most powerful of your many enemies! Before this night is through, Siscoi will be destroyed or damaged so badly that he will be of no further use to your cause.'

The Fiend laughed again. 'It will not happen, witch, because this boy, upon whose scrawny shoulders rests your slim hope of victory, is a coward. He has already fled in terror from my servants, and will do so again!'

Did he mean when I was down in the cellar of the Fresque house? I'd panicked and run, true, but later I'd gathered my courage and returned. I was about to protest when Grimalkin smiled at me and laid a finger against her lips, indicating that I should not reply.

'In the midnight hour this boy will do what is necessary!' she said.

'Then here is something for him to think about. As I warned you, Thomas Ward, your brother James is dead. My servants cut his throat and threw him into a ditch. You will never see him again in this world.'

The Fiend was the Father of Lies but my instincts cried out that he was telling the truth. My heart felt as heavy as lead. I had lost my brother.

Grimalkin lifted up the head by its horns, then moved towards the forge and held it out over the glowing coals. Soon the Fiend started to scream, and a smell of burning flesh filled my nostrils. It was a long time before she stuffed the mouth with nettles and twigs and returned the head to the leather sack. Finally she handed it to Alice to hide with her magic.

We set off for Mistress Fresque's house soon after eleven. Our intention was to disrupt the ritual of the witches and, if possible, kill them all.

We climbed up above the town and started up Bent Lane, beneath the arch of trees. It was very dark, but my eyes were gradually adjusting. 'Won't they sniff us out?' I whispered.

The Pendle witches had their own defences against detection; seventh sons of seventh sons also had immunity, but these Romanian witches were different. Who knew what powers they might possess?

'Alice will take care of it soon,' Grimalkin told me. 'She will cloak us. Our attack will come as a complete surprise.'

I shivered. It was good to have someone so formidable on our side, but the thought of Alice's power made me increasingly uneasy.

Suddenly we heard something large lumbering along beside us.

'It's a moroi!' said Grimalkin, drawing a blade.

'As long as we stay on the path, we're safe,' I told her. 'Save your blade. I have weapons of my own, but they aren't made out of metal. Judd Brinscall taught me an easier way to do the job.'

So saying, I reached down and plucked two big handfuls of grass, then tossed them towards the outline of the huge bear. Instantly it dropped down on all fours and sniffed at the scattered grass.

'It's counting!' I said. 'Romanian elementals are obsessive – it is compelled to count and re-count every blade of grass. It can't move on until it's finished.'

We left the trapped moroi and continued along the path until the house loomed up before us.

Alice held up her hand, signalling that we should halt. Then she began to mutter a spell under her breath. Instantly a cold shiver ran the length of my spine – a reaction to the dark magic that was being used.

At last Alice fell silent, sucked in a deep breath, then pointed towards the door. 'It's done,' she said softly. 'We are cloaked – hidden from enemy eyes.'

Avoiding the tree that grew up out of the path, we approached the front door. I remembered how Judd had dealt with doors, using his boot to break it down. But this was a house where daemons had lived, and it was shrouded with illusions. Stealth was a better option here. We hoped to take the witches by surprise.

The door was locked, but my special key made short work of it, and moments later we were in the library. It was just as I had first seen it with my master. Above us was the atrium, lined with books right up to that spectacular conical roof. On the ground floor, one book caught my eye immediately. I walked up to the shelf and pointed it out to Grimalkin and Alice. It was the *Doomdryte*.

'We need to destroy it now,' I told them. 'According to Judd, it's the source of power for the house – it makes the illusions possible.'

'No,' Grimalkin said firmly. 'There is no time. Such a book will be defended by powerful spells. And do you want to alert our enemies? Alice will counter the illusions anyway. Later I will penetrate its defences and then burn this house to the ground.'

'If you do, seize the *Doomdryte* and give it to me or my master to burn. We have to be sure. We need to see it destroyed with our own eyes!'

'I will do as you ask,' Grimalkin said. 'But first we must deal with our enemies.'

I opened the far door, and instead of steps leading down, we saw a small unfurnished ante-room and, on the far side, another door, which was ajar.

Through the gap, we could make out five witches standing in a large room. The furniture had been pushed back against the far wall so that the floorboards were clear. Two were standing guard, arms folded; one was staring directly at us, so it was fortunate that we were cloaked by Alice's magic. The other three wore expressions of intense concentration and were behaving most curiously. They were crouched on all fours, facing each other, their noses almost touching. Twigs were tangled in their hair, but not randomly; there was artifice in their arrangement. The head of each witch was adorned with a spiky pentacle. There was blood in amongst the hair – evidence that they had been driven into their scalps as part of the ritual to summon Siscoi.

Grimalkin stepped forward, preparing to attack, but then she halted and stretched out her right hand, as if encountering some invisible obstruction. She turned back to face us, clearly annoyed. 'There is a defensive barrier,' she whispered.

Alice came alongside her and stretched out both hands. 'It's strong – very strong,' she said. 'Ain't going to stop us, but it'll take time.' She began to chant under her breath, but she wasn't the only one.

The lips of the three crouching witches were moving too, but no sound could be heard. Instead, something thin and white emerged from each of their mouths –

three needle-sharp pieces of white bone. Suddenly the three witches scuttled backwards, moving in tandem, as if controlled by a single mind. Next they spat out the pieces of bone, which fell so that their six points formed a triangle. It seemed impossible that such large objects had been able to fit in their mouths. Immediately this process was repeated, and a second triangle lay on the floorboards touching the first.

When this procedure happened for the third time, I realized their intention: to create a five-pointed star, the inner symbol of a magic pentacle.

'Quick!' I hissed at Alice. 'We need to stop this before it's too late!'

She nodded. Despite her power, the combined spells of the Romanian witches were proving a match for her. There were beads of sweat on her forehead. Grimalkin was now gripping a dagger in each hand, tensed for the attack. But she had to wait.

As the fifth bone triangle fell into place, the three witches let out a whoop of triumph. Then, with the knuckles of their left hands, they rapped in unison three times upon the wooden floor. The pentacle of white bone began to glow; it floated upwards, spinning and growing steadily larger as it did so.

The bone pentacle must be the portal. Siscoi was about to use it to enter our world!

At that moment Alice finally broke through the barrier holding us back, and Grimalkin ran forward. The cloak that hid us from the witches' sight gave way at the same instant, and the two guards threw themselves between Grimalkin and their sisters. They were strong and fierce, but neither of them was a match for the witch assassin. Blood sprayed upwards as she jabbed and slashed; there were brief screams, and then they were no more.

I was already hard on Grimalkin's heels. Rather than rising up to meet us, the three remaining witches scuttled towards us on all fours, claws and teeth ready to tear us apart. I stabbed downwards with my staff, taking the nearest through the heart, pushing my blade deep into the wood beneath the twitching body.

I looked up. Grimalkin had killed one and was busy dispatching the other, but the spinning pentacle was directly above her. Within it I saw the bestial, scaly face and arms of the vampire god, lips drawn back in a snarl to reveal needle-like teeth and long fangs. He seemed to be immersed in a thick, viscous red liquid. What could it be other than his favoured blood? There were many different domains within the dark, each shaped by and suited to meet the needs and pleasures of its owner. What could be more appropriate here than an ocean of blood?

There was a sound like water falling over a great cataract down upon rocks – but it was blood. It surged out through the mouth of the pentacle and crashed down onto the floor of the chamber, directly in front of Grimalkin. Within it we could see Siscoi twisting gracefully, mouth wide open, razor-sharp fangs ready for the witch assassin.

CHAPTER 25
THE MIDNIGHT HOUR

For a moment my heart was in my mouth. Grimalkin seemed as good as dead. But Siscoi appeared to pass right through her, before soaring away to disappear through the far wall. He was still in spirit form, I realized, and as yet could do nothing. But he was on his way to the offal pit, where a new host body lay waiting to be possessed. It was less than twenty minutes to midnight.

'We're too late!' I cried.

Grimalkin was standing there, covered in blood, as if transfixed. Even she knew that our cause was lost.

Suddenly I heard a voice in my head. There was no mistaking its owner. It was Mam!

Hesitate and you will all be destroyed. Take the fight to the god! Deal with him before he emerges! It is your only chance! But only you can do it, son. Only you can slay the vampire god and hope to survive!

Of course, I could not actually kill one of the Old Gods. What human could hope to do that? But I knew what Mam meant. If I could slay the host, then Siscoi would be unable to use it and the immediate threat would be gone.

'We need to kill the host in the pit before he gets out!' I shouted. Then, without further explanation, I turned and sprinted out of the house, with Grimalkin and Alice at my heels. As we ran down the path, we saw the moroi, snout to the ground, still counting the blades of grass. Before long, I headed into the trees and realized that there would be no difficulty in finding the offal pit: the beam of dark red light was visible beyond the trees ahead. When I reached it, I saw that the stone lid of the offal pit had been dragged to one side. That would save us time and effort. I threw down my staff and pulled off my cloak. I would use the Destiny Blade and Bone Cutter against Siscoi.

Grimalkin placed her hand on my shoulder. 'No!' she said. 'I will kill him, not you!'

'I heard Mam's voice,' I told her. 'She said that only I can do this deed and hope to survive.'

'I will come with you anyway. I cannot let you face Siscoi alone. Even your mother cannot tell Grimalkin what to do!'

I shook my head. 'No. If I die, you must fight on. You must continue to keep the Fiend's head away from his servants for as long as possible. With Alice's help you may still eventually find a way to destroy him.'

'Only the three of us working together can hope to achieve that,' Grimalkin said firmly. 'We need to survive, and in order to do so must stand as one. Alice will guard the entrance to the pit and, if he gets past us, attempt to blast Siscoi with her magic. We two will go down, but I will leave Siscoi to you. The moroi guarded the area above ground; it may well be that other protectors of the host wait below. The stone has been removed.'

I nodded in agreement. Her words made sense.

Alice came to my side and gave me a hug. 'Oh,

please be careful, Tom. What would I do if anything happened to you?'

'Be ready, Alice, in case I fail. Above all, stop Siscoi. Don't let him get the Fiend's head,' I urged her.

'I doubt if I can stop him, but I'll try, Tom,' she replied.

I walked to the edge of the offal pit and looked down. Part of me thought that I was probably going to my death, but at that moment I accepted it calmly. It was my duty: this was the task for which my master had prepared me; all my training had been to this end. Sometimes, I knew, in order to protect others, a spook must make the supreme sacrifice.

The light shone up into my eyes, dazzling me, and I was forced to turn away. I would have to avoid looking into it directly.

I glanced up, gave Alice a smile, nodded to Grimalkin and then entered the pit feet first. To one side the opening was broad; I chose the other, narrower side. It was like climbing down a chimney, and I was able to use my knees, feet and elbows to control my descent. But the task was made more difficult by the slime that covered the rocks – the residue of the offal and blood that had been tipped into the pit by the witches. There was an awful metallic smell of blood mixed with a stench of rot, decay and putrid flesh. Bile came up into my throat and I almost vomited. I was forced to halt for a moment until my stomach settled. I regretted not cutting a piece of cloth from my cloak to tie around my nose and mouth, but it was too late now.

A light shower of pebbles and soil fell onto my head and shoulders, dislodged by the feet of Grimalkin, who had followed me into the pit. I continued downwards, and soon, below me, I heard breathing and then moaning, as if there was something huge suffering down there.

At one stage in my descent, the red light was partially obscured by an outcrop of rock far beneath me, so I was able to look down. I did so, and instantly regretted it. Immediately below me I saw a gigantic figure, human in form but perhaps twice my size. It was lying on a rocky ledge, writhing and taking deep shuddering breaths – and it was soon clear why. The huge face was corroded, the eyes empty sockets from which matter was weeping. This was the old, first host

– the one Judd and I had damaged by tipping salt and iron down the fissure.

Was this movement the mindless reaction of that empty body, or was it conscious in some sense? I asked myself. Could it feel the effects of the damage like a sentient being? I felt certain that it could.

The minutes were ticking down towards midnight. The new host must lie further down the pit, below this one. I just wanted to complete my task, but something inside me couldn't bear to see such suffering. Once I'd drawn level with the huge figure, I braced myself against the rock with my knees. I wouldn't be able to reach it with the dagger, so I unsheathed the Destiny Blade. I judged the distance carefully, and even though I had to close my eyes at the last moment, I managed to do what was necessary, drawing the blade across the creature's throat. When I opened my eyes again, the blood was gushing down over its chest and cascading into the fissure below.

The huge body convulsed, trembling as if fighting to break free of invisible chains; then it gave a sigh, slumped back against the rock and was still. Whatever life it had possessed was gone. I had performed an act of mercy – but had I also wasted precious time that I needed to deal with Siscoi?

I sheathed the sword and continued down. The rocks were now even more treacherous, coated as they were with fresh blood. At one point, dazzled by the light shining up, I slipped and momentarily lost my grip on the rock face. I froze for several moments, shaking with fear. I'd come close to disaster. Then I gathered my courage and continued my descent.

Soon I reached a wide ledge, where I was able to stand for a moment with my back to the rock and stretch my trembling arms and legs. I could see the next part of the descent below me, but on three sides, shrouded in darkness, were what looked like the mouths of a number of caves. I suddenly realized that Grimalkin had been correct: other entities had indeed been placed on guard down here.

I could hear new sounds – the steady approach of boots, deep breathing, and finally growls of anger. A second later my enemies came into view, their eyes a sea of red points of light glittering in the darkness. The situation reminded me of the moment in the cellar when, faced with overwhelming odds, I had fled like a coward.

But this time I would not run. I drew Bone Cutter, gripping it in my right hand, wielding the Destiny Blade in my left. Grimalkin dropped down beside me, a blade in each hand, and we met them together. I glimpsed teeth and claws, and the stink of rancid strigoi breath washed over me, but I lunged out with my blades, feeling satisfaction as the dagger found flesh – though it was the dead flesh of a daemon. My sword, with its longer blade, was more likely to be successful: I struck the head from the nearest strigoi; it rolled across the floor and fell into the fissure. At my side Grimalkin was slashing to left and right with deadly intent, slicing heads from bodies and driving our enemies back with a ferocity that surpassed their own.

The strigoii were fast, but the fighting was at close quarters, hand to hand, denying them much of that advantage. I struck and struck again until the pressure eased. Then Grimalkin spun me towards the fissure and stood on guard, blades raised to meet the next onslaught.

'Climb down now!' she commanded. 'There is little time. I will hold them back!'

I did not argue. It was surely almost midnight.

Perhaps I was already too late; perhaps Siscoi had taken command of the host. I sheathed my sword and thrust Bone Cutter into my belt before easing myself down into the shaft and continuing my descent.

As I climbed down, the metallic clashes, grunts and screams of the battle above receded; soon they gave way to a different noise. I could hear breathing again . . . it was the new host. This time it would not be blind. The vampire god would already have taken possession of it, and at the stroke of midnight would be free to emerge from the pit.

The sound grew louder and louder, until I could actually feel its breath on my face and hands, and smell its rank fetid stink. Then my feet could go no lower; I was standing on the floor of the pit.

I turned and found myself facing Siscoi.

The previous host had been hard to make out because I had been dazzled from below. Now I could see the source of the dark red light. It was emanating from a huge figure, which I could now see clearly; I knew instantly that the vampire god had indeed taken possession of it. His eyes were wide open and he was staring directly at me.

This host was undamaged. It was seated with its legs stretched out before it, its back resting against the rock wall. The huge body was covered with red scales; sharp talons sprouted from each of its lizard-like fingers and toes. Although even larger than the first host, it was relatively slim and built for speed. The head was hairless and elongated, almost triangular in shape, with a flattened nose, and it had the wide-set, staring eyes of a predator.

How long remained before midnight struck? I wondered. How long before this sluggish entity became a ravening beast that moved faster than the blink of an eye?

The answer to my questions came immediately. The god took a great shuddering breath and moved forward onto his knees, then opened his mouth and showed me his teeth. They were clenched together, the muscles of the throat and jaw bunched tightly. There were four large canines; the rest were like needles – this was not a creature that needed to chew its food. Then the mouth moved, and Siscoi spoke in a deep slow drawl, as if half asleep.

'It is so good of you to come to me,' he said. 'The

blood from your puny body will be my appetizer for the feast ahead!'

I did not reply. My answer was to draw the Destiny Blade and move cautiously towards the kneeling figure.

This was my chance to use my gift and slow time.

Concentrate! Squeeze time! Make it stop!

I took another step towards him, struggling to focus.

Concentrate! Squeeze time! Make it stop!

The vampire god laughed, the sound booming and echoing up through the fissure.

I was desperate now; with the whole of my being I focused on bringing time to a halt. But Mam's gift seemed to have deserted me. If I couldn't employ it soon, my life would be over.

'Do you think your miserable powers will work on me?' demanded the god. 'I am Siscoi, and I have the strength and speed to counter anything you can throw at me. Do you really believe that my master would send me against you without the means to deal with your tricks? His servants have combined together and placed their powers within me.'

Could he be immune to my gift? Was such a thing

possible? The Fiend had been able to manipulate time too, and when we lured him into the pit to be bound by silver spears and nails, only surprise had given me the advantage. If other servants of the dark had similar powers and had somehow transferred them to Siscoi, my situation was indeed hopeless.

But then Mam spoke again inside my head:

Despair, and you will be defeated and destroyed. Above all, you must believe in yourself. If you are truly the weapon I have forged to obliterate the Fiend, then you must prove it now. Otherwise all I have done has been for nothing and you are not worthy to be my son!

The words drove a dagger into my heart. How could Mam be so cruel? Was I merely a weapon – a thing to be used to bring her victory? And after all my struggles against the dark, how could she suggest that I was not 'worthy'? Apart from my recent flight from the cellar, one lapse in over three years fighting the dark, I'd always done my best, whatever the odds against me. Could she not appreciate that? She seemed so very different from the warm nurturing mother I had known at the farm. A surge of anger filled me. I took a deep breath and directed that anger, not against Mam but against Siscoi.

I began to focus again, and now I sensed time slowing a little. The god's eyes flickered malevolently, but I took another step towards him, readying my blade. My concentration became even more intense. The god's eye was moving again, but the flicker had become a sluggish lifting of the upper lids.

And now the ruby eyes of the Destiny Blade began to drip blood. It was as hungry as the vampire god himself! And then I felt a movement at my waist. Bone Cutter was actually moving, twisting as if gripped by an invisible hand. It wanted to join the battle.

I was about to draw the dagger, but then I saw Siscoi's eyes focusing on the drops of blood that fell from the Destiny Blade. Blood fascinated the god; distracted him.

Taking advantage of this, I swung the sword towards his huge head. My aim was true, and had the blade struck home, I would have split Siscoi's hairless skull. But my control of time was not perfect. He was still struggling against me, and he twisted his head away as the sword came down.

I cut off his left ear, and it fell slowly towards the rocky floor, spinning like a red-tinted autumn leaf in the damp chill breeze that heralds the approach of winter in the County.

The god screamed. So loud was his cry of agony and anger that the walls of the pit shook, and small rocks, soil and dust cascaded down.

I took a deep breath and adjusted my stance in the way that Grimalkin had taught me. Once more I tried to focus my mind, but now Siscoi was on his feet, towering over me.

I swung the blade upwards from right to left, aiming for the neck, hoping to sever the head. But now our struggle had entered a new phase; Siscoi's power was waxing while mine was waning. My blade moved slowly, while the clawed hand swept down towards my face in a blur of motion. The god easily evaded my sword, but I felt a burning pain as his talons raked my forehead. I dropped down onto my knees and he lunged for me again.

Once more I failed to avoid him, though I did just enough to survive. This time he used his huge knuckles, seeking to crack my skull open and knock me unconscious so that he could drain my blood at leisure. As it was, I managed to twist away, but the blow sent me rolling over and over until I crashed into the rock wall.

I struggled to my knees, my head spinning, waves of nausea washing over me. I tried to stand but my legs were too weak to support me. Siscoi could finish me off before I even knew what was happening, but his approach was leisurely. He knew that it was all over now. He had won. My control of time was at an end.

But then I heard another voice. It didn't actually appear inside my head like Mam's had. It was a voice from my memory – the voice of Grimalkin, the witch assassin.

Is this the end? Are you finally defeated? No! You have only just begun to fight! Believe me, because I know. I am Grimalkin.

These were the words she had hurled at me over and over again when training me in the use of the Destiny Blade. I remembered that cellar in Ireland where we had first fought – I had been sure she was going to kill me; then, over the period of a week, she had taught me to fight in a way that even the tough, battle-hardened Bill Arkwright could never have matched. She had used these words to goad me on when I had felt too weary to continue.

Once again I recalled her voice:

Get on your feet and fight! Kill your enemy now! Kill him before he kills you! Be like me! Be like Grimalkin! Never give in! Never surrender!

I forced myself to my feet and lifted the blade, grasping it with both hands.

CHAPTER 26
THE SPOOK'S BLOOD

I began to focus on slowing time again. Sweat and blood were running into my eyes, making it difficult to see. I wiped them away with the back of my right hand, before taking my two-handed grip once more.

Siscoi was staring at me, but time was again slowing. I was moving; he was still. Now I would indeed cleave his skull in two – I could do it. I took a step forward, so that my target was within comfortable range. But then, as I began to bring my blade down vertically, he opened his mouth wide. Once more he was challenging my control of time, exerting his own will.

I glanced at the sharp fangs, but they were not the

immediate threat. Something issued forth from Siscoi's mouth, so quickly that I barely had time to react. I ducked to my left, and it just missed my right temple.

At first I thought he had spat something out at me, but I soon realized that this was his tongue. It was at least six feet long, thick and purple, and covered with sharp spines, each like a thin hook. It rasped hard against the rock wall to my right, reducing the top layer to pebbles and dust. Had that made contact with my face it would have ripped the flesh from the bone.

I took three rapid steps backwards. The god's tongue was back in his mouth now and he was snarling. He came towards me, his fingers reaching for my throat, but I swung the blade upwards and made contact with his left shoulder. Once again he cried out in pain.

This time he was hurt. The Destiny Blade had penetrated his protective scales. Black blood was running down his arm and dripping to the ground.

My defences had proved adequate, and I wondered at that. Among Siscoi's powers was his incredible speed, so why did he not use it? It could only mean one thing – he was unable to! To some extent I was *still* controlling time. Faced with such an adversary, I could not halt it, but I was doing enough to make a fight of it.

I readied my blade. Siscoi attacked again and, instinctively, I lunged forward with the sword. I failed to make contact this time, but I did enough to force him back a couple of steps. Then I was retreating just as fast as I could, dodging that long rasping tongue with its deadly barbs. Suddenly I found myself in a cleft in the rock; escape to either side was now impossible. Siscoi's mouth twisted into a smile and he opened it wide. The tongue lashed out towards me in a purple blur. The god had me trapped, with no place to go.

Only one option remained: to advance! I evaded the tongue and stepped in close so that I was less than a foot away from him. Then, before he could withdraw the tongue back into his mouth, I brought the sword across in a rapid arc, cutting right through it. It fell to the ground, where it twitched and writhed like a huge snake, while a tide of blood cascaded out of Siscoi's mouth to splatter at his feet. His howl made the ground tremble and the very stones seem to shriek.

Now was the time to finish him. While he was writhing in torment, I swung the sword at his neck again. But just when I thought I had prevailed, it all went wrong. The god was far from being finished – as I learned to my cost.

His clawed foot arced upwards as if to disembowel me. In avoiding it, I left myself vulnerable to a strike from his left hand, which almost tore my arm from its socket. The pain brought me to my knees. Even worse, the Destiny Blade went spinning out of my grasp.

Siscoi hurled himself at me, still spitting blood. I just had time to draw Bone Cutter and stab at him. I pierced his chest in two places, but he picked me up like a child and carried me towards his open mouth.

His fangs plunged into my neck, but I felt little pain. He began to suck out my blood, and I could feel it throbbing through my veins, the pumping of my heart becoming more and more sluggish.

My situation seemed hopeless but, remembering what Grimalkin had told me, I fought on. I didn't want to die. I wanted to see Alice again, and my family too. The future I had looked forward to – my life as a spook – was being taken away. I struggled to break free, desperately stabbing at the vampire god; but the dagger seemed to have no effect, and soon I was too weak to hold it. It slipped from my fingers, and I felt my heart thudding ever more slowly. I was sinking towards death.

Then I heard a loud scream. Had I cried out? Or had it issued from Siscoi's throat? Never had I heard a sound that was so full of anguish. It was as if the very earth had screamed out in agony.

Then I was falling into utter darkness.

My last thoughts were of Alice.

My last words, spoken inside my head, were to Mam:

I'm sorry, Mam. Sorry for being a disappointment. I did my best. Try not to think too badly of me.

I waited in darkness for what seemed like an eternity. My heart was no longer beating; I was no longer breathing – but I felt no fear. I was at peace, all my cares and struggles left far behind.

Then I heard a sound that I remembered from my childhood: it was the creak of a rocking chair. I saw a glowing figure taking shape out of the darkness.

It was Mam – not the terrible lamia, but the kind, loving mother I remembered. She was sitting in her chair, smiling at me, rocking to and fro as she used to when she was happy and relaxed.

'You are all I ever hoped you would be,' she said. 'Forgive my harsh words earlier. They were necessary at the time. I'm proud of you, son.'

What 'harsh words' did she mean? I felt confused. Where was I? Was I dead?

Still smiling, Mam faded back into the darkness. Now another figure was emerging. It was a girl with pointy shoes, her black dress tied at the waist with a piece of string. Alice.

'I've come to say goodbye, Tom. Don't really want to go, but I don't have much choice, do I? Wait for me, Tom, please. Don't give up. Don't ever give up!' she said.

Where was she going? I tried to ask, but she faded away before I could get the words out.

The next thing I knew I was lying in bed. I was breathing again and my heart was beating steadily. The curtains were open, but it was dark outside. I realized that I was back in my room at the tavern in Todmorden. A candle stood on a small table nearby, and by its flickering light I saw someone sitting beside the bed, staring down at me.

It was Grimalkin.

'At last you are back,' she said. 'You've been unconscious for three days and nights. Despite all that Alice did to heal your body, I feared that your mind might be broken beyond repair.'

I struggled up into a sitting position. I was drenched with sweat and I felt weak. But I was alive.

'What happened?' I asked. 'I did my best. I'm sorry, but I wasn't strong enough. Did you manage to finish him off?'

The witch assassin shook her head. 'No – he was already dead by the time I climbed down to carry you back to safety.'

'He was taking my blood, but I kept fighting to the end, stabbing him with the dagger. I must have got lucky and pierced his heart.'

'That didn't finish him off,' Grimalkin told me. 'It was your blood.'

I shook my head. 'I don't understand . . .'

'Your blood proved to be a weapon – very special spook's blood; the blood of a seventh son of a seventh son, blended with that of your mother, the first and most powerful of all the lamias. To the vampire god it was a deadly poison – just as your mother knew it would be. She appeared to Alice soon after Siscoi died and told her as much.'

I suddenly remembered how he'd appeared clothed in Cosmina's skin – he could still possess other creatures briefly. 'He'll be seeking revenge!' I told Grimalkin. 'He'll be back. We're still in danger.'

The witch assassin shook her head. 'Siscoi is no longer a threat. You did not merely destroy the host; you slew the vampire god himself. A terrible scream soared out of the ground up into the heavens. Your mother told Alice that it was the very dark itself, crying out in anguish at the loss of one of the most powerful Old Gods. You have weakened our enemies. The head of the Fiend has fallen silent again and there is no way to get a response out of him – and believe me, I have been anything but gentle.'

It was astonishing to think that my blood had resulted in the death of Siscoi. Mam would have known about it all along. But a price had been paid. James was probably dead, and the Fiend had ordered his servants to kill my other brothers.

'He'll try again,' I said. 'He said that his servants were more numerous than the stars. He'll never give up!'

'So we must make an end of him!'

I nodded. 'Did you get the *Doomdryte*?' I asked.

'When I went to burn the Fresque house the library was empty. There were no books. No *Doomdryte*. But I burned the place anyway.'

'Then our enemies must have it . . .'

'We must assume so.'

So that was another threat; something to face in the future.

'Where is Alice?' I asked.

'Alice has gone into the dark,' Grimalkin said. 'She has gone in search of the third sacred object.'

It was almost two weeks before I was strong enough to return to Chipenden. During that time Grimalkin cleansed the hillside of the rest of the Romanian entities. Those she didn't kill fled from her. She burned their houses too, with the bodies inside. None would return from the dead. But although she searched for the *Doomdryte*, there was no sign of it.

The County side of Todmorden was also empty, its inhabitants all gone. Somehow I didn't think that they'd be in a hurry to return.

We could have used Benson and his cart again, but I chose to walk, using the journey to re-build my strength, bit by bit. It took me almost three days to get home.

Grimalkin accompanied me, and each night we talked and discussed our plans for the future. It depended on Alice returning from the dark with the third sacred object in her possession. The thought of her there kept me in a permanent state of anxiety. The worst thing was being powerless – I could do nothing to help her.

It was during the first of our talks that the witch assassin delivered another shock to me.

'Alice knows that you must sacrifice her, Tom,' she said bluntly.

For a few moments I stopped breathing and stared into the embers of the fire. 'How *could* she know?' I asked at last.

'As I told you, her magic is very strong. Alice scryed it.'

'Did she see herself die?' I asked, my heart pounding.

'She saw you preparing to take her life, but then the mirror darkened.'

'Darkened? That's good, isn't it?' I said. 'It means the future is still uncertain. Alice once told me that – she said when there are too many variables, the future cannot be foretold so the mirror grows dark.'

'There is another reason for that. A witch cannot scry her own death. But I must know – are you prepared to sacrifice Alice in order to destroy the Fiend?'

'I don't know if I'm capable of it,' I answered truthfully. 'I care about Alice too much. How could I sacrifice her?'

'I have talked it over with Alice. If we can find no other way, she will willingly die at your hands.'

'We *must* find another way!'

'We will certainly try, but time grows short. It is already June.'

We arrived at Chipenden to find the Spook little better. He was walking more easily, but he still looked frail, a shadow of the man who had taken me on as his apprentice.

Later that afternoon we talked, sitting at the kitchen table, watching the fire flickering in the grate. I found it too warm, but my master clutched his cloak about him tightly, as if to fend off the cold.

First we talked of the *Doomdryte*. 'Who knows where it is now,' he said gloomily. 'In the hands of the Fiend's servants, no doubt. The danger is that someone will attempt the incantation.'

'They are unlikely to be successful though,' I told him in an attempt to raise his spirits – although in truth I felt very low myself: my brother was surely dead, and there was no certainty that I would ever see Alice again. Even if she did return, further horror and heartache lay ahead.

'That's true, lad. Do you remember what I wrote in my Bestiary about it?'

I frowned. 'Some of it,' I said uncertainly. 'I know the incantation is hard to complete.'

'Some of it! That's not good enough, lad! You need to be up to the mark. It's vital that you start to think and act like a spook. Come with me!' he said, rising from his chair immediately.

My master led the way to his new library. He climbed the stairs slowly but was out of breath by the time we reached the door.

'There!' he said, pushing it open to reveal what lay within. 'What do you think?'

There was a smell of new wood, and I saw row upon row of empty shelves. 'It's great,' I said. 'Full of promise. All it needs now is books, and lots of them, and then we can call it a library!'

I smiled as I spoke, and the Spook smiled back; he had not lost his sense of humour. He led me to a row of shelves opposite the window. On the middle one, leaning against each other for support, were the first three books in the new library. I read the titles: *The Spook's Bestiary*; *A History of the Dark*; *The Pendle Witches*.

My master had begun the second two while we were refugees on the Isle of Mona. He had completed both before we left Ireland to return to the County.

He lifted the Bestiary and placed it in my hands. 'Read what it says about the *Doomdryte*!'

I flicked through until I reached the right place. 'There's not much here,' I said.

'There's enough, lad. Read the whole section on grimoires aloud.'

'These are ancient books, full of spells and rituals, used to invoke the dark,' I began. *'Sometimes they are employed by*

witches, but they are mainly used by mages, and their spells have to be followed to the letter, or death can result.

'Many of these famous texts have been lost (the Patrixa *and the* Key of Solomon*). The most dangerous and powerful grimoires, however, were written in the Old Tongue by the first men of the County. Primarily used to summon daemons, these books contain terrible dark magic. Most have been deliberately destroyed or hidden far from human sight.*

'The most mysterious and reputedly most deadly of these is the Doomdryte*. Some believe that this book was dictated word for word by the Fiend to a mage called Lukrasta. That grimoire contains just one long dark magic incantation. If successfully completed (in conjunction with certain rituals), it would allow a mage to achieve immortality, invulnerability and god-like powers.*

'Fortunately no one has ever succeeded as it requires intense concentration and great endurance: the book takes thirteen hours to read aloud, and you cannot pause for rest.

'One word mispronounced brings about the immediate death of the mage. Lukrasta was the first to attempt the ritual and the first to die. Others followed in his foolish footsteps.

'We must hope that the Doomdryte *remains lost for ever—'*

'That's enough, lad,' the Spook interrupted. 'So you see the danger? The Romanian entities used only the power emanating from the book to feed their illusions. What if the book was used in the way it was intended?'

I shrugged. 'It seems unlikely to me that anyone could successfully complete that ritual.'

'How unlikely? The Fiend and his servants grow ever more desperate, and that means desperate measures will be employed. I'm worried about that book, and you should be too, lad! It might be somewhere in the County. The threat is very close.'

'Well, talking of books, I've got something to add to your collection!' I said. I opened my bag and handed him three books. They were the notebooks I'd kept during the first three years of my apprenticeship.

'Thanks, lad,' he said. 'This is the right place for them. And you'll be able to come in here and consult them whenever you feel the need.'

'Here's another book,' said, reaching into my bag again, feeling a little nervous. I wasn't sure how the Spook would react. 'Alice was going to write an account of the two years she spent being trained by Bony Lizzie; instead she wrote this, thinking it might be more useful.'

The Spook accepted it and read the title from the spine: '*The Secrets of the Pendle Covens*.' Then he opened it at the first page and began to read Alice's neat writing.

My master closed the book very suddenly and looked at me hard. 'Do you think this book belongs on the shelves of this library?' he demanded.

'It's about the magic used by the witches, and about their strengths and weaknesses. It should help us a lot!' I insisted.

'Well, lad, it's your decision,' said the Spook, 'because the truth is, this is your library. It'll be yours until you hand it on to the next spook. In the meantime, you'll decide what goes on these shelves. My knees have gone and I've lost my wind,' he continued, shaking his head sadly. 'Although you've still a way to go before you complete your time, but to all intents and purposes, from this moment on you are the Chipenden Spook. Start to think like one! I'll still be around to offer advice, but from now the burden of the job must rest on your shoulders. What do you say?'

'I'll do my best,' I said.

'Aye, lad, you'll do your best. That's all any of us can do.'

Once again, I've written most of this from memory, just using my notebook when necessary.

A letter arrived from my eldest brother, Jack, yesterday. He said that James was missing but that they hadn't given up hope. Jack was confident that he would return any day. I don't know what to write back. Is it better to allow him to live in hope for a while? If I tell him what I know, Jack will somehow blame me anyway. He thinks that my job as an apprentice spook has brought nothing but trouble to my family. He is right. I believe James is dead, slain by the Fiend's servants; but for the fact that he is my brother, he would still be alive.

The routine of spook's business goes on, but when the bell rings at the withy trees, *I* am now the one who deals with any problem. Ghosts, boggarts and the occasional witch I deal with alone. My master spends a lot of time sitting in the garden. He looks older and the whole of his beard is now white. He reminds me of the old men I saw as a boy – the ones who used to sit around the market square in Topley village. They seemed to have withdrawn from life and were waiting for death, just content to observe and remember. I think John Gregory is also waiting to die, and that saddens me. It is one more burden I have to carry.

Judd Brinscall has taken the three dogs with him and gone north of Caster to set himself up in the watermill. He has taken on the territory that Bill Arkwright once covered and is now busy ridding the area of an infestation of water witches. I've done my best to forgive him for his betrayal of the Spook, but I still can't quite get it out of my head. It will take time.

As for Grimalkin, she is on the run again with the Fiend's head, still pursued by his servants. I offered to lend her the dagger: she had once refused the Destiny Blade, but now she accepted Bone Cutter. She will give it back when Alice returns from the dark with the third weapon so that all three sacred objects are finally in my possession.

Our fight against the dark continues – but I miss Alice. And time is running out. It is now early August, and I've just turned sixteen. I am in the fourth year of my apprenticeship to the Spook. It is less than three months till Halloween, when we have one chance to complete the ritual and destroy the Fiend for ever. Each morning I awake full of hope, thinking that this will be the day when Alice returns from her quest in the dark. As the hours pass, my mood slowly changes. Hope gradually gives way to despair. By dusk I am choked with grief, convinced that I will never see her again.

Even if she succeeds, it is only then that the horror truly begins. Mam's letter not only explained how I must sacrifice Alice; it revealed other aspects of the ritual. One requires the use of a living skelt. I have a strong sense of foreboding about the creature – images and references to it keep cropping up. And it bothers me that its head decorates the hilts of the sword and dagger.

I think about the task that faces us. If we fail, the Fiend will eventually win and a new age of darkness will begin.

Knowing nothing of the ritual and what it involves, my master is chiefly concerned with the whereabouts of the *Doomdryte*, the evil grimoire that we saw in

Mistress Fresque's library. He is right to be worried. In the hands of our enemies, that book could be very dangerous indeed.

Despite all that's happened, I'm still a spook's apprentice – though I must start to think and behave like the Chipenden Spook. I must anticipate the time when John Gregory will no longer be here – even to offer me advice.

Thomas J. Ward

YOU CAN READ MORE ABOUT
THE DARK CREATURES IN THE WORLD
OF THE *WARDSTONE CHRONICLES* IN

THE SPOOK'S BESTIARY

TURN OVER TO DELVE INSIDE . . .

Strigoi and Strigoica

Strigoi are masculine; strigoica are feminine. These vampiric (blood-drinking) daemons live in Romania, mostly in the province of Transylvania. Often content to exist for years in spirit form, many eventually choose to possess the living; when their host dies, they move on to seize another body. Others prefer to animate the dead and choose a corpse soon after it has been buried.

These daemons enter a living host through a cut or wound: Romanians are so fearful of this that they will endure the pain of cauterization – the wound being burned with a hot poker to seal it against that threat. The dead have no defence, and strigoi and strigoica follow worm-holes into a corpse.

Strigoi and strigoica daemons often work in pairs. One animates a living host, guarding and protecting the other during daylight hours. Many live in grand, isolated dwellings and have accumulated wealth acquired from the living hosts they have possessed.

Once clothed in human form, living or dead, they exist on a diet of human blood, but sometimes eat raw flesh, hearts and livers being considered particular delicacies.

It is the practice of Romanian spooks to dig up bodies one year after they have been interred. If decomposition is underway, the corpse is considered to be free of possession. However, if it has changed little – and especially if the face is pink or red and the lips swollen – it is deemed to be possessed by vampiric daemons and the head is cut off and burned.

There are many ways to deal with strigoi and strigoica, both the living and the dead: they can be decapitated, a stake driven through the left eye, or they can be burned. They can also be kept at bay using garlic, roses, and the same method employed against water witches – a salt-filled water moat. Only a daemon possessing a dead body can be destroyed by sunlight.

A Strigoi

Moroi

These are vampiric elemental spirits found in Romania. They are sometimes controlled by the strigoi and strigoica, but even when operating alone are a considerable threat to travellers. In their disembodied form they inhabit hollow trees and clumps of holly. However, they often possess bears, which crush and lacerate their human victims before dragging them back to their lair. Sunlight destroys them and they are only at large after dark.

Moroi have one significant weakness: they are compulsive in their behaviour and often linger close to their lair, counting holly berries, seeds, twigs or even blades of grass, wasting the hours that would otherwise have been used to hunt human prey. By the time they have finished counting, it's usually almost dawn – which can be the most dangerous time of all for unwary humans because the creatures are desperate to drink blood before the sun rises.

This weakness is exploited by Romanian spooks, who always have a pocketful of seeds or berries. Threatened by the moroi, they cast these towards it. Rather than attack, it is forced to begin counting again.

THE SPOOK'S BESTIARY

AS TOLD TO JOSEPH DELANEY

Dear finder of this book,
What you hold in your hands is my BESTIARY – my personal account of the denizens of the dark I've encountered, together with the lessons I have learned, and the mistakes I have made. I have held nothing back . . .
By possessing this book I am counting on you to continue my battle against the dark. Do not let me down.
Yours,
John Gregory

A complete guide and companion to Joseph Delaney's phenomenally successful Spook's stories, this fascinating, lavishly illustrated Bestiary is a replica of the Spook's own notebook; John Gregory's life's work and findings.

'The illustrations . . . are stunning. It is a brooding and eerie collection of stories for reading in one sitting or dipping into.'
Jake Hope – *The Bookseller*

ISBN: 978 0 370 32979 6